_To_

Kim e

Enjoy

Ann x

The Lost Window

Part One of the Symm Saga

Summer

The Lost Window

Published by WordPlay Publishing Limited

www.wordplay-publishing.com

Acknowledgements

Christine and Terry, for your helpful comments;

Carol, for help with the editing;

My English and Spanish friends who have always thought of me as 'a writer' and not just a wannabe; especially Sole, Jan and Mike;

and finally to:

Michael (and Ian) for making my dream come true.

Dear Readers,

All of the characters in this book are my creation and from my imagination, the names of these individuals are however not made up, and almost to a man/woman or any thingamebob, the name of a member of my family, a friend or pet (here or gone).

The characters do not in any way mirror the real person's personality. I just wanted to have their name in print with mine and there is no detrimental or underlying meaning if the book name is a baddy or goody!

I just wanted the opportunity of naming the best of my life and bring them into the make-believe of my other world.

This has, with this book and its next three, taken over, and set me off on a fantastic journey.

Enjoy the ride, I am!

AEM x

Dedicated to the loves of my life

Bill, Adam & Tristan

My late Mum and Dad

and

Alan, miss you lots sweetheart. x

The Lost Window
Contents

Chapter 1

Tom and Kristy

"Welcome to London Mr Davidson. May I take your bag for you?"

A tall, nondescript man, wearing a chauffeur's peaked cap came forward quickly and broaching no argument to his question, took the small executive suitcase from the smartly dressed businessman's hand.

"Thank you, 'arley."

The elderly man said, dropping an 'h' in his heavily accented English, whilst surrendering his case. He smiled to himself, as he looked his driver up and down, and taking in the rest of the of the man's ensemble, which in truth had little resemblance to a uniform, consisting of jeans, white t shirt, lightweight taupe jacket with a new pair of the latest designer Gucci trainers. "You are well?"

"Very well sir, thank you!" he grinned familiarly as his voice slid into its natural cockney accent, which also dropped an 'h' or two, when the occasion arose. "Gotta be 'onest though, I can't wait for the football season to start, it will be great to see the 'ammers at Upton Park again and playing well. I really miss the atmosphere of a large crowd and supporters going crazy!"

Moving forward they walked side by side through the throng of bodies in the crowded arrivals concourse at Heathrow airport, their long strides covering the distance steadily and at an unhurried pace.

"Yes, well let us 'ope the 'olidays 'ave improved their form on that of last year. Not that I follow West 'am's progress when I watch CNN, at 'ome, of course!" They

1

shared a knowing look and laugh together and he continued "and Ellie is ….!

Without warning, a sudden loud crash of what sounded like a pile of crockery hitting the floor, had the men turn their heads immediately to their right, reacting instinctively to the unexpected sound.

As one, they turned in the opposite direction, both sets of eyes on alert and analytically scanning the teeming crowd, as was their way. Looking for some hint of recognition in every face they saw, and both hoping that they themselves, would not be recognised.

It had been a reflex response to a startling noise and they moved quickly to an alternative exit leading to the parking concourse. The businessman immediately took back the case as if it were featherweight, thus allowing his companion free use of both hands, one of which he immediately placed in his right hand pocket without removing it, as he followed closely at the rear.

By mutual consent they both automatically bypassed the lift and took the 'up' escalator to access the parking levels, back to back one man checking in front, whilst the other was scanning the populace behind them.

Reaching the top level, the chauffeur took the lead and headed through the menagerie of vehicles, heading for the farthest side of the parking level, which contained only a few cars and continued on to the only one facing out towards the exit.

"We're getting jumpy in our old age!" The chauffeur chuckled, as they proceeded at a slower pace. "Got to admit though, I could do without all this cloak and dagger stuff nowadays!"

"Better safe than sorry, eh Splash?" he smirked, at using the nickname of many years. The businessman's voice had now dropped any pretence of an accent and speaking in a much more recognisable higher pitch and tone, " and *you* give up your calling. Nah! That's never going to happen now is it?"

A minute later they reached the outside of a newly customised black saloon and when close enough, the chauffeur activated the electronic car key which was in his pocket and opened the doors. Swiftly taking the case back from his charge, used his foot to activate and open the boot, not even waiting to see his passenger get inside.

When he was sitting in the driver's seat himself however, he looked up at his rear view mirror and winced on seeing a young blond woman behind him, just the other side of a ground-breaking paper thin bullet-proof partition. Luckily for him, it was between himself, his passengers and the verbal fireworks that were about to explode.

"Crap!" he cringed visibly, realising only too late, that in the confusion he hadn't warned the man of the additional passenger. Well that information was now clearly not moot and definitely shelved.

He closed his door firmly, pressed the start button integrated in the centre control, leaving his only action, to press the new silver button next to it. This initiated the windows to become tinted, in the other half of the car, automatically appearing as if no one was actually in the back and an almost inaudible beep that confirmed the rear of the enhanced interior, was now electronically sealed from any listening devices.

By then he was driving slowly away towards the down ramps, stopping only at the barrier at the bottom, to insert the prepaid ticket and exit out of the airport. He was not looking forward to the torturous drive into

London.

"Well, hello! Cousin Henry, you look very good today!" Kristy Osmundsen looked up into her brother's eyes and grinned nervously at his dour expression. "Well done Tom, you really have got his face down to a tee!"

Looking intensely face to face at his makeup, she proceeded to scan every detail of the disguise.

"What the hell are you doing here Kris?" Tom glanced deliberately to the clear window in front of him, but seeing only the back of the now hatless chauffeur.

"Why didn't Splash tell me?"

"He didn't know," she responded lightly, although not totally unfazed by the rebuke and admitted openly. "I sneaked in via the garage, early this morning!"

"Yeh and that will be a first. He isn't ever that stupid Kris, what on earth are you doing here?" he was not happy, this was a covert operation, no one was supposed to know he was even in England, hence the masquerade, let alone actually seeing his sister until he was ready to. This meeting therefore did not bode well for his composure at present.

"I suppose Ellie told you I was coming?"

"No, she didn't!" Staunchly defending her cousin, but hesitated as it was not quite the truth. "Well, not exactly and not in so many words."

Kristy felt such an idiot now, all her explanations seemed to have dissolved into thin air.

"Oh, okay, yes! But only when I told her, what I am going to tell you!" she swallowed nervously and tried another tack. "You really do look like Henry. So logic says, you must have finally read the book I left you at Easter!"

"Don't change the subject and I don't know what the

hell you are talking about!" he responded defensively.

"Pigs might fly! I only left the book, so you could hide in plain sight when you go out, but proof of the pudding, is now in front of me." Kristy answered quickly, and then gave a crooked smile as she spoke again adding softly, "You take far too many risks, I worry about you and I really do have a good reason for being here!"

The last sentence hit a cord in him, at 15 months his junior, she was his baby sister and she should have no need to worry, unfortunately in their world anything could happen, especially to him, so unconsciously he gave her a smile back and began placating her.

"Lucky our wily cousin and I are the same height and build then, isn't it?" his voice was just a little patronising. "It's the first time I've impersonated him and yes, I'm well pleased with the result!"

He watched as she relaxed a little, at his backhanded compliment.

"The family likeness made his features really easy for me to age 30 odd years, sympathetically. Still, I've got to admit, it was a difficult, somewhat opportunistic move, but one which still had to be perfect to get me through passport control here in the UK."

He ran his fingers through the neatly shaped older hairstyle and loosening his overly long blond mop into its usual chaotic mess.

"Passport! How on earth did you get that?"

"The paranoid goat has gone glacier walking for two weeks and he left Dad his valuables, including his passport, to be put in our safe."

"You robbed Dad's safe?" Kristy was shocked.

"No, I'm just borrowing a passport," he smiled at her, "and now I only have to make sure that my trip is shorter than our naff cousin's break on the

Jostedalsbreen. I left all our dad's millions of kroner in the safe for later."

"Ha, ha, you're so funny today."

"Okay I admit it, the book was helpful!"

"Thanks for the compliment, I think!"

Her face reflected the somewhat less than enthusiastic tribute, considering she had been studying for a BA (Hons) in 'Make Up and Prosthetics' in London for the last year and was clearly now able to bring her expertise to the table.

"Be grateful I'm not chucking you out of the car at this moment," he winked at her, "now hand me the holdall that's by your feet, I need to get my real self together here!"

A truce was now fully in place. How could it not be, he hadn't seen her in four months and she was in her last week of staying in England, before returning to the family home in Norway. She was probably just homesick, he reasoned and realistically she knew nothing of his real motive for being there. Peaceful in this knowledge, he settled back in his seat and starting to undress, whilst waiting for her to comply with his request.

Watching him pull at his neatly tied tie, she lifted a blue sports bag, which obviously contained another set of clothes, up onto the seat between them.

"You are still taking a chance, especially now!"

Ignoring the comment, even though he knew she was right, he immediately pulled the bag towards him, then tugged the zip to open it and looking inside, rummaged through the contents impatiently.

"Where's the cleaning grunge then? I need to get this muck off and be myself again!"

Expecting his sister to find what he wanted, he

pushed the bag slightly towards her, then shucked off the tailored jacket. Quickly followed by his father's borrowed bespoke shirt, as he didn't have one himself that was, he considered, boring enough to match the look he had wanted to achieve.

She groped around inside and handed him a tube of cream, a cloth bag containing wet wipes, some wads of cotton and a towel, that their cousin Ellie had obviously put together for him. Shaking her head at his cavalier attitude, Kristy hung his suit jacket on the only hanger in the bag, before hooking it on the hand grip behind her. Then sat back watching her brother's return to the original, Thomas George Osmundsen she knew and loved.

"Hey, this muck as you call it allows you to get around far more safely than you used to, so don't knock it!"

Tom grunted a non-verbal response, neither agreeing, nor disagreeing with what she said, but it only took a few minutes for him to scrub away the perfectly aged face and hands. When finished, he resumed stripping down to his underwear, changing into his own well worn jeans, aqua t-shirt and old trainers out of the holdall, stowing everything he had worn, excluding only the trousers, which he gave to his sister to hang with the jacket. All the rest, including the cleaning paraphernalia was tossed unceremoniously back in the bag and placed back on the floor.

By that time they had left the airport's perimeter and were gliding down the M4 motorway, towards London. Tom now more comfortably dressed and in the comfort of the new car, relaxed back into his seat.

"Now tell me little sister, why are you here now? It had just better be vital to world peace," he joked, although even he couldn't hide the slight tremor in his voice, as he fastened his seatbelt.

Seeing Kristy in the car was a shock and one that need not be anything other than, one sibling wishing to greet another, but then she would have waited at their uncle's for that. No this needed to be something very important and he didn't like it one bit.

"I would never, ever, have gotten up this early in the morning for anything less."

"That dear Sister, I figured out for myself. You have never been an early riser, but then people change. I rarely see you, to know nowadays," he admitted and ruffled her hair the way he used to when they were children. "So, fess up!"

There was a lapse of half a minute, before she finally spoke again.

"I think I may have found one of the Lost!" she whispered softly and her summer blue eyes now wide in anticipation.

"And you thought I would be interested. Why?"

He grimaced, his voice was barely controlled and the hairs on the back of his neck rose accordingly. This was not what he expected and his stomach churned at what was coming next. He instinctively closed his eyes, his mind then going off at a tangent, as he tried to think ahead of what she was about to tell him and only opening them as she touched his hand.

"You know I would never have come to you, without thinking this through. I am fully aware of the risks you are taking to be here, for whatever reason yourself, but I just have a feeling that we have to recover this Lost. It's as if finding this particular sentinel is of paramount importance to us all." Her chin quivered as she finished in a rush.

Tilting up his head, he looked at her now expressively

worried face.

"But why should I want to find it?" he asked, his tone edging convincingly to disinterest.

"Because that's what you do! Well, you help find the Stolen and you get them home safely!" Kristy immediately retorted, in a firm no nonsense voice.

"Oh, I do, do I?" his voice held just a hint of a humour, so as not to betray how deeply her words were affecting him.

"Yes, you do!" she said confidently. "Do you think I am some kind of ignoramus Tom? For heaven's sake, I've known about every one since the Lokkint Blue, and I mean every *one!*"

His features didn't change at this piece of information, only giving her a nonchalant 'don't know what you're talking about, shrug', which prompted her to continue.

"Ok, I'll indulge your scepticism, brother of mine." Gulping in some air to clear her head, and staring straight at him, she again spoke decisively. "I was there, the night of the equinox storm and watched when you all came in the 'posh' dining room at home, through the French doors around 10 o'clock." Kristy's stated precisely and her eyes teared up, "and I almost cried out when Dad stumbled in so suddenly with Walt, but to be honest I didn't recognise them at that point. Walt was taking most of Dad's weight, because he could hardly walk, and they went straight through to the kitchen. Then you came in next, holding the Blue in your arms, followed by Johann and Bjorn, who looked far worse for wear than you did, if that were possible! All of you were a mess, soaking wet with blood everywhere and I could see that it was difficult for you to stand. I wanted to yell and tell you I was there, but I was too scared and shaking. You put the Blue down gently on the dining room chair, and you stood there staring at it, before Walt came in and gathered it up to take it upstairs."

The silence in the car was deafening and Tom suddenly began to snigger,

"Good one Kris almost had me for a minute!" Blatantly, he shook off her retelling of the actual event.

"Damn it Tom! So I was only 13, but I wasn't either deaf or blind. I thought you were going to die, you looked so awful!" Angry that he wasn't, even now, taking her seriously after clarifying what happened.

"Where were you then, when I committed this supposedly wondrous act?" he asked, trying to control the turmoil of feelings coursing through him, as she had pinpointed the moment to perfection.

"I was hiding behind the yellow brocade Queen Anne chair, the one by the bay window. I'd stolen half a chocolate cake from the fridge and I was stuffing my face, because mum said I was putting on weight and she'd stopped me having chocolate on weekdays," she smiled, at his incredulous look. "Hey, I was a teenager and I loved chocolate, what can I say? Anyway, that was my favourite place to hole up, as hardly anyone ever came in that room voluntarily!" Looking at him fiercely and morally hurt he wasn't acknowledging the truth. "I suppose that's why you chose it, being so near the harbour and facing away from the rest of Nåletre Eiendom." She named the estate that their house was a part of.

Tom cringed, what to do, tell her she was dreaming, but her face was so earnest and she did say one of the Lost. Taking a deep breath he admitted defeat, as he

10

realised he now had to find out what she knew.

"So you have known all this time, I always wondered why you never questioned Dad's sudden, so called, illness or my injuries, but then you were such a quiet child." He said almost to himself.

"Finally!" she sighed. He'd actually acknowledge she was telling the truth and she relaxed back in her seat. "What I remembered most about that night was what you said when Walt took away the Blue, you called after him. 'If only they didn't know what we look like, Splash, it would have been a bloody sight easier!' Do you remember how Walt turned back and said, 'Get used to it Sir Goldilocks, you have started now, so there is no going back and next time wear a bloody hat to hide your famous halo.' I love it when he calls you that!" she involuntarily giggled,

He made a face at the reminder of his and Walt's friendly name calling, nodding distractedly, but her words were ringing loudly in his head. As a consequence, he was suddenly transported back there, to that night and in that very room, as a wave of memories assailed him.

Of course he remembered, and the first thing he recalled vividly was the awful pungent smell under his nose of the sea sodden clothes and blood, lots of blood, thankfully mostly not his own. His mind suddenly conjured up the bloody-sea salty mixture dripping onto the dining room carpet and he shuddered.

It had been his first rescue and he could summon up every minute of the four days of careful reconnaissance to rescue the Lokkint Blue, which could have ultimately ended in more than the one fatal loss to their group.

He was 14, big for his age, but he was still young and

very inexperienced in everything that had occurred. Their father had unfortunately had his leg badly shattered and the rest of the team were severely smashed up in the chase, when their speedboat was rammed into some rocks, losing one of their own. Erik Röhn died, crushed between the boats in the mayhem and the rest of them had been extremely lucky to save themselves after the skirmish, which was both scary and painful. Let alone managing to rescue the precious Blue as well.

With that in the forefront of his mind, his brain tumbled back to her question.

"Oh, yes I remember!" his voice hardly above a whisper, but seeing her earnest look, brought his thoughts rushing back to the here and now.

The hardest thing to take in was the fact that she had known his deep secret all along and he smiled indulgently. All these years of trying to keep the families extracurricular recovery business under wraps, and she already knew.

Furthermore and totally unexpectedly, he had, what in the movies is often referred to as a light-bulb moment. Selfishly now, he realised, and not having put two and two together at that or any later time, why she had insisted on learning everything she could know about make up.

Back then, he had put it down solely to a little sister's whim. Didn't all girls go through the dress up and make-up stages, but he knew now that this was not the case with Kristy. She had been unobtrusively feeding her knowledge to him for years, allowing him to think it was his idea to go out in different disguises, as normal days also held their many hazards for him, that she actually did know about.

At first merely adding glasses or a hat, then suggesting colour contacts and skin tones, he had thought he was just indulging her, but had found the looks he was achieving very useful and in his six further forays, very useful indeed. She had done this without anyone's recognition of her true objective, least of all their parents, as she fought hard to get where she was today.

Both parents, for different reasons, had been against all suggestions of her learning a trade, as they called it, although he now realised that hers was more a vocational expertise. He was amazed as he grasped all she had done with her life thus far, the only motive being to learn the skills to keep him safe. Incredible!

"So after that night you decided to help me!" his voice mirrored his disbelief and she smiled at him and nodded in admission, "..........and in the following years too, I believe!"

At last he believed her and was taking her seriously.

"Just wanted to make sure you were not disadvantaged, out there in the big bad world!" she declared cheekily.

He inclined his head. "Well, if that's the case, I wholeheartedly agree, you must have a very good reason." his affirmation was said gently and he breathed in deeply. "I doubt I would be here today, but for you, so how could I say no, sis!"

"You think?" She smiled and her beautiful face shone at his words.

"Yeh, I really do!"

Fissions of love went from one to the other as Tom finally admitted defeat, he took her hand and grinned, the way he used to, before he was a little too tired to think, let alone feel.

This was mainly due at this point in time, to information received only a few days earlier of a trade happening here in England. A known disreputable Squirrel[1] was travelling to Europe from somewhere in the Pacific to sell one of the Stolen, to an equally notorious Magpie[2], which had instinctively put his team on alert. This had set in motion arrangements that had involuntarily hastened his arrival to London against his own needs to stay partially hidden in Nåletre Eiendom and only a more urgent message yesterday revising his options, brought forward the journey to this morning, rather than later in the week.

"So now you have a captive audience, you had better tell me everything you know!"

He leaned back into the soft leather car seat, engaged his seatbelt to match his sister's and still holding her hand he felt the tension leave her body, as she relaxed and moved a little closer to him. His eyes closed, as she began her story and with every word his heart beat faster.

For what she was relaying to him was unbelievable and actually much more alarming than she realised.

[1] Squirrels steal, but will trade to the highest bidder.
[2] Magpies collect to keep, and the 'Stolen' are often, lost forever.

Chapter 2

Rosie/Buddy

Rosetta Jayne Martha Norton had always struggled with her given name, but by the time she went to school she had managed to get both her mother Lisa and her late grandmother Violet, to come to a mutual agreement and call her by the shorter version, Rosie.

Her dad Dave, brothers Michael, older by three years and Jack her twin, along with her grandad Bert, always called her Buddy and for some reason she loved them for it.

The Norton's lived in a 1950s semi detached house in Welling, Kent, whose exterior of a rambling rather shabby dwelling, belied the interior chic inside. Although their spectacular rear garden had been a favourite with Vi and she had often called it, their family's hidden treasure.

"You ready yet, Buddy?"

Mike Norton leaned casually on the doorframe of his sister's bedroom, as both Rosie and her best friend, Vicki were sitting on the unmade top bunk.

The room smelled of shower gel and perfume and both girls were already dressed in their signature clothes. Rosie's, strawberry blond hair tied back with a blue scrunchie and wearing, in varying shades of aquamarine, striped leggings, a short navy skirt and pale blue blouse.

"I called from downstairs, but you didn't answer!" he said indulgently.

On first hearing his voice, Vicki had turned and

jumped straight down off the bed, looking embarrassed by his intrusion, even though the door was wide open. She turned her back to him and quickly picked up an oversized grey t-shirt nightshirt and rammed it in her black rucksack, which was on the bottom bunk.

At her reaction to his voice, Mike's eyes lingered a little longer on Vicki, as her usual shiny brown shoulder length hair was cut to just below the ear and was now striped with a deep shade of poppy red, from the crown to the nape of her neck.

This distracted him for a minute, but then nothing about Vicki Giacomelli was expected, except perhaps the way she was dressed in her customary Goth look. Made up of the usual black jeans and t-shirt, which for the life of him, he could not remember a time he had ever seen her in any other colour, since she moved up from primary school, and only when she was obligated to wear school uniform. Maybe the hair was the start of some colour coming back into her life he mused. He rather liked that idea.

Knowing he was staring, he quickly diverted his eyes to look at the rest of the room, which in truth looked like a bomb had hit it, after what had been an obvious sleepover. This was a first for his sister, as ever since she was four years old, she had made her own bed and the small third bedroom was always sickeningly tidy.

This in itself had wound Mike up no end, as it was the benchmark their mother would measure all her children by and in which, while sharing a bedroom, Mike and Jack failed miserably. Now he was not living at home, he gave way just a little to sentiment and thought it was probably just a girl thing.

"Oh, hi Mike! I'm running a bit late this morning, sorry! I was working into the night putting the finishing touches to the next chapter, with Vicki's help." Rosie muttered in a sleepy voice, folding her own pale blue nightie and putting it under her pillow, before descending more sedately down the ladder, "It's the longest chapter I've written so far and I needed to get it right for today."

"No gain, without pain, eh!" Mike said in a deep 'over the top' actors voice, whilst stepping forward into the room, then lowering his tone to add, "but let's be honest Buddy a few kids from the west-end aren't going to eat you. I bet they wouldn't even notice if anything was wrong?" Laughing indulgently at his own words.

Vicki turned to face him and lifted her eyes up in despair.

"What's that for?" he asked, as he caught the action.

Totally confused by the look, he turned his head and only then seeing his sister's thunderous expression out of the corner of his eye, he involuntarily took the same step back.

"What the hell do you mean they wouldn't notice anything was wrong?" Rosie snapped. Her mind instantaneously wide-awake and her voice now as clear as a bell, she stepped deliberately round Vicki.

"They aren't stupid, you know! They're good kids with a few differences that's all!" she shook her head, "and just one last thing. What I write, is never wrong!"

"I didn't mean you write things wrong, I was just saying ……."

He backtracked, as he was intelligent enough to know he was just digging a bigger hole for himself, looking at her now glowing face. In this instance, discretion being the better part of valour, he turned quickly back into the hallway and checked his watch.

"Time's getting on. I'll meet you at the car then, shall I!" They heard him call on his way downstairs, "... and hurry up about it!"

Rosie immediately sat back on the lower bed, and knocking the back of her head on the top bunk in the process.

Vicki stood laughing at what had happened, before making her own observations to her best friend.

"Ah come on Rosie, did you see his face, you scared the daylights out of him and he didn't mean anything!"

"Yeh, I know!" she admitted grudgingly, rubbing her head. "A bit like mum and dad, I suppose. As lovely as they all are, they really don't get it, even after all these years. You know last week mum said, they were talking about sending me to agricultural college, so I can get a 'proper' job." Bending two fingers on each hand, she waved them up and down in the air to signify the inverted commas.

"She didn't, really! That's for farmers isn't it?" Vicki's eyes looked up to heaven. "Although, I must admit, to understanding their reasoning. You can't blame them being proud of the fact you have green fingers and their garden is a real picture. You're a miracle worker as far as they are concerned and they can actually see what you can do! Come on Rosie you are Welling's answer to Charlie, oh what's her name? The one on telly!" Trying hard to remember the well known TV gardening presenter.

"Anyone can do what I do in the garden, if they really tried!" she mumbled.

"I doubt that, but I'll go along with you on that one. The fact is that your writing is just way too clever, for want of a better word. They just don't understand how good you are, do they?"

"Duh, you think?"

She got back up and bumped her head, yet again. "Ouch!" Then taking in a deep breath, dipped her head as she rose up and stepped away carefully from the bunk.

"Well, once you have your book published, I bet they will be the first to say, 'I always knew she was a talented writer!' or words to that effect." said like the good friend Vicki was.

"Yeh! You're probably right, but somehow I'd like them to come to that conclusion without having to borrow my kindle to read the actual printed words. Hold that thought, I will have to get it in paperback for my lot, they are so archaic!"

She wandered over to the window still rubbing her head, looking out on to the lawn below. "Anyway, gardening is just a hobby. Ok so I like it, but Vicki, writing is something I have to do!" her voice suddenly filled with emotion.

"I know!" Vicki whispered sympathetically.

"It's a part of me that seems to take over, almost as if it's the other half of me," she turned back and gave her an awkward smile and asked. "Do they think its fun, spending most of my time in front of a damned computer screen? It's really hard work!"

"Yeh and don't you love every minute of it!" her friend said irreverently, but knew more than anyone how hard it was for Rosie to live with her talent.

"Of course I do, but I wouldn't tell them that and you know what! My so called west-end kids know the story backwards and the characters far too well," she boasted proudly, "they would soon tell me if I was wrong!"

Vicki just smiled, whilst she took her own things, hair brush, nail file and nail varnish off the dresser and they joined the nightdress in the rucksack. Then watched as Rosie picked up the three sets of collated pages next to her printer and handing one of the freshly printed copies of the completed chapter to her. Vicki stowed it carefully on top of her clothes and zipped the bag closed.

Looking up, they both laughed.

The two girls were poles apart in every other aspect of their lives, except for their friendship, which bridged all their dissimilarities.

Their mums, Lisa and Diane and her mum's best friend Pam, were friends since all three families moved into Poplar Place, coincidently on the same day 15 years before.

After Rosie's birthday last year, it had been Pam who suggested she should read for a small group of different needs children from the local school, near to where she was the manager of a branch of Senots bookshops in London's Covent Garden.

A couple of months earlier, Pam had set up a reading room, on a mezzanine level, where she provided a quiet haven for her customers to read and relax at leisure. This was where she had gently encouraged Rosie into showcasing her stories of the Springer family and all their adventures.

So for just under a year now, on every other Saturday morning, it was used as, Rosie's Reading Region or the 3R's.

After the first reading, a couple of the parents asked if they could bring along older and younger siblings. Within four sessions word had got round and they had reached 12, if not eager kids at first, at least they were sitting still marginally longer at each visit and on the third every other Saturday, she had a final attentive audience of 14.

It was a special time for Rosie, as she loved to read to her gang (as she called them) and watch their young faces as they got involved with the characters, yet more importantly, began to read books on their own.

An obvious development which raised its head as the readings progressed and something that Pam had championed after about six months was that Rosie should have her work published, so other children could benefit from the tales.

At first Rosie wasn't keen and it had taken a further two months to convince her, that her work was good enough to publish. Pam was now in consultation with a small self-publishing house called Wordplay in Spain. She was good friends with the ex-pat owner and writer Michael Barton, who was helping lots of new authors get their books published after many years of rejections, for most of them.

She even went so far as to volunteer to pay for the printing herself, as she was so convinced Rosie's books would be bestsellers. She had gone this route because she had been working in the book business for years and knew herself how difficult it was to get even a good book published.

"Rose.....ee, move yourself!" Lisa Norton's voice reverberated up the stairwell into the room, stretching her name as she called and made both girls jump, then added "Vicki your mum's just driven up!"

Rosie hurriedly thrust the other two copies of her work into a brightly multicoloured folder, ready to take with her. One was for her grandad Bert and the other one for her to read at Senots.

"OK mum!" she yelled back through the doorway.

"Thanks Lisa" Vicki called at the same time.

"Crap!" they said together.

Looking deliberately round the chaotic room and laughing. They immediately started to straighten their duvets and pillows. Rosie threw clothes into her linen basket and dumped crumpled sheets of paper in the bin, before she picked up her folder again and her shoulder bag. Vicki had already grabbed her rucksack and they made their way out onto the landing.

"Rosie, you do know that your brother is hot don't you?" Vicki threw away the line, heading for the stairs. "When he isn't being dumb that is!"

"Oh, you have got to be kidding me, right!" Rosie stopped dead and looked askew at her friend.

"Don't look at me like that! I'm not the only one! Half the girls in class think he's gorgeous!" she chuckled out loud at Rosie's expression.

Mike had taken to picking both girls up from school in their last week of term. He had returned early from University and drove a classic blue Volkswagen beetle, a gift last year on his birthday from their grandad. Who'd had the car from new, but decided at his then advanced age of 79, he didn't want or need to drive anymore and the fact that his eyes were not as good as they used be, had nothing to do with it, of course!.

"Talking about me again Vicki Giacomelli, that's what I like to hear!"

A voice swung both heads round to face Rosie's twin brother Jack, who was standing outside his room near the top of the stairs and blocking their way.

"In your dreams, she was talking about our older brother. You remember him, the one with the brains!" Rosie sparked back.

"Come off it, he works in a care home with smelly old people, that's not exactly a stepping stone to being another Doctor Miracle!" he sneered.

"Oh grow up, you know as well as we do, it's just work experience until he goes back to Uni, and don't you dare, let mum and dad hear you talking about Sunnymead like that either, you know damn well, Nanny Vi, had excellent care while she was there. Anyway, you can talk! Your room stinks and if mum and dad don't recognise the smell, I do," she took a deliberate breath " and I might just .....!

"Tell them?" Jack sniggered. He was about the same height as Rosie, but almost the same build as their older brother. "You keep your *nose* out of my business!"

The air seemed to crackle round them and seeing what was potentially about to happen, Vicki pushed between the two of them.

"No she wouldn't say anything, but I might Norton," she said firmly. "Get a life, why don't you?"

"I have a life, thank you!" he jeered, but still didn't move.

"So do toads, but you don't hear them bragging about it either." Rosie's pithy response came from behind Vicki's back.

"Anyway, I have to get downstairs today, not tomorrow." Vicki made to move forward. "I'm working at mum's salon this morning and she's outside in the car waiting for me. Maybe I should call her?" Leaving the sentence open, but putting her hand in her pocket and drawing out her iphone, making her intention obvious.

Jack slinked back, a look of pure loathing crossing his face. Diane was a formidable woman with bright natural auburn hair and a temper to match. Remembering only too well, the run-in with her just two nights earlier, when she had found him at the top of the road, well after midnight and literally frog-marched him back to his house, before he had a chance to leg it.

"I better let Buddy and Giac, (making it sound like jerk), go then hadn't I!" his mouth curled in a surly grin as both girls swiftly pushed passed him and headed down the stairs.

"What is it with him Rosie, he's definitely getting worse!" her friend whispered. "I'm assuming it's cannabis in his room?"

"Haven't got a clue, and I have no idea what it smells like anyway!" she sighed "He's been more secretive than ever lately. You must have heard him talking on his mobile late last night, he does that nearly all the time, now. I just don't understand him anymore."

"I can see that," she agreed, "but, not knowing what pot smells like, is nothing to be proud of Rosie! You really have to get out more!"

They were still laughing when they reached a bright and spacious extension that was the kitchen/diner, to find Rosie's mum Lisa doing the ironing and singing along with a DVD, on the TV at the end of the breakfast bar.

Rosie and Vicki shared a smile at what the DVD was playing, as it was Lisa's all-time favourite film 'Love & Miss Behavin' the musical karaoke version. Seeing the girls in the doorway she quickly put the film on hold and still holding the iron, turned back to them, noting their amused look at what she was watching yet again, but made no comment.

"Hi, you two! Rosie, tell Pam I'll see her for lunch Tuesday, will you love. They changed my shift on Monday at the museum and I forgot to ring her last night. Give Grandad my love and tell him it's lamb tomorrow for lunch, I know he can't get his teeth into beef now, so that should make him happy." Even what she said, was in a sing-song way.

"Will do, mum!" Rosie responded and wandered over to the French doors, which were open wide, and even this early in the morning, bringing the sunlight right through into the house.

"Hi Dad!" Rosie moved to one side, as her dad walked in through the doors carrying, a half-finished bacon sandwich in one hand and a huge mug decorated with 'Buddy's Dad♥s his garden', half full of tea.

"Hello you two, finally found your way down have you? Your breakfasts are on the worktop." Dave nodded in the direction of the breakfast bar and the girls rushed to get their own hot bacon sandwiches wrapped in foil and a paper napkin. He had made them earlier, so they could eat on the way out, knowing both would be demolished, before reaching their respective lifts.

"Thanks Dad." Picking up both the sandwich and carton of orange juice, Rosie passed Vicki hers, then snatched her recharged smart phone off the worktop and put it in her pocket, before picking up her own.

"Thanks Dave, I love your bacon butties!" Vicki turned back giving Dave a broad smile.

"That's because your mother can't cook, but she's a marvel at burning!" he laughed at his own joke.

"Isn't that the truth?" The girls said in unison, slipping the napkin and carton into their bags, tore the foil off and started to eat their favourite every other Saturday breakfast, as they made their way out of the room.

"Oh, and say hello to Diane for me, Vicki." Lisa said, as she pressed the play button again on the remote and waving the iron at them both as a farewell salute. "Have a nice day sweetheart and be good!" and within the same breath began singing at the top of her off key voice to "Leave London in winter."

"Hope your kids enjoy today's chapter Buddy," her father said.

Rosie gave her mum a wave and called, "Me too!" To her dad and at the sound of a car horn outside, they quickly made their way down the hallway and out the front door.

"I love your house and your mum is so funny!" Vicki mumbled, as both were munching their sandwich and walking down the path.

"Funny ha ha, or funny peculiar? Although I must admit she does seem a bit distracted lately! But Mum's mum, I'm sure she's good, and at least she didn't mention agricultural college again." Rosie sighed, grateful for the reprieve, whilst chomping through her sandwich.

"Look, stop worrying Rosie, it isn't gonna happen!"

They had reached the gate and could see Mike talking to Diane, as she waited in her car further down the road and Vicki opened it, holding the sandwich and her rucksack in one hand.

"It isn't their fault they just don't see it and look I'm sure they'll come round some day." She elbowed Rosie in the ribs with her free arm, before transferring the sandwich back and looking down the road to where Mike and Diane were.

"By the way have you mentioned Jack, to Mike?" Taking another bite, into the nearly finished breakfast.

"Are you crazy?" Rosie looked incredulously at Vicki, "Not unless I want to start World War III, between them. It's bad enough that Mike has to stay at Uncle

Rob's during the holidays, because Jack packed up everything of his and insisted it went in the loft when Mike left. It's not fair for him to have to deal with dickhead's behaviour as well, now he's home. He definitely has enough on his plate with University and it is positively for mum and dad to sort out." She murmured softly as they were now within striking distance of the man himself.

"Hello girls!" Diane called from inside the car "Come on Vicki get a move on, I've got a 9:15 perm coming in and she's always early and," checking her wrist watch, "we are definitely running late!"

Starting up the silver/cream mini, Vicki scooted round to the passenger side and got in, throwing her rucksack on the back seat.

Diane leant out of her window and called out.

"I can't wait to read Vicki's chapter tomorrow, Rosie. You do a good job love, I'm getting a real addict and I'm really proud to know you!"

With that she gave a quick beep on the car horn, and shooting off at speed, up to the main road with Vicki's arm waving goodbye out the side window, still with a crust of her sandwich in hand.

"Me too!" Came a familiar voice behind her "Really proud!"

"Honest to god Mike, you made me jump!" Rosie exclaimed as she turned to face her older brother, and hit him on the arm making some of her sandwich fall on the pavement. "Well, if you're so proud, why the hell don't you read any of my stories?"

She bent down and picked up the bread and small piece of bacon and threw it over the hedge into their garden.

"Who said I never read any?"

He got in his side of the car and she opened the passenger door, throwing her own bag into the back and after pulling the front seat forward, climbed into her spot on the back seat behind him.

Mike leaned over and closed the door before starting off, following Diane's more modern mini, but not at such an urgent pace.

"Nobody!" her tone admitted. "But you never asked to read them either?"

She finished her own sandwich as quickly as she could and put the foil neatly folded into the backseat rubbish bag and took the carton of OJ out of her bag, stuck in the straw and slurped the juice, right next to his ear.

"I've had my juice already thanks!" Mike smiled as he looked up at her in the rear view mirror. "Oh, come on Buddy, I've read every chapter since the first week silly girl! Grandad sends me his copy when he finishes it and it's me that keeps them safe up in Cambridge. He's always worried mum would put them all in the dustbin, when she goes round his place, on one of her cleaning forays."

They had both lost a number of things to the dreaded dustbin, when their mother was in cleaning mode, so what he said made perfect sense.

The car stopped at the top of the road and Mike indicated right, waiting for a bus to pass before turning and carried on down the street indicating right again. Reaching the turn-off into the beginning of a crisscross of roads in a small housing estate, where they would finally end up in a cul de sac and their grandad's small bungalow.

"In my, not so humble opinion, I think you are really good Buddy. I'm in awe, and I'm sure that's why I never commented!" he was glad his face was turned away from her, as he blushed at what he said. "It's hard to admit that your little sister knows lots of words that I sometimes have to look up in the dictionary!"

"Yeh, thata be right! This from the man now at University who got four A* AA levels." she said proudly, not mentioning the additional five GCSE A*'s and three A's he had earned when he was younger.

"They my love, as you know were for Chemistry, Physics, Maths and Human Biology, not much of a story in them, now is there?" he smiled shrewdly. He was studying Medicine at Cambridge University and loving it.

"Point taken! So which characters do you like the best?" Rosie asked him, and smiling to herself. Mike was her hero and ever since she was a little girl, she had thought he was a superstar. She missed him a lot while he was away.

"Just checking to see if I really did read it?" Mike chuckled. His baby sister was growing up.

"Well maybe?" She didn't disagree that she was, and put her empty carton in the rubbish bag.

"Ok, I love Maddison, there you go, I've said it! She is so bright and bubbly and of course Alfie, reminds me of me when I was young, but lately I have a soft spot for Laura and Paul! Especially now, as they have to study so hard for the competition. You really do have a fantastic imagination Buddy, just thinking up all the things they have to do. Where on earth do they come from?"

"Honestly, I don't know! It's just here in my mind." she quickly dismissed his question shaking her head, "and you never said a word, I thought you didn't care!"

"Of course I care dummy, but I suppose it's my age.

You have to remember, us guys are a bit lame at the emotional contact bit, until they finally get to …. well give me a number, why don't you?"

By then they had nearly reached their destination and could see Grandad Bert step forward from his front porch, always the early bird, waiting for his lift to the train station.

She kissed the back of her brother's hair and then hit his shoulder. "Yeh, I had noticed and I think it might be 65 or even a bit more?"

"Hey Bud, not that old!" Mike chuckled, as he drove to the bottom of the blocked end and turned round, stopping the car in front of Bert, then leaning over to open the passenger door for him and the old man slipped into his seat.

She smiled as she sat back and hugged her bag to her chest, content in the afterglow of Mike's praise.

"Hi, Grandad!" Rosie said, and realising he wouldn't hear her clearly, she moved forward again, so her face was in line with his ear and she wouldn't have to repeat herself.

"Hello you two," The pensioner smiled, slamming the car door and both Mike and Rosie felt the vibration go through them. "See you're taking care of Bluebell! (his name for his old car). Are these new seat covers Mike?"

"Yeh, grandad, got them in Bexleyheath last week. Snazzy enough for you?" Mike responded, as he had replaced them with exactly the same colour and pattern as the originals.

"Not bad son, nice and cosy," he moved his thin octogenarian body from side to side, testing the comfort factor. "Well let's get this wagon rolling, Mike. Buddy and I have business in town."

"See what I mean, we never get old!" Mike smiled back at Rosie, as he started the engine and moved Bluebell forward and towards the end of the road.

"Grandad, how are you feeling today?" Rosie asked, she was always concerned about him since her grandmother had died, a little over a year before.

"Good thanks Buddy, never felt better. Well apart from the knee, still giving me a bit of gyp, but I don't suppose I can complain." He rubbed his left knee to indicate where the pain was.

"Just getting ready to play Long John Silver in panto aren't you grandad?" Mike said cheekily.

"Don't take the Mickey, Mike!" he smiled at his eldest grandson "It's not nice to make personal comments to us old un's!"

"Grandad, are you coming back to the book shop straight after you finish lunch with Aunty Lool? I'm only asking as this week's chapter is longer than usual, so I think I might be a bit later than normal."

"Me sister is fine, in small doses, Buddy! So I'll come at the usual time if it's alright with you. I'd rather sit in the store with Pam and people-watch, for a while," her grandad replied then asked. "Been working hard, have you girly?"

"Yes, but it's been really interesting, especially now the competition has started, you'll enjoy this chapter!" she grinned at Mike's head. "Both of you!"

"I told her, I read your copy." Mike informed him.

"About time! Should have done that, ages ago. She needs to know people close are interested, even if you are away at school." he stated.

"It's Cambridge University, grandad!" Calling it school just didn't cut it for Mike.

"Still a bloody school though, ain't it, still learning,

just in an older, posher building, so don't you get uppity with me, son!" The old man ordered.

"No grandad, wouldn't dream of it!" Both, Mike and Rosie beamed broadly at the old man´s words.

"Too ruddy true!" Bert smiled, and more than happy to have the last word. "How's your uncle Rob doing by the way? Is my youngest still seeing that divorcee from round the corner?" he winked at Rosie, as he asked.

"Yes he is. Hilary's nice and she can cook as good as Nan did." Mike indicated left and stopping at a zebra crossing to let half a dozen young boys in football kit, cross and heading for the park across the road. "I miss her apple crumble though!"

"So do I son, so do I!" Bert said. "Still at least we don't have to worry about her apple pie."

"No, you're right, her pastry wasn't feather light, I agree!" Mike nodded.

He and Rosie screwed up their faces, remembering how unyielding their grandmother's pastry was.

"Feather light it wasn't. I'd say it was more like a blooming building brick, me self!" he leaned back in his seat, remembering a bygone age and his wife of 50 years. "My Vilie just didn't have that light pastry touch, but her crumbles however, were legendary!"

Rosie just grinned at the pair of them. She loved them both so much and enjoyed listening to their banter back and forth.

Time flew and within just a few minutes they had reached their destination and stopped in the road, just outside Welling railway station.

"Here we are, you two! Remember, I don't finish until late today, so I won't be able pick you up!"

"That's all right son, Buddy and me will catch the bus, otherwise we like to walk, don't we girly?" Bert answered for both of them.

"I like the bus better, but if it's a nice afternoon, I don't mind the walk." Rosie admitted graciously.

"Good!" Again, glad he was having that last word.

They both got out of the car and waved, as Mike honked a response on the car horn, heading down to the traffic lights, Sunnymead Old People's Home, and work.

"C'mon Buddy, the train's due in 10 minutes." Bert took her arm and marched into the station.

Pointing to his watch, had them walking quickly to get their tickets.

Bert enjoyed his every other Saturday trips to London with his favourite granddaughter, especially as she had a talent he was so proud of.

Chapter 3

Tom and Kristy

As Kristy finished her account of events from the previous day, she hadn't realised how tightly she was grasping Tom's hand within her own and slowly relaxed the hold. Wishing he would say something to either confirm or invalidate the statement she had just made.

Tom sat staring for a while at the back of his driver's head, thinking distractedly that his friend could do with a haircut.

"Well, I admit everything you have told me points to it being one of the Lost, but you can understand my concerns Kris. I have to be very sure of the facts, before taking this task on. You know full well, I am not here for sightseeing on the London Eye!" he turned towards her and asked her slowly. "Are you certain that the information is legitimate?"

"Positive!" she nodded in response.

"You didn't see the actual speakers. It could have been planned, to draw me here at this particular time."

Which in this instance would not have been implausible?

"I never thought of that, but no, I don't think so. It was pure fluke that I overheard what I did yesterday and it was so vague, only someone who is Symm, could have put two and two together. To be honest at first I didn't get it myself, but there were so many familiar coincidences with what I knew and it grew quickly into something more concrete," she rummaged in her handbag for a tissue and blew her nose, "and I know the voices, I've lived next door to one of them for a year, remember, and they were speaking the truth as they knew it, I have no doubts on that!"

Neither spoke for some minutes, as Tom digested the information and Kristy waited for his verdict at her disclosure.

"As we both know this isn't an exact science! I shouldn't even contemplate continuing investigating, unless of course, I have a lot more time and information. Here's the rub, I don't have a lot of that, either way. I always knew there were 'Lost' out there, but it seemed like they were in a fairy tale, and it is almost impossible to recognise any of them here." Tom was speaking his thoughts out loud, rather than to her.

"But it could be?" Kristy was taken aback at the suggestion that it might not. "You must have seen a lot of the other existing sentinels over time, so it could be possible for you to recognise a new one," she pleaded. "Please try!"

Fortunately, Tom's career in rescuing was as single minded as his father's before him, and he took pride in having a hand in liberating the vulnerable within the Symm.

He sighed "Oh I don't know, the timing is off, isn't it? To be honest, I'm not used to winging it, as Dad does all of the planning for getting back one of the Stolen! I already have so many other responsibilities and this additional venture is on top of everything else....." and left the sentence unfinished.

He sat up straight and faced her.

"Until a couple of days ago, Kristy, I was not even sure of the location chosen for the selection of the new influx of the Cliquey. The competition is my first encounter with the actual process, and it took me a while to figure out, albeit a little late, that it must be here in England." He sounded disgruntled at the admission. "It is not altogether a coincidence that I am here, too! I should have been more discerning!"

"That's hardly your fault" she exclaimed loyally, "You can only do your best!"

"Thank you sweetheart, for those kind words, but in the last couple of days I have seen an inordinate number of new little gems, that I haven't recognised and all of the contestants have excelled in the selection process. It's a huge gathering, and I counted an inconceivable amount that have come here to watch the competition!"

He unconsciously tried to stand up in the moving vehicle, suddenly wanting to pace, but within milliseconds his seat belt held him firmly in his seat, just as the car came to a stop at traffic lights. After a short pause he resumed speaking again.

"We are going away from the point here Kris! By what you are telling me, once I have confirmed it's genuine, and I cannot guarantee I can! I will have my work cut out, finding out its history." he nodded sagely. "The other real danger of course, is that someone will already be on its trail. Not something I would want happening just yet, I'm far from ready and you know as well as I do, it's imperative I find it before either a squirrel or, heaven forbid, a magpie gets wind of it," he emphasised, "it will be totally defenceless against their tactics!"

"I know that, but no, although this has been ongoing for a while, I just don't think it has been discovered yet. Although you're right it is only a matter of time!" she shook her head and then took back his hand, "which is why I knew it was urgent. I'm so sorry that you only know where it is going to be today, I was hoping I could manage to get more than just the time and place."

Her look of desolation knocked Tom for six, as it was now obvious, she was blaming herself and that hurt.

"Hey, that should be enough!" Being more than generous, as he stared passed her and out on to the London streets through the tinted windows.

"It'll be just fine, I'm sure we will find it, but it does beg the question. What the hell do I do with it then? Turning back to her, "By the way does Harley know where we need to go, would Ellie have told him?."

"Harley? Oh don't tell me!" she suddenly looked up at him, shaking her head, "... and you must be Davidson!" I thought Lewis and Hamilton, last year were bad enough!"

His expression reflected that the name combination was not common knowledge and she smiled broadly.

"But yes, I should imagine Ellie would have kept Walt in the loop. She wasn't really happy about me coming here anyway!"

"Oh, so why did she let you?" he made a face.

A moment ticked by before Kristy disclosed her cousin's words.

"What she actually said was, 'Better to be out there doing something, rather than sitting at home worrying that if you hadn't done it, chaos might ensue!'," she screwed up her face as she quoted verbatim. "Then I made her promise not to tell her dear beloved husband, where I was until after we reached the airport."

"She certainly has a way with words, does Ellie!"

Tom ran his fingers again through his hair and leaning forward, pressed a button that lowered the partition between the two men, making eye contact with Walt in the rear view mirror.

"It seems we have to make a detour to Covent

Garden, before lunch!" he announced.

"I know, I'm sorry Tom, I meant to tell you of the added company! I've already spoken to Ellie, she's just leaving home and will meet us at the Portrait Gallery to stay with Kris and we should be there in about 20 minutes."

"Not your fault Splash, our next project isn't due until tomorrow or even later anyway!"

He was hoping to have a few hours to himself, but this was only a small spanner in the works. Anyway it might not even be anything to worry about and raising the panel again, he turned back to his sister.

"All sorted then!"

Kris stretched over and gave him a grateful kiss on the cheek.

"Before you say anything else, I know I can't come with you, even though I really want to. Anyway I haven't told you the best news. I have my first real paying job, I'm an assistant, to the make-up assistant," she grinned at the title. "I'm going on a photo shoot for 'Fashion: Picture Perfect' (naming a magazine, as if Tom would readily know the name, which he didn't) in Trafalgar Square, isn't it fantastic?" Kristy looked ecstatic.

"Well done you, a proper job," he actually looked envious for a fleeting moment, "and of course, it will be safer if we are not seen together."

"Good that's settled then!" Kristy added, "and let's face it Tom, you are the only one who could recognise this little gem anyway and Walt is probably the best person, apart from you, who would be aware of a squirrel or a magpie hanging around," she added confidently.

He tipped his head to one side.

"Quite right, I am unique!" his words heavy with irony, "but you know what, Kris! Something about this doesn't make sense. It's almost as if this particular Lost, wants to be found!"

"No I don't believe so! I thought about it too, but honestly I just think that it really doesn't know that it's lost," she said in amazement. "Why would it?"

"True, but I've only ever helped those who were stolen, and now you have directed me to a Lost, which is a whole different ballgame! I can only hope I will be able to warn it in time!"

Tom was well aware that the, ignorance is bliss, theory might work for some, but for one of the Lost, as they were not aware of 'The Symm' it could be precarious, to say the least.

"Luckily I made sure I wasn't followed and no one knows I'm in the country," smiling broadly he added, "and it is most fortunate that our grandad's sister has such a handsome looking son. So even if anyone was watching the airports, I still have the advantage!"

They smiled at each other and settled down in their seats for a couple of minutes, before Kristy spoke again.

"Tom, just one question. Why do I keep seeing a kaleidoscope of coloured dots in my head? Ever since I overheard the conversation, I've have a funny sensation going through me every time I think of this Lost, it makes my heart flutter as if I have a connection."

"Well, maybe you are feeling the gems presence! With so many in the area, it would be overwhelming, especially when you are 18. I remember last year I began noticing an assortment of sensations too, and we know there are lots of colours. I've seen gems in the rarest pinks, or darkest violet, greens and blues of different shades and there are the different ambers and browns," he was thinking out loud. "I don't think I will ever get over how many colours there actually are!"

"I can only guess at that one, but I expect you will recognise, the one I mentioned." She murmured confidently.

"I still can't promise!" he whispered, "but I will do my very best to try!"

"Please, keep yourself safe." She felt the tears rise to burn the backs of her eyes at the thought of its outcome being otherwise, and smiled as he gave a short nod.

"Thank you!" she whispered back.

Safe! How did he know if he would be out of harm's way on this one, as most of the time he didn't even know if he would be alive at the end of a rescue, least of all safe. Unfortunately it wasn't something he could acknowledge to her, what else could he do? It was anyone's guess, how it was going to pan out and he'd had extremely close calls before, as she had seen for herself.

It was part and parcel of the role he had chosen, he supposed. Finding one of the Lost was important, and actually imperative to their way of life. He had to try. What choice did he have? None, none whatsoever!

"Oh, I forgot to ask, how are the wedding plans going, by the way?" Kristy said, bringing him back to the here and now with a bang.

Grateful for the change of subject, Tom smiled warmly.

"Let's say, I'm glad I'm here, rather than in Norway, at this moment in time." He grinned back.

"That good eh?" his sister commented.

"An understatement, Mum is causing havoc with all the preparations, but I'm glad I'm not with Nicola, she says her mum is twice as bad as ours!"

Grinning Kristy repeated the age old family saying.

"Well, 'It is our Symm to carry the burden of the world!' quote unquote and anyway it's the end of an era." Her future sister-in-law was everything Kristy wanted to be: brainy, independent and beautiful. She could see no bumps in the road for them relationship wise.

"Honestly Kris, I'm terrified. I still can't believe it!"

For the first time since the engagement, he was admitting his feelings.

"Stop worrying, Nicola is perfect for you and just remember that you only have a very short time limit. You're leaving it really late as it is!"

"I know! Circumstances have made it difficult, you know that!" he nodded guiltily.

After that, the conversation settled down to the mundane, trading family and friend's gossip, along with what wedding preparations had been arranged for the following month. Half an hour later, traffic being what it was in London, they finally reached Trafalgar Square.

Walt stopped the car at the mouth of Irving Street, off Charing Cross Road and helped Kristy to retrieve her makeup case, hidden from sight under a blanket, from the boot, before asking her for Ellie's spare car key fob, which he knew was the only way she could have entered the car.

Returning the key she gave him an, 'I'm sorry' smile, kissed his cheek and then turned round and walked away.

Walt took a moment to watch as she headed round the corner of the Portrait Gallery. Smiling gratefully as he saw Ellie, slipping unobtrusively into the mainstream of people behind Kristy, and giving him no indication that she knew, or even saw him. Once out of view he spotted a traffic warden descending on him for parking on a double yellow line, and immediately re-entered the car. Within seconds he was heading up the road towards Leicester Square tube station and then turned east to Covent Garden.

Tom had stayed in the car, thinking deeply about the last 60 minutes and trying desperately to plan the next step.

He already knew it was dangerous for him to be there, but knowing didn't change the fact that he could be nowhere else under the circumstances. He had expected to have had time to plan a strategy with Walt and his uncle Trevor, on how they would take back the new Stolen and he hoped this Lost, was not going to cause too much time and trouble.

What he was now about to do, unscheduled as it was, rarely happened in his life, although sometimes when he was on a rescue, it was scary, but then again also exciting. On this thought, a tingling went through him of trepidation and anticipation, both of which were certainly thrilling sensations; albeit not something he should dwell on now.

Within minutes the Audi headed down the backstreets to Covent Garden and Walt conveniently found a parking space just being vacated by a red Clio, the young owner of which gave him a thumbs up as he went down the road. Once parked up, he lowered the partition and turned to Tom.

"Remind me again how long have you got now before your 20th birthday." Walt asked.

"Just over four months." Tom smiled philosophically.

Their birthdays were in fact 12 years apart to the

day and both knew it.

"I hope me 'art can take the strain!"

The ex-bodyguard commented as he placed a New York initialled baseball cap, low over his eyes and handed a similar one to his passenger. They then exited the vehicle and Walt secured the car, with both men proceeding to walk down a side street and which led directly into the Covent Garden area itself.

"Hey, just remember Splash it's me, they're after!" he threw his arm across the older man's shoulders, "I thought you realised, I'm the prize, not you!"

"Really, I could never see the difference me'self." Walt patted his coat pocket reassuring Tom of his loyalty, "but Betsy and I, are always at your service anyway Majestet, or is it still Sir Goldilocks?"

"One day I will come back to haunt you for that name, but at this moment in time, I am really grateful for you being here, Walt!" Tom responded with a genuine smile.

Walt countered the compliment by slapping his own hand on the younger man's back. He was now part of the family since marrying Tom's cousin Ellie last year and had previously, not only been this full grown boy's minder for six years, but his faithful friend. They had made a good working team over time, even though Walt had moved to London and Tom rarely left Norway, both men now realised how much they missed one another.

Talking while walking, Tom explained exactly what he needed Walt to do. He didn't have to recap Kristy's account that she had given to him, as he knew only too well Ellie would have relayed this information to her husband, but it was still crucial to form some sort of strategy and it felt good to discuss the pros and cons of the operation, just like old times!

Chapter 4

Rosie and Bert

Rosie handed Bert his copy of her chapter, as they stood waiting on the platform and just before a woman hurried up to them, a little out of breath.

"Hello, Mrs Walsh" Rosie's warm smile, welcoming the older lady as she stopped beside them.

"Blooming buses, decided to play at who can go the slowest, this morning." She wasn't moaning exactly, just philosophical at her tardiness.

Rosie and Bert travelled up to London on the same time train, as Mrs Walsh, every other week. Although the lady herself travelled up every weekend; to help in her daughter and son-in-law´s café, just off Haymarket. Her every other Saturday, meeting with Bert and Rosie had become a regular joy for her.

"So another chapter finished then?" she smiled knowingly at the teen.

"Yeh! I´ll let you know when the book's published," she replied cheekily.

"Oh, Rosie, published well goodness me. I didn't realise you were publishing it, congratulations. You must be dead proud, Bert?"

"I´m proud of all my kids!" he said, albeit to himself, as the two of them were now chatting, and mainly about Mrs Walsh's new baby granddaughter, Emily.

The 9:34 train to Charing Cross sailed into the station, stopping with the carriage doors right in front of Bert, who pressed the open button and escorted the two ladies on board, and following them to their seats.

Settled down, the two ladies conversation did not stop until three stations further on, then the talk suddenly ceased and both turned to look at Bert.

"What?" he stared back at them sternly.

"Your turn grandad!" Rosie smiled at him.

"Well, if you two insist!" he smiled back at them both, and joining in on their usual Saturday banter.

He was always busy, seeing a selected band of gradually depleting friends and going to adult learning classes.

He was getting really good at Spanish, most of the words he could get, the accent he couldn't, OAP yoga, good for his muscles. He also took a drawing and watercolour class too, but only because he was the only man in it and he enjoyed the company of the ten old dears who also attended, as they treated him like royalty. He thoroughly revelled in the attention especially as they vied to give him the best of their advice accompanied of course, by their even better, home-made cakes and since his Vilie had passed away, there was nothing keeping him at home anymore, anyway!

His rendition of his week ended just before they reached Waterloo East station, and his bus to the Elephant & Castle where he would visit his ten years older sister, Lily (although all the grandchildren, for some long ago reason, called her Auntie Lool).

Before leaving Buddy however, he had once again confirmed their arrangement to meet again later at Senots, as he liked to escort her all the way home. Rosie carried on in the now, not so crowded carriage to the next stop, Charing Cross with Mrs Walsh and coming out of the station, they said their goodbyes.

Rosie waved, then turned right and made her way

into her favourite restaurant just off the Strand, for her regular two weekly, strawberry milkshake. Then continued on the short walk down the Strand to Covent Garden, where her every other Saturday job, began.

Senots was a smallish, but well thought out establishment, set in one of the rows of buildings in the centre of Covent Garden, with one entry/exit door and one exit only door on opposite sides of the building.

Pam had made every inch a used space and even Rosie's Reading Region on the mezzanine level was quite cramped, especially now that the children had reached 14 in number and a full house this week. This didn't seem to put them off, in fact she thought that they actually enjoyed the cosiness, it was more like reading at home and didn't have a normal library atmosphere.

Just an hour later, Rosie was settled in an olive green overstuffed armchair at the back of the 3R's and in front of her gang of young appraisers, placing a huge cup of milky tea on the side table, which would be left, and stone cold, before she finished her reading.

She had spent half an hour chatting with Pam, giving her mother's message, and although had no news on the progress with the publishers, they chatted about their week, before Rosie was ready to start.

"Right, everyone settle down, Jessica, please take that chewing gum out before I start, you know the rules and Duggy go sit on the blue cushion and let Carmen sit on the red chair. I've had Pam fix it so it doesn't squeak now, so she can jiggle as much as she likes. OK!"

Carmen had trouble sitting still for any length of time, and seemed to settle better in a chair, than on a cushion, but never got there in time to find a free chair for herself.

Duggy gave the little girl a high five, as he vacated his seat with no argument and he sat down on her cushion.

"Oh thanks Rosie!." The tiniest girl of the group climbed into the largest chair, her auburn curly hair pushed back with a pink sparkly headband and she brought her little legs under her, and she looked as if Christmas had come early, her face beaming back at the young woman in front.

Smiling to herself, Rosie scanned the group whilst taking out the typed pages from their usual place in her folder, as she had done every second and fourth Saturday for the last 11 months (excluding holidays). She deliberately took her time to allow for the restlessness to stop and as she shuffled the pages straight, she looked over to the top at the variously shaped and coloured eager young faces

She still enjoyed reading to them, even though she hadn't been at all willing at first. She knew Pam had manoeuvred her into accepting the challenge, working with this small group called "BOOTE-OK" (Best Out Of The Extra-Ordinary Kids), who were a real eclectic mix, but after all this time she admitted to herself, she wouldn't be anywhere else. The ones, who had been there at the beginning, were some who found reading a challenge, but now the number had increased as siblings became involved, it was just like family, everyone at a different level, but Rosie's stories brought them all together, nicely.

"One last thing …., has everyone been to the loo?" She tried not to grin at this question. It was her usual final appeal, and an immediate unanimous yes, in a mixture of defined and lacklustre replies came from this week's full group, now sitting around her.

"Good! Now we all know Gracie and Max were luckily enough to go on holiday to Florida for three weeks and they need to catch up on what happened in Summer's - Chapter 5."

She turned and looked around the faces in front of her.

"OK, now let's see who will be able to give the gist of what was in that last one, so we can remind ourselves what the story is about."

Before anyone had a chance to put up their hands, Rosie zeroed in on a pretty Asian girl of about 12 years of age, a couple of cushions away.

"Narinder, how about you?" she asked.

This petit girl was the shyest of the group, but over the months they had been together, she was blossoming and Rosie was determined that today, would be her graduation into the mainstream ensemble.

Beautiful brown eyes looked widely back at Rosie and she winked at her, making the little girl relax her fear and replaced it quickly with a broad smile, then she nodded.

"I think I can remember," she voiced her soft reply.

"Of course you can, and I'm sure that the rest of the team will help out, if you don't. Won't we guys?"

Her hand turned up and moved her fingers back and forward several times to indicate a 'come-on' movement to encourage a positive response.

"Sure," said several voices.

"No problem," others said.

Enough answered, to prompt Narinder to stand and thread her way over to where Rosie sat. When she got there, she leant rather than sat on the arm of Rosie's chair and the usual spot for this part of the reading. Her face was pale, as she looked around nervously, but

Rosie's hand crept over and came to rest on hers, giving the young girl, enough courage to start.

"Well, everything was so exciting for Laura, and you know she won her place at the Seasons Global Academy competition several weeks ago. She and Paul were the only two candidates from the whole of the UK and as they came from the same school, it was the first time ever that this had happened. They were in the news all over the world, especially as Paul was the second youngest competitor too and they had to travel round to tell the UK what had happened. They went to all the major cities, like Edinburgh, Belfast, Cardiff and lots more, I can't remember the names of all of them, but it was a lot." She turned her head to Rosie to see if she was doing alright.

"Well done Narinder," smiling back at her and urging her to continue, "go on sweetheart."

"Well, Paul was in a really bad mood when he got back from touring. He didn't like the travelling as much as Laura did, so he asked Maddison to help him with practising his low profile selections, for his assessment. He was at it for ages in her back garden, because he wasn't concentrating. When he finished, after he had managed to do them all perfectly, they went for a walk down to the boating lake in Damson Park. That was where he asked Maddison if she would write to him at Rainbow House, it was the Academy's nickname, if he got a place there. She said yes, and they kissed."

A sigh came up from the girls, while the boys made a resounding yuck sound or thereabouts, and Rosie put a finger to her lips for quiet.

"Oh, I missed the best bit, I should never have gone on holiday!" 13 year old Gracie wailed, her face wilting visibly with disappointment and everyone laughed, until

Rosie called for quiet again.

"Anyway!" Narinder continued boldly, "Laura and Paul had to go up to the huge Seasons Global Hotel in town, the night before the competition and to get them signed in and they were really nervous. They had dinner in the hotel's posh restaurant with Paul's parents and met some of the other competitors, but didn't have much time to talk, because they had to go to bed early. I think that was all?" Looking back at Rosie, her little face unsure if it was or not.

"You haven't said about Alfie and what a pain he was, because he was bored that day. You also forgot that he found that dagger by the lake." Joe called out.

"Oh, sorry!" Disappointed she had missed something, she gamely carried on, "Yes well! Alfie was, as Joe said, a bit annoyed, because Paul didn't take much notice of him. So all day he sneakily watched Maddison and Paul as he worked at his competition pieces, and then followed them down to the lake. By then he was even more bored, but didn't know what to do with himself and when he saw they were going to kiss, he turned round ready to go home, only to trip over a large stone hitting his head on the way down and nearly drowned in the shallow water of the lake. But when the cold water had scrambling out, he saw the handle of a very old dagger poking out of the mud"

"Was he alright?" Max asked.

"Yeh, course he was!" answered Jess.

"He just got all muddy" called Kevin in the front.

"......and the dagger had a black shiny handle with a dove engraved on it too!" As another descriptive phase was thrown into the mix from Lacy-ann, at the back.

"The blade was huge!" Joe pitched in.

"No it wasn't! Rosie said it was curved, not big!"

Another voice corrected, which sounded very much like Kevin again.

"Well, it could have been huge and curved." Joe added sulkily.

"Guys, this is Narinder's rendition, not yours! You are only helping her...... right?" Rosie stopped them before the helpful information, got too out of hand.

"Right!" A few called back.

"Sorry Rindy, you carry on." Lacy-ann said. "Don't take no notice of them lot."

"OK, thank you. Yes, it looked really old and dirty, so he took it home, washed it in the bathroom, and then hid it in his room, in his secrets box. Because of the dove motif, he went to find out if it was in his lost treasure book and see who the dagger might have belonged to."

She stopped her narrative, looking out to her audience, she scanned the group and said proudly.

"It belonged to the Earl of Bexley's family and was lost in the battle of yellow-time many, many, years before!" Then turned to Rosie and asked, "Did I miss anything else?"

"No that was about right, except for finding the dagger bit." A sulky voice came from the front.

"Joe, that's enough!" Rosie warned softly, and turned back to her storyteller. "Well done Narinder that was just great for a first attempt. A round of applause you people. You all know how difficult this is!"

Narinder pushed away from her place and went back to her flowered cushion on the floor, flushed with praise and enthusiastic hand claps.

"So now we can all follow the story, are we ready?"

Smiling as they all nodded in agreement and taking the first page off the pile, she nestled down in her own armchair.

"It's a bit longer than usual, as there is an awful lot going on and I didn't want to leave anything out, so we might have to have a drink and biscuit break halfway through, alright with you?" she asked.

"Yeh, Cool!" came the consensus of replies.

"Then I shall begin".... and she started reading the latest chapter of her book 'Summer' to them.

Chapter 5

The Book

Summer - Chapter 6 – Rainbow House

The Seasons Global University Auditorium was huge, (*as big as the O^2 or a small football stadium. Rosie informed them in a stage whisper*) and in Maddison's eyes, she had never seen anything so wonderful. The journey from their home had taken a little over an hour and her mum Jackie, dad Stan, with her brother Alfie, were as excited as she was.

Laura was already there, of course, having made the journey with Paul and his parents the evening before to register and stay overnight in the multi-storey 1,800 roomed, Seasons Global Hotel, to prepare for the competition.

Paul's parents, Ron and Janis Ray, had decided to make a night of it staying up in town, having dinner with the two contestants and then afterwards, went on to see the gardens around the hotel and auditorium.

The following morning, like clockwork, the Ray's had met all the Springer's at the designated meeting place, the rendezvous arranged well in advance by Ron and Stan.

They all congregated outside the lobby of the Seasons 'Rainbow 7' entrance, as it was the last rainbow in the series. This proved to be the easiest location of all, mainly because the puddle, just to the right of the entrance, had multi-coloured balls rolling along in the seven coloured rainbow channels and ended at Rainbow 7, where the queue was routed around it. This allowed the general public to enter the building with a modicum of decorum in pairs and not en masse, like the other six manic entrances.

As Maddison and Alfie waited their turn, they became mesmerized watching as each ball dropped and then disappeared in what appeared to be a golden pond of water, although it had no obvious depth. It did however fix their interest as it seemed so magical.

Within a short time of queuing, their entire group entered the building and inside the first hall, both the youngsters were stunned at the lavish decorations representing every world continent.

They walked through this area into the next, where they were met by a bevy of helpers, one of whom zeroed in on their group, dressed in a flowing rainbow coloured dress.

"Welcome, welcome, to the Seasons Global University Auditorium, please accept this gift of a Rainbow lily pad. It has the layout of all the exhibits, entertainment and extras. The screen has an amalgamated intelligence with information on all of the exhibits that are being displayed here today and are linked to all members of your group, so no one can get lost. If you have tickets to the competition, please remember to put either your relative's name or your seat number, into the pad which will give you precise instructions on how to reach your destination and the time the arena opens for the competition." The girl said in almost one breath.

"Thank you." All said in unison. Alfie was given a green pad and Maddison a violet one, all the grown-ups were handed smaller hand held pocket sized versions in red.

"You are most welcome, enjoy your day."

Ushering them through the main doors, she quickly

turned back to greet the next group.

Alfie was enamoured with the pad and quickly ran his hand over the screen.

"Dad, what's my seat number? I want to put it in. Can we have a look round before the competition starts?" Taking a deep breath, he added, "It's fantastic here!"

"Of course we can, that's why we came early. We have over two hours before it begins Alfie, where do you want to go first?" his mother asked him.

His head was roaming from the lily pad to the signs in the foyer "Well I think I would really like to go and see *everything!*" Nodding at his answer "Yeh, I don't want to miss a thing!"

"Everything!" Both adults said at once, their faces mirroring the regret of asking the question in the first place.

Seeing their expressions, Maddison smiled.

"Why don't I stay with Alfie and you can take a leisurely walk round and look at what you want," looking up at her parents "and we can go anywhere we want and see *everything!*" she turned and asked, "is that all right with you Alfie?"

"Yeh, Maddi, I'd like that!" he answered abstractly, still looking at the lively interaction of people in the hall around him.

"Are you sure?" Stan asked Maddison, and both children nodded. "Okay then go, enjoy yourselves. It appears these pads are linked with you both, why don't you take a good look round, but keep in touch." Stan informed them.

"Send a message where you are, every half an hour and make sure you follow the pad's instructions to get you to your seats and in time for the competition." Jacky warned them both.

"I'll put the seat information in, via my pad for you." Stan began entering the information.

"Thanks Dad." Maddison gave him a wink, before she kissed them both and deliberately took Alfie's arm and walked him quickly away from the four grown-ups.

Within a few of seconds, they entered a third huge hall, with a long row of booths giving detailed information of every aspect of the Seasons Global Academy and all the exhibits. Most of which were surrounded by interested individuals, in some places three or four deep, and they decided to by-pass all of them as time was at a premium and they wanted to see the actual exhibits themselves.

It was their first real taste of freedom and they were glad they could roam around on their own. With having Laura and Paul in the competition, it made this an extraordinary occasion and they were determined to take in every second of the experience.

The contest was only held every four years, with each continent taking turns to present it in their various locations and in all the years it had been held, it had never been in the same place twice, until now. This year it was Europe, and the UK had been chosen to host the event for the second time, the last time was many years before.

For Maddison, it was exciting to be in this position to see and experience all of the Academy's work from around the world. Although she was somewhat relieved that she wasn't old enough, by two days, to enter the competition herself. She was, in truth, a bit of a home body and really didn't feel confident at entering a competition which, if she were chosen, could whisk her away at the end of it, to be enrolled in the Academy for four years, then posted to one of the their satellite

Universities or work stations, anywhere in the world.

Allowing themselves some time to acclimatise to the vast crowd around them, Maddison and Alfie wandered at first, into the smaller areas that were displaying exotic plants, tree production and near extinct fauna and flora species. Alfie's first love was insects and of course, his all-time favourite, small mammals on the verge of extinction, so they spent a longer amount of their time looking around these areas and soaking up everything that was being shown.

Maddison had initially tried making sure that they spent only around 15 minutes in each area, but after the first hour, she realised that if they kept to that slow pace, they would hardly see a quarter of it. Finding a drinks stand she bought two cold raspberry juice apple cups, Alfie's favourite, and from then on in, they continued looking round a little quicker.

Eventually they gravitated to the huge arenas which were producing: hurricanes, earthquakes, volcanic eruptions and tsunamis, all in smaller versions of course, but none the less totally incredible.

This led them to the sea creatures section, some of which were from the bottom of the Pacific, near the Mariana Trench and Maddison was in her element, having a real interest in this area.

Unfortunately it was something that wouldn't interest Alfie and so for him, she sought out the baby blue whale, swimming in the largest fish bowl they had ever seen and situated right in the centre of the exhibition hall, with several other marine creatures dotted around the area. The baby was beautiful to see up close leaving Alfie to study the whale in detail as she went back over to the other exhibit, but not before giving him strict instructions not to wander off. When finished he was to go over to the Trench stand and wait for her at the entrance/exit.

"Leave it out Maddison, I'm not a kid anymore. Go, enjoy the deep, deep blue sea. I'll be fine."

"You're sure? I'll send Mum and Dad a message to let them know where we are."

"Whatever!" he said, and stepped forward to take his place in line behind some foreign tourists, who in turn, faced him so they could practice their limited English.

Turning round quickly, Maddison got only a few yards towards the exhibit when a huge mass of people came out of the Pacific Area.

"Sorry!" A voice said, as a boy of a roundabout the same age was pressed into her, as he tried to avoid the oncoming populace "Crowded here isn't it?"

Maddison looked up into his face, they were both being pushed in the opposite direction to where they were walking and the boy, gently pulled her to one side allowing the majority of the line to pass, so they could turn back.

"Thanks, it is a bit!" Maddison agreed, as they dodged and weaved, to travel back on themselves.

"You going to the Hawaii booth?" he asked, keeping by her side as best he could and deflecting the crowd away from her.

"Mariana Trench! I always wondered what was really on the sea bed" They slowed, having nearly reached the entrance.

She was able to see him properly then and he was just a bit taller, but not much, and had a kind of dishevelled mousey hairstyle, making him good looking in a rugged kind of way.

"Me too! Are you here on your own? I'm with a school group."

His eyes dipped down, as he thought this was a really uncool reason to be there.

"My sister Laura is taking part." Maddison tried not to make it sound too important.

"Cool!" he shuffled a little. "My name's Tristan Kane, by the way. So you'll be seeing her in the competition then?"

"I'm Maddison Springer, and yes, my brother Alfie and I are looking round the exhibition before we go in. I left him at the blue whale. Are you seeing the competition too?"

"Oh no, we only came to see the exhibition, competition tickets cost a fortune."

"I know, we were lucky as Laura got four tickets free. Did you have to come far?"

They were now at the Mariana Trench entrance.

"Essex. I won a competition at school, I didn't know I was that clever!" he said cheekily. "But I expect I'm not, as another 29 got to come too!"

"What kind of competition?" she smiled up at him.

"Oh the usual, you know?" he laughed, "Why do you want to visit the exhibition? What do you expect to see here? Then we had a test, which consisted of a 100 questions about the exhibits!"

"So what did you say?" she asked, curious to know what he thought, as they joined the end of the queue.

"I can't remember to be honest! I just wrote what I was feeling at the time, which was basically, how bored I was in the class, and how it would be nice to come to London for the first time! Then somehow, I scored 99 questions right," his face showing that that was not something he was expecting.

"Wow, well that was brilliant, but you sound surprised."

Was all Maddison could think of to say as they carried on through the archway to go down into the gloomy subterranean exhibit, housed in a cavernous hall.

"Gob smacked! I have never scored in any subject anywhere that high, ever!" he laughed again, not admitting the fact; he had deliberately put answers that he knew were wrong, but were marked right. "You don't mind me coming with you?"

"Of course not, I'm glad of the company."

It was nice to have someone her own age to talk to and he was so unlike Paul and she had known him all her life. Tristan was yes, different, as in a 'poles apart', kind of way. She smiled at her own comparison and giving him another sideward glance, admitted to herself that he was also a bit hard to figure.

The next ten minutes went very quickly, as they were chatting about the strange luminous creatures scurrying across the ocean floor, while trying to absorb as much of the information as was given on the audio descriptions. Maddison however, was ever conscious of Alfie being on his own, and knew she had to go back to him and after a further five minutes, told Tristan she had to leave.

Disappointed, but agreed that he had probably seen enough bottom feeders to last a lifetime, they moved to the exit.

Just as they were coming out of the darkness, a voice suddenly echoed around them and Tristan's pad lit up flashing red, as it was coming from within his orange lily pad and turning heads towards them.

"Kane, we are waiting for you in Section 12, I do not have time to ask you again." Tristan visibly cringed.

"Damn! Sorry, looks as if I have to go!" he looked

embarrassed by the call and tried to hide the pad in the front of him. "Nice meeting you Maddison Springer, it was a real pleasure!"

He obviously didn't want to go, even Maddison could see that and was smugly pleased, knowing she was the reason for his feet dragging.

"Kane?" The high pitched voice although now slightly muffled, echoed round them again. Shrugging his shoulders he smiled at her and reluctantly headed out towards the Sections marked 10-11-12 across from where they were standing.

Maddison's eyes followed him and whispered, "and you Tristan Kane, a real pleasure."

Looking at her own pad, there were thankfully no messages, so she headed back to the blue whale exhibit and found Alfie walking in her direction. Once reunited the siblings made their way through the natural phenomena portion, only stopping to see the earth, wind, and fire shows, before spending a little time in the geology sector, to buy some small crystals and rocks for Alfie.

When they finally reached the Aurora Borealis zone, Maddison was tired, but happy, as this was the last area on their list of 'must sees'. It was her own and Laura's favourite school subject. She had wanted to see this particular area the most, so she could read the northern lights close up in all their glory.

Both sisters had studied them on a much smaller scale, with both being extremely good at translating the nuances of the colours and movements within the spectacle. In fact, Laura had mentioned, maybe a hundred times, that she would like to be a teacher of Aurora Borealis (Northern Lights) language (ABL). Of course, only if she was accepted into the Academy, but she didn't think they got a choice of what they could do.

As they entered the ABL amphitheatre, both stood mesmerised, watching the giant semi-circle vista, dance with a replica Northern Lights. The magnificent panorama was big and beautiful, especially as it was the first time she had actually seen them close up and not on a school screen in her classroom.

Of course these views were only a representation, but even so, they were enchanting and she was able to read them easily. The word formations were in this instance, welcoming all the visitors to the exhibition as they streamed before her and she was captivated, because she was able to read them all fluently.

Alfie however, wasn't so keen, but stayed by her side as she walked from one to another and just as she was about to leave, the final panel caught her attention as the lights suddenly changed completely and somehow focusing the glow directly in front of where they stood. They immediately became distorted and completely revised to another configuration as Maddison stood transfixed, trying to read what was within the fluorescent green glow of the curtain-like formation and to actually define the new message in front of her.

'She is ailing and there is little time, siblings of the 36th partaker. You must both take up the challenge when the soft face of night calls and you must help the starling find its way.'

A vague sentence at best and one which disappeared as suddenly as it appeared and another view became visible and mundanely similar in content to those she had read before.

Maddison looked furtively around, but no one was looking as bemused as she felt. Alfie was still playing with the piece of garnet she had bought him at the geology booth and was taking no notice at all. Why should he, his knowledge of ABL was almost zero anyway and didn't start language classes until next year at school. She even checked her pad, but there was nothing other than a detailed description of the Northern Lights themselves and no mention of anything else that would help her.

"Quick, come with me!" Grabbing Alfie's arm, she ducked and dived back past others who were entering, literally dragging him with her and walked up to one of the attendants of the stand, who was on sentry duty at the entrance.

"Excuse me, but could you play that last message at the end, before this one, I mean, again," she pleaded. "I'm not quite sure I caught what it said!"

"Sorry love it's on a loop, you would have to wait another 12 minutes before the last one comes back up again, but I do have a copy of what they all say here," he smiled down at her, taking a folded green sheet of paper, he placed it in her hand.

"It's for people who don't read ABL," he said helpfully, handing another list of translations to Alfie, they both thanked him politely.

Without looking back, and hoping Alfie was still following, she walked out of the entrance and over to where there were some seats facing an advertisement board to view other exhibits. Sitting down, she scanned the words she had been given.

"Well what was that about, you have never had any difficulties with ABL and you're even better than Laura." Alfie complimented.

"I just thought I saw a message that was for us," she looked perplexed. "It somehow felt that it was, anyway!"

"Us? Really, what did it say?"

This caught his attention. Alfie was now very interested, as being the youngest, he was never included in what was happening to either of his sisters. Maddison was saying 'us', which included him too and he sat eagerly beside her.

"She is ailing and there is little time siblings of the 36th partaker. You must both take up the challenge when the soft face of night calls to you and help the starling find its way." Repeating the message verbatim Maddison looked anxiously at Alfie as he examined the information the attendant had given him.

"Nope that isn't here, but I agree it does sound as if it was for us," nodding his head, wisely.

"Really?" Maddison looked down at him, her face with a look of astonishment. "You really think so?"

"Nah, it's someone playing a joke, probably somebody who wants to feel very important themselves, on a day like today."

Sitting back in their seats, he took out the garnet again and began throwing it up in the air.

Maddison looked at her little brother with an amazed look.

"Ok! Who are you and what have you done with my dimwit of a brother." Her voice, was soft with light recrimination.

Alfie dropped the rock and stared at her

"Very funny, I do have a brain you know, Maddi." He stated.

"Oh Alfie, I'm sorry," she was mortified. "I know, it's just that you surprised me, with your quick thinking and I forget how much you are growing up!" she complimented.

"Thank you, I think!" Giving her a wink and a cheeky smile.

She hugged him to her, but wasn't sure if she really believed herself, what if anything had happened in the last five minutes.

Putting on a serious face, Alfie spoke again to her. "Let's look at this logically though! If it isn't a joke and you definitely think it was for us and no one else saw this and thought it was for them?"

She nodded and mouthed, "I do." Waiting to hear what else Alfie thought.

"But, it did mention siblings of a partaker, which we are, and the 36th partaker must be Laura, well what does that conjure up?"

"That our Laura is getting a place in the Academy for sure and will be the 36th chosen!" Maddison concluded.

"Right, so who is ailing? he sounded a bit worried then. "Do you think it's Laura?"

"No, of course not, Alfie. The words say, 'She is ailing' first, and if Laura is the 36th chosen, then it's logical that it isn't her."

"Good!" he gave a sigh of relief, "so how do you explain what just happened?"

"I can't!"

Just then the pad activated itself and a message telling them to head towards their seats, came flashing up on the screen.

"Look it is almost time to meet mum and dad, so let's go see how this plays out for Laura shall we, and not get worried about it until we know it's for certain, ok?.

"Good idea" Alfie said a little apprehensively, and then added. "Exciting, isn't it?"

In her heart Maddison could not agree with him, but gave him a strained smile. "Could be!"

The sudden tinny voice on the tannoy sounded loudly to reach everyone above the noise.

"The Competition will begin in 30 minutes. If you have tickets, please take your seats. For those who don't have competition tickets, the exhibition will be open until 11pm and the exhibition hall itself will be closed promptly at 11.30pm."

A few more booths caught Alfie's eye on the way to Level 4, but Maddison managed to get them to where their parents were waiting at the entrance of the Green section on time and followed them to their seats a few minutes later. Maddison sat at the end of the 21st row in seat 821a, next to Alfie and their mum and dad were sitting next to Paul's parents.

They had pretty good seats too, on the side, and about half way up. Alfie recounted their visit to all the exhibits, and on agreement with Maddison, the ABL exhibit had been given a very brief account. He kept the conversation going until the majority of the 20,000 seats around them were filled.

Without warning the auditorium lights suddenly dimmed and a hush came over the hall, as a huge channel of light appeared in the centre of the stage and a voice swiftly vibrated through the air.

"Welcome everyone!"

All eyes focused immediately on the stage to an attractive young woman, dressed in an outfit of pale rainbow colours with a bodice which looked as if it were raining over the rainbow, but neither the material nor floor appeared to be wet. Her hair was glossy brown and hung in gentle curls to her waist and tied with a rainbow ribbon to keep it in place.

Her voice was beautifully modulated and resounded round the gargantuan hall.

"My name is Noelia and I am spokesperson for The Seasons Global University or as you all know it, 'Rainbow House'!"

Loud cheering and clapping came from all over the auditorium, Noelia allowed the interruption and smiling broadly, she continued.

"We are happy to announce the start of our four-yearly competition for choosing junior trainees, out of the thousands of applicants from all around the world, and the final wonderfully gifted applicants, who won a place, are here today!"

Another round of applause erupted again from the audience in front of her, but this time raising her hand to indicate quiet, she continued.

"This contest has been arranged with just one end in view, to find the best of the best, in the formation of: fauna/flora, aqua/air creatures, natural phenomena, elements/ matter, small and medium land creatures. This year we have added leviathan creatures...

*("Levi ath ans? What's that when it's at home?"
asked Jess*

*"Well it's a large creature," Rosie replied. "like say......
a whale for instance!"*

*"Well, why can't you say a whale, we all know what
that is." Kevin added.*

*"But I like the word, it means more than whale, it's
kind of a description of something as big as a whale, or
elephant, just a massive creature."*

*"That's silly, how can we figure out what it is?" Jess
answered.*

*"She's right you know!" a familiar voice drifted up
the stairs to the landing above. "You'd be better off
calling them monsters. Kids like the word and they can*

visualise anything they like then."

"OK, thanks Pam!" Rosie grabbed her pen then scribbled out the word and replaced it quickly with – monster and read the sentence again.

This year we have added ~~leviathan,~~ I mean, monster creatures and last, but not least reading and understanding the language of the sun."

"Everybody happy with that?" The kids cheered and a hand rose with a thumbs up from the stairwell.

"So can I get on with the story"?

"Yeh!" Came a chorus of agreement.

"Noelia continued ....)

"Every contestant has the opportunity of producing flawless creations, in fauna, flora, natural phenomena, and discovering their aptitude with puzzles within each of the six practical areas. Their aim is to achieve this, with their first attempt, and the configuration will be judged solely on how well the candidate has chosen and produced their handiwork."

Moving across the stage, she pointed to the panels hanging above her head.

"The process is overviewed by two experts in the area of choice and elimination is instantaneous, but only at the end of the sixth segment."

She continued walking to the opposite side of the stage in what could only be described as a graceful gliding stride and coming to a stop in front of a full rainbow archway.

"Mistakes will only prove costly to those who make them."

Disappearing through the portico, just as the atmosphere became electric and an audible sigh rose from the listeners in the auditorium, the minority of whom were family members of the entrants.

The opportunity to join Rainbow House, had been the dream of most youngsters worldwide over the last 1,000 years, with the academy only adding female contestants in the last 100 years. It had become the premier college for innovated training in every field of study and the entrance of which was only allowed by competition. This was strictly controlled within age parameters, when the contestants reached between the first day of reaching their 16th birthday and the last day of their 19th year.

Suddenly all eyes were drawn back to Noelia, who had appeared again, in her original position and was continuing with her dialogue.

"As you can see the stage is arranged into seven areas, each one is designated an individual colour. Six sections are positioned for working, but the violet zone however will be used as a final waiting area. Each candidate can be seen in every one of the sections and you the audience, will be able to follow the journey of individual candidates, by inputting their number or name, into the screen on your lily pads, or activate the larger screen on the back of the seat in front of you. An overview is also given on six large screens set around the hall," and she pointed to all the screens, individually.

"The areas are divided into the six categories I have just described, but he violet section will remain shrouded to give the competitors time to rest and will eventually be revealed only when all the winners, who have succeeded to reach this area, are put to their final test." She took a deep breath, and it seemed almost as if the audience themselves joined her. "This year all areas will have individual force fields available to surround the working area. Previously the organisers had found that some of the natural phenomena and creatures that were created, accidentally escaped from their areas before the judges could progress the candidate. We have now proved this will be the best way of keeping control of any rogue elements."

Another round of applause broke out and again her hand indicated silence.

"I now have the greatest pleasure in introducing to you all twelve of the specialist judges. Some of whom you will yourselves have heard of, others you will not, but I can assure you that each and every one is qualified to judge in this exciting competition."

She took a step back and looked towards the right side of the stage.

At that precise moment several individuals entered through the archway Noelia had exited just minutes before, and went forward to stand in the spotlight of centre stage. They were in pairs and dressed in the colour that matched the zone, they were obviously going to be judging in the contest.

Noelia began to read from the top of her rainbow coloured lily pad display.

"Flora will be completed within the **green zone** and will be judged by the well-known judge Steven Baker and of course you all know Margo Powell!"

The two judges stepped forward and gave a confident wave to the crowd. A thunderous applause broke out as the audience recognised Margo, considered the queen of flora, having been in the public eye for her work with extinct plants from around the globe. Only a little less familiar in appearance was Steven Baker, his name however was equally famous for having written most of the world's school reference books on the subject, over the same period of time.

As the applause died down, they took a step back and Noelia continued to introduce the rest of the twelve.

"Aqua and land creatures will be within the **indigo zone** and may I introduce for the first time in this category Ang Dickinson and John Webb, two of the Rainbow House senior lecturers in the subject.

Again the applause resounded around the hall, intermittently spaced with the introduction of each new pair.

Jan Wilks and George Fife for elements and matter - **blue zone**,

Eileen Read and Eric Shields small and medium land creatures - **red zone**.

James Modlock and Wendy Harvey - natural phenomena - **orange zone**,

Dawn Dunsford and Chris Corbett - Insects and levi .... (*oops sorry!*) monster creatures - **yellow zone**.

"Last, but not least, I have the greatest pleasure to introduce, Carolyn Saxby and Fred Burgess judges for almost a half of a century at Rainbow House, who will have the final place overseeing the **violet zone** and the reading of Aurora Borealis or Aurora Australis."

The older pair raised their hands to the deafening applause, which she allowed to go on much longer than the other pairings. In fact joining in for a time herself, until she realised the competition had to start and she waved her hand across her lily pad to alter the screen.

"Positions please experts."

She instructed, looking up towards the back screen now of the twelve faces, each edged with the colour of their chosen speciality and were highlighted on stage in their elected colour

"Candidates, one to six, please enter centre stage and let the competition begin."

This time the audience did not applaud or acknowledge the candidates entry onto the stage, in any way. It was tradition that silence was now foremost, allowing each entrant to concentrate without interruption and the atmosphere was now tangible, but calm. The contest had begun.

Maddison's head was suddenly filled with thoughts of Laura and then of course Paul, and with it, the face of Tristan Kane came in a flash, but was gently pushed to one side, although not before she had reflected fondly on their short time together.

Alfie elbowed her and brought Maddison's mind back into focus

"When is Laura due on?" he whispered eyes glued to the stage. Maddison checked her pad, and scanned the page of information on the contestants to find that Paul Ray, was 59th and her finger followed down the list of names to Laura Springer, 75th, she audibly sighed. "A while yet, Alfie."

She was wondering how Laura was at this moment in time, she wasn't good at handling stress, and so today would be a real challenge for her. Although it wasn't as if she wasn't ready, Maddison had watched with admiration, as her 18 months older sister, had improved over the last couple of years in school and had also won every competition she had entered. Today was different however, today would be life changing and Maddison knew how much Laura wanted this opportunity, as she would then be in control of her own destiny.

Chapter 6

Jaime

High over the auditorium, in a prominent and well placed soundproof booth, two of Rainbow House's faculty, were looking through the floor to ceiling window giving a panoramic view over the vast hall below.

The stage was now a hive of activity and the seats were still filling at a rate of knots, luckily in silence for the competition had just begun, but neither of these activities, holding their attention, as they scanned the space directly in front of them.

"How many did you say there were again?" The younger one asked, as he squashed his nose to the glass.

"Over 50 attached to participants, but there are well over 200 in the auditorium. I keep losing count, as they keep coming and going." He was also close to the glass and his glasses kept tapping at window as he moved his head. "This is the highest number of gems in any competition since it started," sighing as he licked his dry lips.

Cupping both his hands whilst resting against the glass, the other tried concentrating harder to see into the gloom. "I can only count about 60!"

"Look down at the front, the lights are masking their brilliance," pointing to an area near the stage where the most activity was. "Did I tell you we have something of a coup this year, it appears there are more than 20 quarter days this time, too!

"Really?" his eyes widened then turned away from the window and focused on his associate. "Perhaps the two are linked!"

"I suppose there is a faint possibility!" The older teacher crossed the room and poured a single glass of red wine, "They have been around so long, I wonder which came first, the chicken or the egg?"

"Does it matter?" Not taking offence at the gesture of not being offered a glass of wine, the younger, leaned back against the window. "I have never fully understood their meaning!"

At that point the door to the room opened and several other colleagues entered, ending any private conversation between the two and they both stepped back into their seats. The others were taking their places in the other dozen or so, large comfortable stuffed chairs, around the room.

A voice next to the wine drinker, gabbled excitedly. "Hello Hubbard! What a turnout eh! I get a real buzz watching the contest. Those offspring really have wild imaginations! Do you remember that time when a plague of locusts swarmed through the auditorium in Salt Lake City?"

As he received no comment back, the speaker immediately turned to his other side and repeated the question to his opposite neighbour.

Jaime purposefully directed his eyes more keenly to the stage and focussing longingly on the objects of his desire, as the multi-coloured gems flitted across the auditorium. He still did not know what they were exactly and he had never been that interested until recently. He knew only that they belonged to certain individuals within various families, all over the world.

He had begun to read up on them before the competition, but there wasn't much information, only that they were more common in youngsters, who also had the brightest colours.

As he watched them flying in all directions around the auditorium, his hand reached into his pocket again clasping greedily the object that had caused the flutter of anticipation earlier and had now made his heart beat faster at what could happen today.

If his plan was going to work however, he needed to be backstage, to see who was getting the most passes in the competition and equally, who amongst them had little gems. For that was his goal, today he intended to capture one of the gems, if he needed to and only if he could figure out whether or not he had one already.

His head ached in confusion and without a word of goodbye to his colleagues, he got up out of the chair and left the room.

No one noticed his leaving, except his younger associate, who only registered the exit momentarily before looking back at the stage and became once again, engrossed in what was happening there.

Chapter 7

Tom and Rosie

Tom stood holding a huge coffee table picture book of London, trying to blend in and pretending he was scanning its pages. He leaned on the wall, just by the side of the staircase, watching as the children poured down from the upper floor, chatting ten to the dozen about the story they had just heard. Luckily he had caught almost the entire tale himself, along with several parents, who had also been engrossed, but they were now chatting about how good it was and wasn't Rosie the best writer ever.

Hearing this, his stomach churned and his head pulsed fitfully. Yes, the writing was very good and she had written the story in concise detail of what had happened. She definitely wove a magical world, which described the characters skilfully and with a vocabulary, he could only imagine.

He should know, he had been at the competition, as she had, so he knew exactly what had taken place, albeit from a different perspective. Knowing the, now made it imperative that he warn her and then somehow get her to stop writing. Well, at least reading the story, as inevitably someone would put two and two together, realise who and what, she was.

This book made her vulnerable, especially now that there was a certain amount of public exposure happening, he shuddered at the thought and tried to stop himself thinking of what she had written, because it wasn't a story as such, not really. He felt a slow icy feeling trickle down his spine, it was now getting far too dangerous for her and with no one concerned for that part of her life and she would be easy pickings.

He had to help her!

Turning he hesitated as he put his foot on the bottom step, there was something about her voice that made him feel protective, as if she were family. At first he had thought she was just one of the Lost, as she obviously had no idea what she was seeing, but her work was far too intricate, her story woven in such a way as to believe, perhaps she actually could hear what was being said and if that were the case, it could only mean one thing.

She was Primera. Tom knew they existed, of course, but there were so few of them and he had only heard of a handful being around in the last century, well what he knew of that is, whether a squirrel or magpie had collected any others was anyone's guess.

Slowly he mounted the next three steps to see the older woman who had been sitting on the penultimate stair during the reading. She was now talking softly to the girl, Rosie, as they were putting the area back to its original state. Blocking his view of the girl, he stopped dead on reaching the top step as he heard the words.

"Oh, Rosie, that was fantastic, this storyline is so exciting, I loved it, and guess what? It's the best news! Just after your break I had a phone call from Michael in Spain and he says he can get the book to press in a couple of weeks and he likes your title: Seasons of Equilibran. Summer will be second after Spring with Autumn in four months time, so it gives you time to finish Winter.

"He does? Pam, four books!" Rosie was putting the last of the cushions in a store cupboard at the rear of the room, "He doesn't think I'm too young, does he?"

"Michael read the work on its merit, silly! He already knows you're only 16 years old. He sounded really excited and said you bring the Springer's to life!" Going up to her and giving her a hug,

Tom audibly groaned, at the news and both of them turned to face him.

"Are you feeling all right, young man?" Pam enquired, immediately putting on her customer services voice.

"I need to sit down."

He wasn't joking either, he'd missed breakfast getting up early to create his disguise, then fallen asleep on the plane Along with what he had just heard, his stomach suddenly began to churn and he had lost what colour he had in his face.

Pam came forward and quickly guided him to the armchair Rosie had recently vacated and then rushed down the stairs, saying something about getting some water, as she never put it up there until after the reading, in case the kids decided to help themselves and spill it on the carpet.

"Have you eaten?" Rosie asked quietly.

She was now standing in front of him as Tom looked up, taking in a shocked breath and just as Kristy had said he would, he recognised her immediately, it really was uncanny.

"No, but I'm fine, honestly, I just had some news that was a little troubling." An understatement, of course, as what he had just heard, was totally unexpected and had so many implications.

"You look very pale, let me take this book. It looks as if it might fall out of your hand and land on your foot. It's a monster, isn't it?"

She smiled at him, as he automatically gave her the

'Highlights in pictures of London' coffee table hardback and leaned back in the chair.

"I was looking for a little light reading." His smile was lopsided and forced, as she leant the book against the leg of the armchair.

"You missed out on that then, didn't you?" her laugh was sweet and natural. "If you want London landmarks, you'll find the tour guides closer to the front of the shop, unless you're looking for a present, then there are some other good picture books in the aisle downstairs, to your right, and they aren't quite as heavy!"

Pam came back with the tall glass of water and just as quickly left them together, as she heard her name called from the shop floor.

"Thanks!" he drank down the water in one go, trying to think of an opening to ease the conversation forward and to where he needed it to be.

"I was wondering could I ask you, was it you reading the story to the kids just now?"

"Er, yes, why do you ask?" She quickly withdrew into herself. It was fine for children and parents to ask her questions, she had got used to that, but a member of the public. No she wasn't ready for that just yet!

"I only caught the last of it and I wondered whose book it was?" he lied and he mustered up his most winning smile. "I'd love to get it for my young cousin. I'm sure it would be just what she would enjoy."

"It isn't a published work!" Rosie blushed with embarrassment.

"Really, well that's a shame."

He was floundering, finding out that the work was actually going to be published, had completely thrown him, but somehow he had to learn more about Rosie, if he was to be able, to help her.

At that moment out of nowhere, it seemed, a boy of about nine years old, thumped up the stairs, in a way only boys of that age could, threw his arms round Rosie as she kneeled next to Tom and almost knocking her over in his excitement.

"Bye, Rosie, I wish you could write quicker and we could come every week!" he spoke in a high pitched squeaky voice, and Tom recognised the little boy from his questions at the reading. Rosie hugged him tightly, smiled at him, and then blushed deeper as she looked up guiltily at Tom.

"Joe, come on I have to get home." His mother called from the downstairs level and he immediately disentangled himself from Rosie and grabbed the book he had dropped.

"See you in a couple of weeks!" he waved back at her.

Then he thumped down to his mother, clutching, Rosie noticed with pride, the book title was she had recommended at the end of the session. She could now see for herself that Pam's original plan for the kids was actually working.

Losing what balance she had on her heels, she sat down on the floor with a bump and called after him.

"Bye Joe!"

So that was Joe, Tom smiled, yes a very distinctive voice, as Kristy had said.

"You wrote the story?" he was looking at her as if it wasn't true.

"Yes, so what if I did?" Scrambling upwards and on to her feet.

"No reason.... Erm! He hesitated. It was totally unlike him to be so stumped and at a loss for words.

"Look I'm 16 and have been writing for almost all of

my life. It's what I do," she finished and then walked towards the back of '3R's' to pick up her folder. "No that isn't true. It's who I am!" Holding her head high and daring him to contradict her.

"Wait, please, I didn't mean to offend you!" he called after her.

"Well you did," she still had her back to him. He hadn't really offended her, but she was so embarrassed with talking to him. Worst of all, he was really good looking, blond longish hair, blue eyes that sparkled and a smile to die for, but it felt so weird talking with him, he must be at least the same age as Mike.

"Then I apologise, look let me make it up to you, I saw a coffee shop round the corner, may I buy you a drink?" Seeing her hesitate on the top step, he crossed his fingers behind his back that she would turn round and talk to him. He needed time to get to the bottom of her past, but somehow he knew it would not be that easy. She didn't even know the Symm, what it was or who they were, and the most important point, what she was going to have to do to stay safe and sound.

"No, thank you" she said primly, but swung round, "I don't even know you!"

"Well that's easily remedied. My name is Tom Osmundsen. I'm an environmental science student (for want of a better description) from near Bergin, Norway. I am here on holiday to stay with my uncle and aunt, who are looking after my sister, while she studies in London. They have two young children Ellie and Francesca, and it's Frankie that I would like the book for!"

That was as close to the truth as he could think of in a hurry, he hoped the two women in question would never find out he had reduced them to children, for his own purposes.

"It isn't a book!"

"Really, what are you holding there then?" he queried.

"It's just a chapter!" Unconsciously moving the folder behind her back.

"Chapter 6, sounds seriously book-like to me!" Giving her, one of his most encouraging smiles.

"You didn't just catch the end of the story, did you?" she said accusingly.

"Honestly, No!" he shook his head, "I came in as the little girl was finishing telling of the last reading. I sat on the steps with a couple of the mums, who whispered to me that it would be worth my while to stay until it was finished." He added honestly.

"They did?" She looked totally surprised. "Seriously?"

"Yes they did, very seriously!" This time his voice was very positive. "I was glad when the kids voted not to have a break and you read it all the way through, I was enthralled."

"I thought everybody dropped their kids off and left to do shopping and such, while I entertained them."

Rosie turned her back on him and looked up at the small window above her head, her chapter now clutched tightly to her front.

"My goodness, you have such a cynical view!" Tom gave her a crooked grin as she turned back to him.

"No just a practical one, I'm afraid, but I love to read to them, so I didn't mind at all!"

"Had you noticed how quiet the whole store was while you read?"

It had been the first thing he become aware of himself, along with her storytelling voice which was captivating, he realised the atmosphere changed after only a few minutes and he, like the rest of the audience were drawn into the story as she saw it.

"No, it never entered my head, I always knew Pam was there, making sure the kids didn't puke on the carpet and I was too engrossed in the story, to be honest!"

"So was everyone else!"

Thinking to himself, 'including me, even though I was there myself for most of it.'

She turned her head round as the doorbell rang, her eyes travelling down the stairs at the sound.

"Not once did the bell go," she smiled at him, "I realise that now. Wow!"

"Yes wow! Now will you please come and have a drink with me? I missed breakfast and now lunch, listening to you!" Chiding gently, and for good measure his stomach rumbled at the plea.

They both laughed at the coincidence.

"OK, I'd like that. I'll just tell Pam where I'm going, as my grandad, picks me up soon and I don't want them to worry." She smiled apologetically at him

Standing up Tom realised as they faced one another that she was quite tall, but still not reaching just above his shoulder and he could hardly take his eyes off her own, the colour was so vibrant and so very familiar.

"Fine, I'll just pop this baby back where I found it and wait for you at the door."

Picking up the book from the floor, he turned and allowed her go in front of him.

"OK!"

She preceded him down the stairs and hurried to Pam's office. Throwing open the door she sailed into the room on a fluffy cloud.

"I've got a date for coffee!"

"The Scandinavian boy with the big blue eyes and matching t-shirt and was mesmerised by my favourite storyteller on the bottom step. Then threw himself at you, just a few minutes ago?" she chuckled.

"You noticed him then?" Rosie grinned.

"Nah, not really!" Pam winked at her. "Not my type!"

"His name is Tom Osmundsen and he's from Norway, on holiday. He is staying with his uncle and visiting his sister who is studying here!" she blurted out.

"Wow, his whole life story, it must be serious." Pam still couldn't hide her grin.

"Oh Pam do I look alright, he is so....o good looking!"

"That I did notice!" she smiled up at her protégé. "Go, enjoy yourself Rosie, you spend far too much time at the keyboard as it is. Take a break for yourself, for a change. I'll give Bert a cup of tea when he comes to pick you up and I'm sure there must be another story from the Norton's family album, which I haven't heard at least 100 times."

"Thanks Pam, I won't be long I promise, but first I'll go to the loo and freshen up. We're going to Tea and Symphony!" slipping her folder, on top of Pam's desk.

Five minutes later Rosie, found Tom sitting on the second step of the mezzanine staircase waiting for her.

"Good, you came!" Tom got up immediately and opened the exit door for them.

"Of course I did, why?" Skirting passed him onto the cobbled street outside.

"Well I thought you might have changed your mind!"

Following closely behind her, and letting the door close quietly on its own.

"No, not me, it's not in my nature." Rosie felt ten feet tall as she slowed to allow him to walk beside her.

"Good, that's what I like to hear, Rosie Norton!" he acknowledged.

"You know my name!" she was quite astonished that he should.

"Oh yes, and you know mine!"

Tom grinned deliberately winking at Rosie and held out his hand so she could put her own, inside his.

Strangely his touch sent a tingling sensation up her arm and as they walked leisurely round the corner and to the coffee shop, she was noticing other unexplainable sensations coursing along her body too.

"Strange, it feels like I am walking along the road with Mike or Jack," she thought and smiled. "Safe!"

Tom could feel the Symm cascading from him to Rosie, but his mind went off in a tangent remembering and rethinking Rosie's story, just at the point where Laura makes her first appearance, as he hadn't seen that part himself.

Chapter 8

The Competitors

Behind the scenes, Laura however would have had Maddison really worried, as she certainly wasn't feeling at her best, in any way.

For the last ten minutes she was throwing up in the girl's bathroom, along with several other contestants, who were also reacting in much the same way.

When she finally stumbled out of the cubicle, she went over to the row of washbasins, turning on the tap, she cupped her hand under the water several times, as she rinsed out her mouth and finally threw some over her face, unfortunately most of it going into her eyes.

Blinded, she realised she didn't know which way to go to find something to dry herself with, and feeling her way along the marble counter she came to the end, without success. Suddenly a towel forced its way into her hand, she sighed with relief.

"There you go." A soft accented voice pronounced.

"Thanks!" she mumbled.

Drying the excess droplets away, she turned round to see a beautiful round face with large oval shaped brown eyes and with such a broad smile, she weakly smiled back.

Then a shudder of fear gripped her and she automatically looked down at her dress, checking to see it was clear of any water, she sighed with relief that it was still spotlessly clean. At this point in time, Laura looked as white as the dress she was wearing. Like every other girl there, she was dressed in the pure white flowing outfit cum uniform, which had been made of some special material that was water and dirt resistant and now she had proved it really was.

"Are you okay now?" The other girl asked.

"Happens in every round I've been in, this last one was the worst though!" she whispered nodding her head.

"I hyperventilate with a vengeance myself! Would you like something to drink? There are loads of reception rooms nearby, but I found one a bit less inhabited than those near the stage. I hate crowds!" she spoke quickly in short sentences, but was smiling at Laura in a friendly way.

"Thanks that would be good!" Laura said a little clearer, although her voice still sounded raspy and she felt a little unsteady. Making her way to the door, the other girl opened for her and they both sauntered along the corridor.

"I'm Sun Ya, by the way and number 73. What number are you?"

"75, I'm Laura. That sounds like we might be in the same set. Oh and thanks for the towel."

"You are very welcome!"

Laura was steadily regaining her stability as they continued to the end of the passageway.

"Where are you from?" Laura asked.

"China originally, but my family live in Petaling Jaya, Malaysia." Sun Ya replied.

Laura gave her a very puzzled look.

"How about, Kuala Lumpur!" she added, as she gave the name of the main city.

"Right, I know where that is, but that's some journey!" Laura had never been outside of the British Isles, herself.

"Ah, it wasn't too bad. It took a lot longer to get

here, than Dad anticipated, as Mum wanted to stop in Dubai for shopping. We did that for a couple of days and in the end dad got fed up and left her there with my sister. He and my little brother brought me to London, to register. I can only hope the shopping didn't stop Mum and Su Ling from being here on time!"

Stopping abruptly outside 'Waiting Room 25', she took Laura's hand and turned into it.

"You're getting a colour back. What about you, where do you come from?"

They moved into the room closing the door behind them.

"In Kent, just outside London. Not far really and nowhere as exotic as you!"

They each collected a juice from a counter by the entrance, as a low steady murmur of voices sounded like the buzz of bees on a summer afternoon. The room had about a dozen or more other tables, most of which had two or three occupants.

Sun Ya looked round and immediately a boy stood up from a table in the middle and waved at her, which prompted her to pull Laura in his direction.

"That's Kawiti, we did the last part of the trip from Dubai together. He came from New Zealand with his Mum and Dad and little sister" she whispered, "He is really funny, but don't tell him, I told you!"

As Laura and Sun Ya made their way over to where Kawiti was sitting, they passed a table where a striking young man of Native American heritage with long straight black hair, sat staring at them as they passed.

Sun Ya smiled at him, but he gave her no response, his eyes were set on Laura, who dipped her gaze away as he stared right at her. She could almost feel his eyes follow her, until they reached Kawiti who was sitting just two tables further on and sat down with their drinks.

"Hi Kawiti, this is Laura, she lives here in England." Sun Ya introduced them.

"Laura, that's a nice name! What's your strongest fabrication then?"

"Not backward in coming forward is he!" Laura commented. She sat facing him and took a sip of her grape juice.

"Not that I've seen since I met him," Sun Ya laughed, "my favourite is small mammals by the way. Kawiti is into the whole spectrum, especially natural phenomena and all creatures large and small."

"I like flora too," Kawiti added. "But then all of the categories are fun."

"Oh, I do flora best." Laura stated proudly, "the rest I'm passable at!"

"Hey, don't put yourself down, you would need to be more than passable, otherwise you wouldn't have made it through to where we are today!"

Holding his drink up in the air, over his head, Kawiti looked to see if there was any juice left inside the carton.

"Ok, so I'm good at all of them!" she said blithely, smiling broadly.

"As are we all, my friend! We just have to be more than a little special today!"

With this he threw the carton over arm into the rubbish bin five tables along and close to the entrance. All three had been watching the stunt, as it entered safely inside the bin, but it was only Sun Ya who noticed someone new entering the waiting room.

"Oh boy, Laura, look at him!" she spoke softly, behind her hand.

A hush came over the whole room as a tall, aristocratic, athletic looking blond, came through the door and scanned the area obviously looking for someone and finding the smouldering Native American, walked across to him and sat down.

Both Laura and Sun Ya sighed in unison.

"Isn't that Prince Thorlief?" Laura whispered to her new friends.

"It sure is, wow!" Sun Ya acknowledged "I never thought I would see him in person. To think I had a Season's Royalty calendar on my wall for about three years, I kept changing the dates so I could keep the pictures. He was Prince December." she sighed.

"My sister Maddison and I both had posters up on our wall too, how cool is that! I didn't know that they allowed any Season Royalty to enter for a place here, surely he and his family have enough to do in winter, without putting studying at Rainbow House for the next four years into the mix!"

Kawiti laughed at their reaction, pushing his gold framed glasses back on his nose, a habit which Sun Ya had gotten used to, in the last couple of days.

"Oh, he is eligible all right, just like any of us, but I heard his family had to get special permission though, as he won't be allowed to serve in the southern hemisphere and must always put his duties to winter first."

"How does he know all this?" Laura turned to whisper to Sun Ya.

Shrugging her shoulders, she smiled back and shook her head at the question.

"They are certainly a pair of hunks. Don't you think Laura?" Voicing her own thoughts

"Well , the prince is anyway!" Laura said, more or less

said to herself.

"What if by chance we all got in, you could be sharing a room with him Kawiti, and Laura and I, could come and visit you." Sun Ya said looking at him expectantly.

"Yea in your dreams, if he gets in, he will most certainly have a room to himself. He won't be mixing with the likes of us." His voice had an edge of distain.

"Why ever not?" Laura asked.

"Well, the obvious reason is that he is Royalty, and possibly because he has a little gem!" Sun Ya stated.

They all turned to look at the object of their conversation and sure enough above his head floated a bright clear sky blue gem, glittering brightly.

"But I have one too! Although, I'm no princess!" she laughed at her own joke.

"You do?" Sun Ya looked at her in surprise. .

"Sure, but mine is probably following Maddison, my sister! No cancel that, Dusky is hovering over by the door. I don't understand the significance of them myself."

"You named your little gem, how cute!" Sun Ya cooed.

"No, my sister did!" Laura followed her little gem around the room and saw a tawny coloured one, a little further along the wall.

"I'm no prince either, and I hate to say this, but the brown one is mine." Kawiti said, turning back to them. "That's a coincidence, all three of us in the same room."

Sun Ya began scanning the room again, and then elbowed Laura to get her attention.

"I think it's four, look just behind the head of the dark haired guy with the prince."

Floating above him was now a brown orb flecked with gold.

"Well, I like the Prince's better it's the colour of a

summer sky." Laura said whimsically.

"You know the percentages against this happening are quite phenomenal. There are so few little gems in the world now, and in the competition today there are just 59 contestants that have them." Kawiti said.

"And you know this how?" Sun Ya asked smiling broadly.

"I ask questions, and I get answers!" his face was beaming, "and the fact that we are here together in the same room is pretty extraordinary. We have to find out what numbers they are!"

"Why?" Both girls said together in astonishment.

"I don't know why, I just know we have to. I'm 76, Sun Ya is 73 what about you Laura?

"She's 75" Sun Ya answered for her.

"What about birthdays?" he probed again.

"What about them?"

They again said in unison and both girls looked questioningly at him.

"Well, what are they? If my guess is correct, we were all born on quarter days!" he said smugly.

"Actually no, I wasn't" Laura, shook her head.

"Sorry me neither, but yes Prince Thorlief is. I remember that information from the calendar!" Sun Ya answered.

"Damn! That's my theory out the window. I always thought that the two were connected in some way." Kawiti said.

"Really! How?" Laura asked.

Before Kawiti could answer a now familiar robotic voice vibrated round the room from the amplifying system.

"Would numbers 37,38,39,40,41 and 42 make their way to the waiting area B5 and numbers 43,44,45,46,47 and 48 to waiting area B6!"

"Well only another 20 or so, to go before us." Sun Ya reflected.

Two boys and three girls left the room unseen, as all three sets of eyes rested again on the Prince and the American, who were still talking in low tones.

"He looks like a prince, don't you think?" Sun Ya asked.

"The other one doesn't" Laura immediately put in.

"Hi Laura, can I sit with you?"

Paul Ray suddenly appeared beside Laura's chair, making her almost jump out of her skin. "I tried to find you earlier, but met up with a crowd from all over. I was next door, but the last two guys have gone to the waiting areas. To be honest, I hate to be on my own at the moment, I still have a few to go before I get called."

"Sure Paul, you don't have to ask, let me introduce my two new friends."

Paul sat in the vacant chair between her and Kawiti.

"This is Kawiti and Sun Ya. Paul and I go to the same school." Laura explained.

"What number are you?" Kawiti said pointedly.

"59!" Paul replied, automatically, raising his eyes to Laura in question.

"Well at least it isn't 99." Sun Ya smiled at him.

"I'd be a basket case by then, especially if I were alone!" he admitted candidly.

"Hey, no negatives today, alright!" Kawiti smiled.

"I can live with that!" Paul agreed.

"What do you know about little gems?" he asked.

"Where did that question come from? Because by coincidence the other group I was sitting with were talking about them too."

"Really, what did they say?" Sun Ya asked. "Do you have them in your family?"

"No, not now, but we used to, according to my grandad. He says we had them for generations, but ours disappeared in the years of the red phase, and one of the guys I was just with said his family lost theirs in the white phase. There were a lot lost then I think. Anyway we had five in our room down the corridor, three looked more or less the same hazel colour, one was a really shiny blue/grey and a girl who was sitting with us had a violet coloured one with tiny flecks of silver all around the edge."

"Oh, that sounds nice." Sun Ya said enviously.

"There must have been thousands in the past, but for one reason or another they have disappeared." Laura was saying.

"We seem to be recouping though!" Kawiti mused.

"We are?" Paul voiced.

"Isn't it strange that we have four little gems here now with us and another five just down the corridor?" Kawiti continued his musings and stared closely at the gems.

"Well, no one knows how many there are in the world and given how many of us there are, I should think there could be lots more." Laura stated.

"That's the point, there were lots, but now there are fewer than 10,500 worldwide. I read about it when I was studying and there are always the quarter days."

"Oh, I was born on 21st March, so yes I'm a quarter day" Paul volunteered, glad to be included.

"See, it isn't just coincidence" Kawiti turned round behind him, let's go over to the Prince and ask him if he knows anything?"

"Are you out of your mind?" Sun Ya instinctively

grabbed his arm and held him in his seat.

"What are you going to ask him first? Do you know how many little gems are here?" Laura whispered, glaring at him across the table in horror.

"Well that's a start!" Kawiti was smiling at them both.

"He will think you are mad!" Sun Ya stressed.

"Actually, I don't!" Both the Prince and his companion were standing on the other side of Paul. "May we join you?"

Sun Ya immediately dropped her hold of Kawiti and Laura sat up straight her stomach turning over, but this time, in a nice way.

"Sure, why not" said Kawiti, quickly before the girls could get a word in, and moved his chair out to allow them to bring another two seats, into the circle and sit down.

"Why not, indeed!" Laura whispered to herself.

"So do you know why there are little gems?" Kawiti pressed.

"I know that I should, but I'm sorry I don't. As is mostly the case, we take them for granted." He turned to the American. "What do you say Amitola, do you have any ideas as to what they are?"

"Our ancestors have always offered up that the gems are the souls of past lives, and are looking over us." He again spoke directly at Laura and not to the rest of the company.

"That's basically what my family says too!" added Kawiti sulkily.

"I've always found them intrusive myself," said Laura turning to Thorlief.

"How, so?" Thorlief said, looking at her for the first time.

"Well. erm......, they are always there!" she stuttered.

95

"Really, mine comes and goes. Sometimes we don't see it for days" he answered.

"Ours is always with us, every day, since Maddison came!" she said quietly to herself.

"Maddison?" Amitola questioned.

"My younger sister, but I don't honestly remember it being around when I was little. When Maddi was born, it was there and didn't leave either of us at all, then."

"Did it change colour?" Kawiti asked.

"I can't remember, I was only little" she said.

"Does it do anything else?" Amitola spoke, again only to Laura.

"Such as? It's a little gem, what else it could do?" she said contemptuously.

"Ours flashes on and off" Kawiti provided.

"They all do that!" Thorlief added.

"Some it appears, more than others." Amitola observed.

"My sister actually talks to ours." Laura said, and turned to her left "Doesn't she? Paul."

"Yeh, she does it all the time. It's as if it understands her too!" Paul added.

"The point is, does it reply?" Sun Ya cheekily asked.

"Ha, Ha, very funny, but I sometimes think it empathizes with situations that are happening around us. I can remember in the preliminaries, it kept flickering every time I came first, like it was excited for me." Laura admitted.

"Mine did that too." Thorlief said to Laura and she blushed, but not revealing that he had been taught to interpret the meaning of most of the simple flashes, by his father.

"I never knew that a gem could be shared within a family." Amitola pondered.

"Oh yes, if it isn't with Maddison, it's with my younger brother Alfie, and then it flits around the whole family." Her hoity-toity look, had him smiling at her.

"Would numbers 49,50,51,52,53 and 54 make their way to the waiting area B2 and numbers 55,56,57,58,59 and 60 to waiting area B1.

"Oh it's my turn." Paul pushed himself from the table and gave Laura a kiss on the cheek.

"Good luck!" The whole table called after him, he waved giving a rather weak smile and left with another two girls from the tables at the front of the room and headed for their waiting area.

"He seems so young!" Sun Ya said as they all turned to watch Paul leave.

"He is young! Only 16. We go to the same school and he is dating my sister Maddison, they're in the same class."

"How good is he?" Amitola asked her.

"Brilliant! Even though he is the second youngest in the competition, he will certainly hold his own, that's for sure" she said proudly.

"So back to the question in hand, are you a quarter day?" Kawiti faced Amitola.

"Yes, actually I am!" he acknowledge, leaning back in his chair and still watching Laura.

Suddenly it dawned on Laura and she too turned to Kawiti.

"So are Maddison and my younger brother Alfie!"

"Well that's a heady combination" Sun Ya mused.

"What are your numbers then?" Kawiti focused on the two men at the table.

"77." Thorlief informed them all.

"... and I'm ..." Amitola started to say.

"Either, 74 or 76." Sun Ya interjected.

"Yes, 74." he chuckled.

"So who is 76?" Kawiti asked.

"That would be me!" A voice suddenly cut in, from behind Thor.

A little girl the colour of ebony, standing not much higher than the back of the chairs they were all sitting on, came forward smiling at them.

"My name is Juniper, I too have a little gem," pointing to a honey brown gem, now floating just above Laura's head, "and I was born on a quarter day. Oh, yes!, and I am the youngest in the competition, too!." She added with a flourish, and to the amused silence of the group before her. "I am also a bit of an oddity, an augur! (*Someone who can see the future*).

She spoke with a charming African lilt and a broad smile, as all the others stared at her, in stunned silence.

"Wow!" Kawiti looked astonished and for the first time, he too couldn't find anything to say.

"And you are also a Princess to the autumn family in the southern hemisphere. I met your father last year at the pollution conference in India and he told me you were hoping to get a place here! Hello I'm Thorlief. Please sit with us." He offered.

Amitola stood immediately and gave up his chair to her, then moving quickly to Paul's recently empty one next to Laura, who deliberately leaned away, not allowing him to get too near.

"You were listening to what we were saying, so what do you think?" Kawiti asked.

"About what, Kawiti? The gems, the quarter days, or the fact that we are now altogether? Just coincidence? No I think not. All of us has a part to play in the future, some more than others, but each crucial to our world!"

"You've seen our future?" Laura asked sceptically.

"A little, but only enough to tell you that we will be together!" Both her legs, swinging backwards and forward, as she sat on the chair.

"Oh, cool!" Kawiti said grinning broadly.

"You mean we all get into the Academy?" Sun Ya glowed.

"Actually no!" A universal look of disappointment crossed all their faces. "I don't know exactly what happens, but for some reason, I could not see who follows that path!"

Suddenly she pointed at Laura. "I did feel two more will also travel along our road. Siblings I think!"

"Maddison and Alfie, but they are only children. Well, I suppose Maddison is your age, she only missed the competition final closing date by two days. Alfie is just a child only 11 years old, surely you can't include him?"

"I said, I felt two more, I do not know if it is the younger, but when you said the name of the first, I can say she has already been called and knows she has been chosen for this day."

"Really?" Laura was not feeling so welcoming towards this girl. "Then how was she called, as you term it?"

"Father Sun, has chosen her himself, he was sending a message in ABL this morning. She is key to the scheme," she sighed, "but what plan it is, I have no idea at this time."

"I expect it's me that doesn't do well," Sun Ya lamented, "I don't have little gems, nor was I born on a quarter day" she said, resigned to her fate.

Juniper however had other ideas.

"As I said, I do not know the plan, but you are crucial

to it succeeding, in or out of Rainbow House, it will not succeed without you. But what I do know is that you were born on 21st December, a quarter day!"

She almost put a "Ta Dah!' after she told them.

"How can you not know your own birthday?" Amitola asked.

"Well, maybe it was because the nuns at the orphanage told me I was born on 25th December." She smiled at him "They called me Mary, but when I was a year old, I was adopted and my parents moved from China to Malaysia. They changed my name to Sun Ya."

"So now you have two birthdays" Kawiti said, nudging her in the ribs, "Well done you!"

Making Sun Ya feel special, rather than an oddity, she smiled shyly back at him. "Yes, yes so I do and one of them is a quarter day!" she glowed, which pleased her no end.

"Would numbers 61,62,63,64 and 66 make their way to the waiting area A3 and numbers 67,68,69, 70, 71 and 72 to waiting area A4.

All of them looked at each other, but it was Sun Ya who actually voiced their fears. "We're next!"

"She is so observant." Kawiti joked, but his face had already lost a little colour.

"Listen, all of you!" Juniper's soft voice instantly held their attention. "We have to pull out all the stops. We are not going to be able sail through this. I haven't seen the outcome, only the beginning of the competition for us, so it doesn't mean the outcome cannot be changed."

"That really isn't making sense!" Amitola said.

"I know, but it's more of a feeling than anything else and something is going on here, that is out of the ordinary." She screwed up her eyes and shook her head. "Something bigger than all of us!"

100

"In what way, Juniper?" Thorlief looked at the little girl with concern, he could see she was suddenly scared stiff.

"I have outside influences coming through to me, which is wrong. I was told, I would not be allowed to augur within the competition arena," Shaking her head again, as if it would clear it. "Oh, I don't know how to handle this overwhelming sensation, it has never happened to me before." She was struggling to stay focused.

"Are you just nervous about the competition maybe?" Sun Ya asked gently.

"No! Well, maybe a little, but it's much more than that!"

Without thinking Laura got up and gently took hold of the little girl's hand, as they could all see now that she looked terrified. Glancing pointedly at Thorlief, he put her other hand in his and nodded that all the others should do the same, until all six of them were holding hands in a circle. The impact of apprehension was felt by all of them instantly.

They each stared at Juniper, suddenly amazed that out of the blue, they were all able to tap into her view of swirling dark shaped colours. Within seconds their joint calming influence was helping and the dark colours began to fade into muted light coloured shades, spinning away from them, until they essentially all felt comfortable again and sat back at the table.

"Oh thank you, I feel so much better now!" The little girl smiled.

"Funnily enough, so do I," said Thorlief.

"Do you think our anxiety was affecting Juniper?" Laura asked.

"Could be!" Amitola joined in, "but if that was the

case, we would have made it worse for her instead of making it better. I think our influence was the fact that we all pulled together."

"Yes, I think you have a point there Amitola, now relax everyone. As Juniper says, we cannot think this is a foregone conclusion and while I was in the circle, it came to me, why I am also here with you." Thorlief reflected.

"You worked hard to get here!" Amitola said loyally.

"I did indeed, as we all did," he smiled "but that is not what I meant, in the last few minutes something has come to mind. Something that has been bugging me for a few months now." Leaning closer he went on to explain.

"I was watching the Aurora Borealis last winter from my bedroom balcony, practicing for today." The envy on their faces made him lower his eyes and gave them a shy guilty look, showing a side of him most would have thought didn't exist, as he continued. "I know! I'm one of the lucky ones that can see it for real. Anyway it was displaying the usual messages, when suddenly. It kind of focused in on me, I know that sounds stupid, but it really did and I read a message that made no sense to me whatsoever!"

The others were listening open mouthed.

"Well what did it say?" Kawiti asked the all consuming question.

"It was weird and when I read it first off, it was almost as if the message knew I didn't quite understand, so it literally disappeared, then came again, so I could translate it properly." Stopping and leaning back in his chair.

"Fine, great, but what the hell did it say?" Amitola urged his friend to tell them.

Taking a deep breath Thorlief quoted the message from memory:

Both must lead:
 Six to bridge the rainbow, but not the
 Five to regain the blue,
 Four to seek their terra crystal, but not the
 Three who travel a route and see below,
 Two to mend the network, but there is only
 One who can free the legacy.'

He looked over to them all, but stumbled on what he was about to say next, and then decided not to continue.

"That's about it! It disappeared as soon as it felt I understood what it was saying, but I was left with no idea of what it meant. I wrote it down, but I couldn't bring it with me, because this so called outfit doesn't have any pockets."

"Is it a prediction?" Sun Ya enquired.

"It doesn't sound like it, it isn't really saying what is going to happen and I thought that's what they did, prophesies predict something don't they?" Amitola said knowledgably.

"It is kind of general." Kawiti agreed, and looking meaningfully at Thor. "It's not at all tangible."

"Yes I agree, but it has the prediction elements, look at six to bridge the rainbow, doesn't that sound like it is something to do with us?" he said hopefully, as he couldn't see any other explanation.

"I understand what you mean, Thor! Yes we are six, I can see your logic," Juniper said, "and the message came with the lights which were how I saw the message to Maddison, but I do not understand the whole. There seems to be another group following the same path."

"I'm only suggesting this might be connected to us, but don't you see the reasoning?" Thor asked.

"I see exactly what it is you see Thorlief, in a strange way it does make sense and as the message says, you will lead us! The thing is, where the hell to?" Amitola smiled at him.

Thor shook his head, "I have been trying to figure that out over the last few months and came up with nothing!"

"Thor, please don't beat yourself up. It's probably because there is nothing to figure out, nothing at all, yet!" Juniper suddenly slid from her chair and stood. "It could be really important later, after we have passed our entrance test, that is the time when it will become much clearer, I'm sure!"

"You think?" Sun Ya said and they all laughed nervously. "No pressure then!"

With that the tannoy suddenly announced "Would numbers 73, 74, 75, 76, 77 and 78 make their way to the waiting area A1 and numbers 79, 80 81 82 and 83 to waiting area A2.

Leaving the group in no doubt that they were now all heading out together for the future, they just didn't know what kind.

"Are you ready?" Thorlief asked and walked towards the door, now anxious to proceed with whatever this quest was, "Come on!"

"Leading us already? Mighty Prince!"Amitola laughed and bowed low as he joined him in the corridor. "The signs are good!"

"Better than good" Juniper added as she smiled up into Thor's face in passing, as she and Sun Ya led them down the corridor.

104

"How much better than good?" said Kawiti. He asked in his usual enquiring way, as he followed behind them, but they were all too confused to comment.

Laura followed Amitola into the corridor, brushing his hand and accidentally touching, they both felt a enhanced tingling sensation at the contact.

"Wow what was that?" she stopped and stared at him. Only to see his reaction was exactly the same.

"I don't know, maybe we have a connection?" he said quietly, as if voicing the question would actually make it so.

"Not in my lifetime!" Laura stepped forward, wiping her hand down her tunic and ran to catch up with Sun Ya.

Leaving Amitola, to follow her with his eyes and with a smile stretching from ear to ear, sauntered over to Thor.

"Tola, what's that grin for?" Nudging his friend in the ribs, "She isn't interested!"

"Oh yes she is. She just doesn't know it yet!"

Chapter 9

Tristan

At exactly that precise moment, Tristan Kane was staring at the door to the auditorium and wishing for the first time that he had a ticket to enter. For some reason he couldn't fathom, he had a craving to be inside and not even because he knew Maddison Springer was there. For the last couple of hours he had been roaming aimlessly around the exhibition with the school party from Colchester Seasons Academy. The only enjoyable time so far, was meeting Maddison and smiled to himself as he remembered those short 15 minutes, then turned reluctantly away from the door.

"Tristan?" his so called exhibition partner Gabriella, whispered in his ear. He had thought he'd lost her, but like a bad penny, she turned up yet again. "No use you looking at the door, it isn't going to open miraculously for you to enter you know!" At least two inches taller, even though they were the same age, she glowered down at him.

"What not even with you standing beside me, and I thought all doors opened for Gaby Munroe?" he said as he made to turn away.

"Most usually do!" she smirked silkily, the innuendo hardly subtle, as she looked him up and down, as if he was a piece of meat on a slab. She could still not understand how he had come first in a quiz at school, one of only 30, of those who won the chance to come to the exhibition. She thought he had fixed it somehow, along with almost everyone else who knew him.

Tristan was thinking on the same lines, but he hadn't,

because he had deliberately put what he knew were the wrong answers, which actually made winning a place to the exhibition his worst nightmare. With having Gabriella as his partner, only exacerbating the pain as she was making sure, every chance she got, to make cutting remarks to him.

"Kane!" his name rang unbelievably clear over the heads of the crowd around him. Gaby suddenly disappeared as quickly as she had materialized and Tristan shrugged his shoulders. A movement to his left had him face Miss Pike as she walked towards him.

"You appear Mr Kane, to have gone missing most of the trip so far! How the hell you passed my test I shall never know? You don't even want to be here!"

She made to turn away from him expecting him to follow and walk, in what must have been the direction of the rest her students.

"I don't know either." he admitted, but didn't move a muscle to tag along. "You're right, I didn't want to come, don't want to be here much, and cannot for the life of me understand how I got 99 questions right, when I deliberately gave the wrong answers to them all!" his voice rose loud enough for her to hear.

Stopping the teacher in her tracks, she immediately swung round to look at him.

"You answered them correctly, by accident?" her tone now amused.

"Well I'd actually call it a major pileup by the looks of things." He said under his breath, but the teacher heard that too.

"Well it worked even if you didn't want it to!" her voice, lowered to barely a whisper, as she had turned back and now stood directly in front of him.

"I don't understand ....!" with his head set awry, he

suddenly didn't look like CSA's albeit clever under achiever, who mostly found himself in detention, rather than in class. His eyes widened as he stared right at her. "It's just come to me! I have to be here don't I? For some bloody reason, I need to be here, at this place and time. Should I be in the competition arena behind that door?" Pointing his finger deliberately behind him and at the entrance to the auditorium.

"You don't have a ticket, Kane." she whispered conspiringly. Her face suddenly crinkled and a wily smile came to her lips.

That was a 'shock/horror' look for him, as she had never smiled at him voluntarily, once, in all the three years he had taken her class.

"Never stopped me before!" he replied, suddenly feeling for the first time that day, this was right.

"Go! I'll explain to the rest of the group. I'll say that I sent you home alone." Her smile looked warmer. "It's not as if they can't wait to see the back of you, anyway!"

"Why are you doing this?" Tristan asked. As much as it felt like the exact thing to do, it somehow felt far too weird for him.

"No idea, just know I have to! Good luck Tristan! Oh, give me your lily pad, you won't be needing it where you're going!" Taking the pad as Tristan gingerly held it out to her, she turned without even looking back and was swallowed up by the crowd.

Quickly Tristan spun round and retracing the few steps to the huge competition doors, he stopped just out of sight of the two female concierges as they stood talking about their love lives, behind a desk on the opposite side. They obviously had nothing to do, as everyone who was meant to be inside was inside and the doors were now closed allowing people out, rather than in.

Tristan, however was concentrating fiercely, as he looked at the small square metal swipe device on the side, he smiled to himself, looked over at the two girls to see if they were watching, then back again at the device and smiled.

A piece of cake!

Chapter 10

Rosie and Tom

Once they reached 'Tea and Symphony 2', Tom led the way into the up market bistro and found a table, as always, furthest away from the doorway. Sitting down he placed her, facing him, and as usual had his back to the wall, looking over to the entrance. Old habits die hard and in this case a definite necessity, if he was going to get to talk to Rosie uninterrupted..

There was a moment of silence between them, with only a soft symphony of classical mood music piped through the sound system, but within seconds a waitress came over to take their order.

"So what would you like?" she asked Tom and ignoring Rosie completely, but he nodded for her to ask his guest first.

Reluctantly the girl turned to Rosie, who immediately asked for, "Tea please, milk no sugar, and a piece of prawn and mushroom ....", before she had finished the order, the girl's head spun round to face Tom's.

"Quiche!" Rosie added, to the waitresses back.

"Tea for me too," he said and smiled again at Rosie. "But I'm starved I'll have anything with cheddar cheese and lots of crusty bread with it!"

"Ploughman's lunch has a bit of cheddar, and four other types of cheese too, but I can give you extra bread." She was about 18 years old and smiled wantonly at him, whilst writing on her pad.

"Great, thanks!" Taking no notice of her at all, he fastened his eyes back on Rosie's own and approved wholeheartedly of how they sparkled with the colour of a dusky sky. Admitting again to himself that even without hearing her story, he would have recognised those eyes anywhere.

The waitress left, asking herself, what on earth could such a good looking guy, see in the silly little girl in front of him, she was barely grown out of her training bra, what a waste!

"You like tea and cheese, I see!" Rosie giggled softly.

"Yes I love both of them! Mum's English! Born and bred here in London, married my dad after, she met him at Glyndebourne, when she went to hear the European premiere of New Year, by Tippet. Years ago!"

Which meant absolutely nothing to Rosie, but she smiled encouragingly for him to continue.

"Dad was on holiday here from Norway and thought he was going to see a rock band called New Year, met mum as he helped her up after she fell over in a particularly soggy part of the car park and wham, love at first sight!"

"That is so romantic, a bit like my mum and dad. Mum was on holiday when she went swimming, then getting out of her depth in a few feet deeper than she could manage safely and dad swam out to get her and helped her back to the beach."

"It happens like that sometimes!" he smiled to himself, remembering saving Nicola when she got suspended against a fjord rock face, on an abseiling weekend over a year ago and he helped get her lines untangled. By the time they had descended to the bottom, they both knew they were meant to be together. This thought made him feel decidedly homesick, for some reason and quickly brought his mind back to the here and now.

"So Rosie, tell me all about yourself?" he asked.

"Well, I live in Kent with my mum, dad and I have two brothers and my grandad and my uncle live just a few roads away," she began, "and most of the rest of our family live around us in Bexley, Orpington and Dartford, all within easy reach!"

"So when did you start writing the great British novel" He smiled indulgently, thinking that this would give him a little more substance to her history.

"Hey, don't make fun of me, you sound like my brothers," she smiled cheekily back at him. "I suppose I started telling stories when I was really little. Mum said I was always rambling on to everyone who would listen about the Springer's, even before I got to primary school."

"Why did you call them the Springer's?" he was curious.

She looked at him as if he was from another planet. "Duh! Because that's their name, silly!" she grinned, correcting him in amusement.

"Oh, right!" Tom responded.

She was so positive that this was what they were called. 'Why not indeed?' he thought. It must be so obvious to her, as she didn't know her history, so would pick things up randomly and the name Springer, was a logical progression to the season they were understandably a part of.

"When I began school and learned to write, I slowly wrote it down in my note books. I still have all ten of them. Pam, the lady who got your water for you at Senots, is my mum's best friend and she got mum and dad to buy me a laptop for Christmas, two years ago. Just so I could write all the stories a lot quicker and .... as they say; the rest is history!"

She was smiling at him as he was listening attentively

to what she was saying. Thinking all the while, how young and so earnest, and how dangerous this was becoming.

"And your younger brothers, do you read to them too?" he wondered.

"*Younger brothers?* Where did you get that idea from?" Rosie sniggered and her face, definitely mirroring her bewilderment at his question. "No, Mike is three years older than me and Jack is my twin and he is older by about a 30 minutes."

"Impossible!" he shot back.

This information was like a curve ball and not what he was expecting at all. His whole body tensed.

"Sorry, what did you say?" her forehead folded in speculation.

"Nothing" he sidetracked, this information was totally out of the blue. "You just don't look like a twin!" Was all he could come up with, on the spare of the moment!

"And what exactly are twins supposed to look like?" she chuckled, "We aren't aliens you know!"

"Well, of course not," his face betraying his blunder, "but I've never met or seen any twins, apart from on TV, so I guess I don't know!" He admitted.

"Really? That's a bit strange," she gave him a long questioning look.

"Strange, why?" He actually swallowed, trying to think of something that would make sense to her.

"Well, twins aren't rare are they? There are loads of us around!" Adding brightly.

"I know that, but I live in the back of beyond and I just haven't met any!" He conceded, and then smiled a bewitching grin. "Until now that is!"

"Oh, Okay!" Accepting his answer, she was so used to

being a twin that she found nothing odd in the situation.

"So what do your mum and dad work at?" he asked, changing the subject quickly.

"Mum works part-time in the London Transport museum over there," she turned and pointed out the window to the building nestled in the corner, "and dad is a bus driver."

"Really, and they don't do anything else?" he questioned, again nothing seemed to add up. "Hobbies, maybe?"

"No, not really, mum loves musical theatre, but sings really badly off key," she laughed nervously, "and dad, well dad doesn't do anything much, got no interests at all really. Likes a bit of indoor DIY, but never gets to the outside, because he is afraid of heights and he likes gardening, but that's about it!"

"Were you adopted?" Tom asked, the words coming involuntarily out of his mouth, because that was exactly what he was thinking. There were no twins, or multiples thereafter in the Symm, not ever. All offspring were charged with their sole obligation, and that first gift they carried could not be shared.

"I beg your pardon?" She looked at him askew, taking in his own shocked expression of concern.

"Well, you obviously have a talent and your parents and siblings don't seem to have ....." he floundered, "I'm sorry I didn't mean it to sound the way that came out!"

Damn it, had he said too much, but it just wasn't gelling, he needed his father there to investigate her for him, and to find out who and what she was. But he wasn't here, so it was up to him to help her. He checked his watch, he had so little time, and it was getting dangerously close to an interrogation, rather than gentle probing. Tom extended his hand toward her, then seemed to think better of the gesture, and yanked his fingers through his hair as an alternative distraction.

Rosie watched his deliberations. She could see it was a new experience for him and she smiled to herself back at him again, but still not responding to his half asked question.

Luckily the waitress appeared with their lunch, putting the plates in front of them and followed immediately with their tea.

The silence grew as Rosie drank her tea, then forked the quiche absentmindedly into her mouth, and watched Tom quickly focusing on making a dent into his own meal.

Rosie decided to make her own decision, and while Tom had his mouth full, she emptied hers resolving to continue chatting to him and clear things in her mind.

"Well, to be honest we are all different really, my brother Mike is at Cambridge University studying medicine, and my twin Jack, is also clever, but lately won't study for some reason. Me, I am hopeless at any subject apart from English language, literature and geography," taking another sip of tea and swallowing, "and we are all different, even in looks."

Tom nodded for her to continue, relieved he was suddenly making progress and speaking to her might ruin the flow.

"Well, you see I have, blondish hair, bluish eyes. Jack has a sandy coloured hair and hazel eyes and Mike has really dark hair and grey eyes, he's the most like my grandad Bert. Mum says that Jack and I look more like her side of the family."

"What about your hobbies. What do you do when you

aren't writing?" he had almost finished his meal, but abandoned his knife and fork and decided to drink his tea instead.

"I love gardening, all the dirt and watching the flowers and trees grow, I think that's the Springer's influence." Rosie coyly admitted.

"How so?" Tom queried, now he was getting somewhere and leaned back in his chair, slowly sipping his now very cool tea.

"Well, everything about them is to do with, how to grow things, because they are in a family that's all about spring. They do so much to help the environment, I love to watch them doing their work, it's really interesting," she took another sip of tea. "I try everything I see them doing and continue it in our garden and they always know when it's going to rain or it's going to be really hot and I tell dad." She admitted and unintentionally realising too late, she had voiced her inner thoughts "but it's our secret, dad's and mine!."

"Secret, why is it your secret, Rosie?" he questioned gently, suddenly she was giving him almost what he was reaching for. "You talk as if you are watching a TV programme!" he sensitively accused.

"Do I? Well I suppose I am. I only think about what's happening when I am asleep, I dream all the stories, and sometimes it's hard to remember everything especially when they are chattering away ten to a dozen to each other!"

There it was at last, she had to be Primera. Tom was stunned as he sat staring at her as his cup of tea was dangerously tipping forward, as he physically froze in front of her.

"Tom your tea!" Rosie called, bringing him back to the

116

here and now.

Tilting the cup back he smiled "Oh sorry! Tell me again, in your dreams, you hear what they are saying?"

"Course I do, I told you, that's how I know the Springer's name, they told it to me!" she was giving him more information that he thought possible. "Well, kind of, when I was little they were speaking, but I didn't understand them, although over time I got the hang of their language, so I expect I get some of the words wrong. What is it they say?" she smiled back at him. "It gets lost in translation and I gave all the family, English sounding names that almost matched their own."

"Bloody hell, so you are Primera! I never thought! Tom managed to get out, but didn't finish the sentence, for the sheer knowledge of knowing the consequences of voicing such information was huge. His half empty cup returned safely to the saucer, he leaned his elbows on the table and watched fascinated as a whole host of emotions were running over her face.

"I'm sorry, what did you say?" She gaped at him flabbergasted and looked more perplexed, as she was telling this virtual stranger her biggest secret. "One of the what?

It was now adding up and suddenly Tom made a decision, his blue eyes narrowed, he was sure of two things, Rosie Norton was extra special and he had to tell her the truth! Well, a version of it, that wouldn't get her running and screaming out the door.

Chapter 11

Jaime and the Box

Jaime Hubbard was a Rainbow House lecturer, and leaving the observation room overlooking the auditorium, he walked the length of corridor hoping to find an empty room. He tried several doors, but none were open until he saw one further along the passageway that was ajar. Looking round, he was able to slip inside unnoticed and into what looked like an office of some kind.

Closing the door behind him he walked over to the window and then took the small rectangular wooden box from his pocket. Holding it again in the palm of his hand, he moved back to the desk sitting down in the room's only chair and placed it within arm's reach on the table in front of him. He rubbed his forehead, as if to ease the tension in his brain, spending a few minutes just staring down at it.

He realised he could still only see what he had seen before, yet had never seen the box before two weeks ago. He knew of its existence, of course, as it had been passed down through his family, father to eldest son, for centuries.

His older brother Donald had been killed in an unfortunate accident climbing in the Pyrenees, only three weeks before, and he had inherited the box on his brother's death.

Much to the torment of his sister-in- law, as it had been passed to him, rather than any of her own children, but as none were old enough to carry the responsibility of the box. It was now his.

118

This fact alone had put her nose out of joint, she had been hysterical when the elders had passed it to him, and he knew full well why.

Donald had called it his money box and had often gloated to him. 'You only need one little gem and you are one of the richest individuals in our world.' and he had become, to all intents and purposes, just that.

Staring down, he studied at the box, taking in every detail. Discoloured with age, and could have been any type of wood, but he thought it must have been oak, although he wasn't sure. It was however visually a masterpiece, having on all its sides carved shapes of circles, stars and triangles, overlapping in minuscule patterns covering the whole area with only the lid clear of any detailed decoration, but for a seven point star, with a tiny hole in its centre. Picking it up yet again, he tumbled it gently in his large hands.

There were unfortunately, no instructions given with the box, Donald would have had directives from their late father on receiving the gift on his 20th birthday. Now there wasn't anyone to help Jaime, so it would have to be pot luck, as to whether he got a gem with the box, or would he have to find his own, but how the hell did he capture one and keep it?

Even with all his family's wealth, he himself had in fact inherited quite a large sum from their father, this box was different. If he followed his self-indulgent elder brother's philosophy of taking what you wanted, when you wanted it, as he always had, perhaps the wealth that his brother had accumulated in his short life, perhaps could be equalled for him.

He had tried to open the box on several occasions since receiving it, but it just wouldn't reveal its secret to him. It was frustrating, more so since coming to the competition and seeing all the gems flying around, it must be possible to capture one, if of course, the box was empty. Logically it should come with one, but what if it didn't, how would he know one way or the other.

Distracted and standing, still absentmindedly turning it over and over in his hands, he looked for something that would help him with his quest, a sign of what he needed to do next. His concentration lapsed for a second, and without warning the box slipped from his hand, dropped onto the table edge, where it glanced off and headed for the floor. Yet, before it smashed into tinder, it suddenly stopped in midair and hovered above the ground.

It must have hit some hidden key on the table, activating the mechanism in the box and before it could be damaged and moved again to settle gently onto the floor. To Jaime's amazement, within seconds it shone a light through the hole of the star carving on the lid and onto the ceiling.

Looking up, it was showing him a view of the face of a strange being with two gems in its head, who was obviously not of his world. Then unexpectedly the hologram smiled at him as in what was obvious relief, and leaning back to show the rest of himself, standing in a room not dissimilar to the one Jaime was in, and waved as if in farewell.

Then it happened, the box unexpectedly sprung open, allowing the leafy green gem within, to escape and he watched mesmerised as it flew around and around his head, flashing on and off and finally shooting off through the window to disappear from sight.

"No, No, No!" he scooped the box up, turning it over and over in his hands, "come back, come back!" he screamed, but his command was too late and quite ineffectual.   Jaime sat heavily back on the chair, tears running unknowingly down his cheeks.

Several minutes passed before he finally put the box back on the table, his emotions barely in control and his mind began to try to figure the puzzle out again.

He was obviously no further advanced than when he entered the room, but his brother was a shrewd operator, he had kept this box and made a fortune all these years. It was now up to him to find out how, and obviously capture a gem, to replace the one he had unfortunately set free.

Yes, it could only improve from now on, couldn't it?

Chapter 12

Tom and Rosie

This was it. Tom took an incredibly deep breath, closed his eyes for a second to concentrate and finally decided that if he didn't tell her the truth, he would lose her, but even then, she might not believe him anyway.

"Rosie, haven't you realised yet, this isn't up to you! In fact you actually have nothing to do with it." He gave her a stern gaze and took in her obvious vulnerability, so again hesitated, before continuing. "We belong to a long succession of people who are of a lineage known as 'The Symm' and you are part of it. In fact, if I don't miss my guess, a very important part!" he smiled a devastating smile which lit up his face, as he looked at her. "Let me explain what actually happens."

She was staring at Tom as if he had suddenly grown another head, but he smiled again back at her and scratching just one of his heads, he was trying to find the words that would make it easiest to assimilate what he was telling her.

"You have an overview of another world, a parallel kingdom of sorts that is ahead of us here, in our time!" There he'd said it.

"Overview?" What was he talking about! These were her stories, stories of life in Equilibran and about all of the Springer family, Laura, Maddison and Alfie. Their adventures and in some cases misadventures, were the product of her mind, nothing more, nothing less, she thought. She stared back at him, but he sounded so sure that he was right that curiosity got the better of her.

"What is this Symm thing?" she asked.

"You have never heard this expression before?" he asked, but hoping it wasn't, because for her to have some recognition at this time would be very helpful.

"Nope, I've never heard anything like that before. All I know is that these are my stories, I dream them and I bring them to life!" she said confidently, her expression challenging Tom to differ.

He smiled indulgently, but it didn't reach his eyes and he shook his head in what seemed disappointment.

"No Rosie, you're still learning and they are bringing you to life, not the other way round." He lowered his voice, "I digress. These are dangerous times, for you to write your chapters, even if they have been well disguised. They could open a very large can of worms, as you will be contacted by others; those who know the Symm, and those who want to......!" Tom suddenly stopped speaking and instinctively looked across to the front door.

Walter was standing just outside and indicated to Tom to finish his conversation, by pointing to his watch.

Tom immediately held up the palm of his hand to denote five minutes more.

Rosie looked up bemused and twisting round to the window following Tom's gaze and she saw a man just turning away. Facing him again, she asked, "Who are you?" her voice was breathlessly soft and very nervous.

Tom brought his face back to look at her and this time his smile was genuine. "You don't recognise me? I'm insulted! I thought once seen never forgotten, I recognised you immediately."

He leaned forward and stroked her cheek in a brotherly kind of way, but Rosie felt the sensation go down into her toes. Well, who would have thought?

"Then you have the advantage, Tom!" she was studying him more intently now, and although there was nothing she could put her finger on, she had to admit there was something vaguely familiar about him, "but, I'm positive we have never met. I just know we haven't!"

"Tell me what colour is Thornleif's little gem, again?" he asked, he had to get her on side as quickly as he could.

"Blue, a beautiful blue," she gushed and made herself raise her eyes to his, "it's almost the same colour .... as your eyes!" her speech stumbled, over the admission.

"And your eyes are the same colour as Maddison's little gem!" he countered as his lashes flickered and faltered slightly, hoping she would get the connection.

At this Rosie then did a double take, suddenly realising his eyes actually did match Thor's gem exactly and immediately moved away from the table slightly.

"It sounds as if your little gem is very special, especially being able to hear everything that happens and having the whole Springer family under its wing. This in itself is something I have never heard of before. We usually have only one charge."

"One charge?" she queried, wide eyed again.

Tom leaned his elbows on the table and watched fascinated as a whole host of emotions ran over her face, as her mind was swirling.

"Rosie, I'm Thor's sentinel, and I was at the competition the same time as you were," he confided, "and I can see everything you see!"

"No! You listened to my story, you know about the competition, from what I read out at Senots!" Reasoning quickly and contradicted him emphatically.

124

"I did listen to your story, it was beautifully written, but it was a documentary, not fiction. Our abilities, yours and mine, limit who we can talk to and in fact hardly any have the exact same awareness as we have. We are a little out of the ordinary, you and me." He watched her shake her head in denial. "Yes we are Rosie, but we are not altogether unique!"

"What ability? I am nothing like you and what the hell are you talking about? I'm just an ordinary girl with an over active imagination!" she suddenly sprouted a quote from a teacher at school, and unexpectedly realised she had believed the woman. "If you know what happened at the competition, tell me something that I didn't write down, something, anything that will prove to me, that you are telling the truth!"

She proceeded to fold her arms in front of her and leant forward, looking every inch a scared 16 year old schoolgirl, determined to face him out. This was a test she was hoping he would fail; otherwise she would have to admit to herself that she was going completely round the bend.

He coughed, clearing his throat, and he hoped he was making a little headway, albeit miniscule, as she was obviously still a little afraid. "You know, I know, don't you Rosie?" his smile almost ruined the effect, "You forgot to add about Amitola falling off the chair, when Juniper joined them at the table!"

"How did you see my dream?" Immediately she came back with, what she again rationalised and several negative emotions tumbled over her and she was now very panicky at his words. "You must read minds!"

"No! Rosie I don't read minds, but I think that some others of the Symm have this gift!" he grinned, but gamely carried on his explanation, "I didn't see your dream Rosie, I saw mine, and that's how I know exactly what you missed out of the story!"

She didn't have the nerve then to look at Tom, tucking in her chin, her gaze now fastened on the empty tea cup in front of her.

"Now do you believe me?" his voice was begging to be understood.

She lifted her eyes and stared up at him hard. Oh she didn't want to, but something in the way he was watching her made things start to slot into place. Her body was tingling, as if she were being awakened in some way.

"Yes, I do, I think!" Looking into those eyes did so much remind her of Thorlief's gem, "but it just feels very weird!"

"I'm sorry for that, I know this is all new to you, but you had to know you are connected to 'The Symm'. Mainly because you could be in danger, especially if anyone reads your story and recognises the implications of it." He moved a little bit closer to her, but she didn't retreat.

"It's not exactly a story though is it Tom?" She admitted. "I always wondered how I could make up such fantastic tales! Especially as I was always right on point as what was going to happen with the weather."

He laughed out loud and Rosie saw for the first time a twinkle in his eye and whilst looking at him, still found something puzzling she hadn't felt before in anyone, even her family. A connection!

"No Rosie, it isn't exactly a story at all, but I want you to know that you are a very important person, with a gift that is truly amazing." He closed his hand gently and covering her own.

"Really?" She said in a self criticising and derogatory

way. "I dream about a place, that others can see too, and write it up as a story for kids! That's truly amazing!" Nodding her head she raised her eyes skyward.

He smiled again. "Yes, well I suppose it does sound a bit out there and possibly not exactly how you are seeing it now. It has far greater consequences, than either of us can imagine!"

"What consequences?" her voice trembled.

"We are part of a line of sentinels of families all over the world, who try and keep the balance in both our worlds."

Tom had never had reason to explain himself before, and he was amazed that what he had grown up knowing about the Symm and yet now sounded so, unbelievable!

"The Symm stands for symmetry and balance in the universe." he finished. "Unfortunately, there are some within our world, who can manipulate sentinels to their own advantage."

"Why would they want to do that?" Rosie now looked scared, "and I honestly don't think anyone could find it advantageous, living in Welling!"

"Ah, but there is great wealth to be had, by knowing exactly where certain events are to happen, or to be found, even in Welling. I should think!"

"You mean like when Alfie found the Earl of Bexley's dagger." Rosie tried to help with this explanation.

Tom leaned back in his seat and gave a hearty laugh at that. "Almost, but not quite. No, more like where weather is going to ruin a crop, or floods, tornados, storms of different elements, where to find, out of reach natural resources, for instance. Oh! Hundreds of things can happen in the world, which will affect lots of different areas." His mind scanned every aspect of his life and sighed. "It is sad, that you have not had the Symm's chronicles taught to you by your family, as one of your relatives would have had, history telling, as their own gift!"

Now admitting to himself, that this was a lot harder than he imagined it would be. It sounded ludicrous even to his own ears, it was a lot different knowing about the Symm, but telling of its fundamental life to someone who had not one iota of an idea of what he was revealing.

"You said family. Do my brothers also have this so called intuition?" she asked earnestly. Could this explain Jack's behaviour lately?

"No Rosie, not like you, but, saying that!" his brow rose up significantly as he couldn't figure out this part himself. "You shouldn't either?"

"Why?" Now she was really interested in what he was saying, even if she didn't quite understand it fully.

"It is only the first born in a Symm family who is able to see what you see. Male or female, it doesn't differentiate. So I am not sure why you have this gift either and what a gift! It sounds very much like you are one of the Primera?"

"This Primera again, what is that? I don't understand? I'm only third born and why does the first born in my family, not have my gift as you put it?" She leant forward, even though they were whispering, she instinctively knew that their conversation should not be overheard.

"Yes you are right he should have. It's a real conundrum and I can't answer you." He automatically looked at his watch, realising he was running out of time.

"You asked me if I was adopted?" she replied

astutely.

"I'm sorry about that, it just slipped out." His head leant to one side and he lifted his shoulders, holding his hands up in defence.

"No, no I can understand your reasoning now," she grinned, "but I really wasn't Tom! Mum gives everyone who wants to listen, the story of me and Jack coming into the world. Usually with all the details, and even Dad adds to the tale sometimes. They weren't even in a hospital either, but they got caught up in a flood in Cambridge and Mum gave birth to us in the house of a friend." Rosie realised she was blabbering. "Anyway, they wouldn't lie, it's just not in their nature!"

"Okay, I see, but could you ask them, if by any chance, they have at least heard of 'The Symm?" he needed to have her family onside. Although it was possible they could also be of the Lost too!

"I can ask, but I don't think so!" Then asking him a question of her own. "Why was it so important for you to find me?"

"You're very sharp for someone so young, but yes I did need to find you to tell you how much danger, reading your book is putting you in. If it was to be printed, or anyone found you, as my sister Kristy and I have, just by accident. There is a strong possibility that you would be kidnapped, by a squirrel!"

Rosie couldn't help but giggle at the thought "A squirrel eh?"

"I know! Stupid name isn't it! But warranted, because those good-for-nothings would squirrel you away somewhere, until they could sell you back to your family or worse still, sell you on to a magpie!" he was so sincere she didn't laugh this time and he quickly began this explanation. "Magpies are few and far between, but far worse, because once you are in their hands, it is very unlikely that you would ever be seen again. They would make you work for them, by using your gift to make them even wealthier, than they are already". It was a shortened version, but one Tom felt would at least scare Rosie enough to be on alert from now on. "Do you understand Rosie?"

She nodded, her face drained of what little colour it had, and she was now really frightened at what he had told her.

"Good girl and I am sorry I'm scaring you. I just didn't realise that you were absolutely unaware of what you were doing. I only wish I had the time to explain everything to you!" he took her hand in his, "Kristy was right, you are something very special, and actually you would like her. I want you to know that you can trust both of us with your life. Kris has certainly saved mine often enough over the last few years."

"How?" Rosie's curiosity getting the better of her.

A loud knock on the door had Tom's eyes looking directly into Walt's, his tilting head swiftly indicating that they needed to move, now.

"I have to go. My mate Splash there, seems to think it's time to shift my butt out of here. Now I have told you, please, you must be vigilant Rosie and above all you must stop reading to the children after today, as this puts you in too much danger. I will try and talk to you tonight and certainly again before I return to Norway."

He rose from the table, finding a £20 in his pocket, placed it beside his empty plate. "And Rosie, the Symm is a gift, remember that, but it can be manipulated right up until you are 20 years old. You must stay incognito until then, but I'll explain the details later." He looked so concerned and honest in his plea. "Promise me you will do this?"

Rosie was shaking, what he said had really scared her, but if it were true, then she was not the person she thought she was, and if she were honest, that petrified her even more. What to do? Looking again at Thorlief's little gem, she stood up knowing in her heart of hearts, that Tom was telling the truth and nodded, "I promise!"

He smiled and gave her a brief butterfly kiss on her young cheek, "Good, I am so proud to have met you, Rosie Norton. I promise I will telephone you at home tonight and try to come to see you in the next couple of days."

Turning quickly he pulled out a squashed baseball cap from his pocket and crossed the café, while he put it on. Moving through the doorway being held open by the tall gangly man in a matching cap, who winked at her.

Tom turned his head to see if Walt was following, but caught the hint of a smirk lurking on his face, "What? What?" he raised a wry eyebrow, as Walt held the door open for an elderly gentleman to enter and immediately shut it behind him,

"Nothing!" he glibly offered and followed his disgruntled charge away from the café, his grin turning into a full blown smile.

Rosie sat back down with a bump, "You don't know my number and you certainly don't know where I live!"

She whispered more to herself than anyone else, then going over in her mind what Tom had told her, as the waitress was already there clearing the table.

Was it true? How could it be? Somehow it felt right, but 'The Symm', what the hell was that? It sounded stupid, but now suddenly somehow familiar and she again didn't know why. At this moment in time having

131

such a wonderful imagination was possibly a curse rather than a help. Her worst thought was, is he bonkers? But deep down inside she knew he wasn't and tried to rationalise what she had heard, but only coming up with more questions, than answers.

"Hello Buddy, miles away you were?"

Bert was about to sit beside her, but, just at that moment what sounded like a gun shot rang from outside, followed immediately by the sound of several screams and shouts outside the café, which brought both their heads round.

Within seconds, another shot rang out and before Bert could stop her, Rosie grabbed her bag and was flying out of the door, looking desperately for Tom and instinctively knowing the shots were connected to him.

Outside, a quick glance to her right saw people running away, but when she looked left and along the cobbled road, just before the museum, she saw the still form of Splash, the lanky man, lying bleeding on the cobbles, but Tom was nowhere to be seen.

Without thinking, she rushed towards him, he was Tom's friend, and she had to do something. Reaching the semi-prone figure she dropped to his side and hastily looked around, trying to find Tom, but a movement from the floor had the man rolling painfully onto his back, and Rosie leant over to speak to him.

"Splash it's me Rosie. Rosie Norton, I was with Tom. What happened?"

She began rooting around in her bag for a travel packet of Kleenex, she knew she had somewhere, and would help stem the bleeding. He was badly hurt, the blood was coming from his shoulder and glancing up, and she saw her grandad who had followed right behind her, even with a gimpy knee.

"Grandad give me your handkerchief, quick!" her voice was positive and clear. Her order had him react without hesitation, pulling out his freshly ironed cotton square from his trouser pocket. She ripped open the Kleenex packet and stuck the whole wad of paper tissues into the centre of the clean cotton hankie and gently placed it over the hole in his jacket shoulder and applied pressure. School lessons in first aid were now kicking in, although she was sure Mrs Balinious hadn't had a gunshot wound in mind when she taught Rosie the basics and would be gratified now, knowing she was the only one in her class who had fainted at the sight of the pretend blood.

"Oh where are you, Tom?" Rosie called gently into the distance.

At that moment Walt turned towards the sound of her voice, his eyes were barely open and he spoke softly in a raspy whisper, "Ah Rosie, the white magpie has him, tell Ellie I am sorry I failed. It happened too fast, his man got a lucky shot in, that's all! I should have seen........" abruptly his eyes closed and his head drooped into unconsciousness.

With that, a young man suddenly appeared and was kneeling down beside her.

"Well done Miss, my name's Terry and I'm an ex-army medic. I'll take over from here for you and the ambulance is on its way." He immediately checked for a pulse while removing Rosie's hand, so he could continue to apply pressure to the wound. "You can go now, Rosie!"

He knew her name and his touch had again felt tingly, like Tom's had been, she looked into kind eyes, as he was smiling at her and she nodded. She knew Splash was in expert hands, for her mind was telling her Terry was another member of the Symm.

Bert helped her up, her dazed expression frightening the pensioner, but nothing had prepared them for the piercing scream that turned them both round to look up and along the cobbled road.

"No..........!," came from two young women as they ran towards them, "Walt, oh my darling, Walter!" The older of the two went to the other side of Splash and fell on to her knees, taking up the hand that was on the uninjured side.

"I'm his wife!" she informed the young man who was tending her husband "What the hell happened?"

"Oh my God it's all my fault." A loud wail came from the younger one. "Where is he?" She almost accosted the poor medic on the ground with her heavy makeup case."Where is my brother?" her voice was on the verge of hysteria.

Automatically Rosie spun the girl round to face her, they were almost the same height and she looked into a duplicate set of Tom's eyes, although these were brimming with unchecked tears.

"Kristy?" She asked gently. "It is Kristy isn't it? I'm Rosie Norton, Tom found me today!" she clarified and moved her a little away from the scene, with Bert hovering nervously at her side, not understanding anything of what was going on.

"Is he safe?" Kristy whispered. "Did he get away, please tell me he got away?"

"I can't tell you that, because Splash told me just now, that the white magpie has him and to tell Ellie he failed and he was so sorry!" she whispered her message, knowing she was bearing the worst possible news, ever.

Kristy's faced drained of what colour she had left in her cheeks and the tears were now flowing unchecked across them.

134

"Oh no! I brought him here to find you. How could I have been so stupid?" Turning away she wiped the back of her hands across her face. "It was me who failed, not Walt and now he could die because of it!"

Suddenly as if out of nowhere, uniformed policemen were swarming around them, escorting them away from the incident, as a motorcycle paramedic came running to Walt, his crash helmet swept aside and was taking instant command of the situation, by asking Ellie and the young medic questions before gently advising them to kindly stand to one side, so he could assess the casualty.

As if in a dream, Ellie wandered over, along with the medic, to where Rosie, Kristy and Bert were standing and stood in front of Rosie

"Excuse me miss, but do you know the victim?" A young policeman had come up behind Ellie.

Rosie looked directly at Ellie and could see panic in the other woman's eyes, but within a second, she shook her head as if to clear it and turning to face him, she became very businesslike.

"Yes I do, Constable! His name is Walter Treleavan is my husband." He took down her name in his notebook, but before he could continue his interview Ellie asked "Could you give me just us a minute? I'll answer any questions after I've had a word here with my friends," indicating the group she was with, "before they take my husband to hospital." She then pointed towards the ambulance, which had just arrived on the scene.

"Of course!" The young policeman took a few steps back, looking closely at what was happening to the injured man on the ground and then watching as the ambulance crew trundled across the cobbles with the mobile stretcher.

"Rosie Norton?" she asked formally "My name is Ellie."

"Yes, and this is Bert Norton, my grandfather."

She introduced him quickly and he nodded hello in Ellie's direction, still not understanding anything at all, of what was going on around him.

Without preamble Ellie looked straight at Bert.

"I need you to do something for me, take both the girls back to where you live. I know Rosie's name, as my husband already text me all the information he had found out about her while she was with Tom, in the coffee shop."

Turning immediately to smile at Rosie and nodding her head slightly in deference to Rosie's position.

"I am sorry we are meeting under such circumstances, but I must be with my husband at this time and I cannot take care of you all!"

Rosie and Bert looked at each other in confusion.

"Kristy will be our intermediary," and turning to face her cousin, "now Kris take care ....."

"I don't need taking care of!" Kristy said flatly.

"No cuz, you probably don't, but Rosie does! We have to get her out of here, in case something else happens. As you said yourself, she is important to us, we cannot lose her, otherwise both Tom and Walt have gone through this for nothing!" she turned back to Bert "Do you think you can do this for me?"

"Course, I can!" Bert bristled, his old spine ramrod straight. "I might be old, but I ain't senile, girly!"

"Good!" The older girl smiled, then turned to her cousin, "Kristy do not do anything stupid, it is now our duty to help Rosie, you and I must keep her safe. Understood?"

"Yes, Mrs Bossy Boots." Kristy hugged her cousin

tightly in her arms, and managed to whisper what Rosie had related to her.

"No surely not? I understand Kris, and I will deal with this information while I'm at the hospital. I'll also inform your mum and dad about Tom, as soon as I can."

The paramedic and ambulance crew had Walt on the stretcher by now and were gently leading it over the cobbles, towards the open doors of their vehicle, which was parked on the adjacent road several yards away.

"Now go before any more police arrive to question you two, go!" Then added as an afterthought "Text me when you get to Welling!"

"Welling?" Kristy asked quietly. "Where's Welling?"

"I have no idea, but I have Satnav. So I'll find it don't worry!"

The policeman called to her, signifying that she follow the stretcher and Ellie hurriedly kissed Kristy on the cheek and turned to do exactly what he specified.

"I'll come with you to the hospital, if I may?" The medic said quietly to Ellie and was by her side as she moved in the ambulance's direction. "We can talk on the way if that's alright? I also have some information that may be of use to you." He gave her a knowing smile.

Ellie smiled back, he was Symm, she could feel it around him and was so grateful, she took his hand and gave it a squeeze feeling the familiar tingle of energy flow between them.

"Thank you, I'm sure it will be most helpful." Turning back to Kristy she said, "I'll get back to you as soon as I can, I promise!"

Seeing both Ellie and the young man steer the policeman towards the ambulance, Bert took both girls by the arm and firmly moved them at a steady pace towards Senots. Once round the corner they could see

Pam was hovering in the shop doorway trying to see what was going on. When she saw Rosie she let out a sigh of relief, and ushered them quickly inside.

Chapter 13

Tristan

Tristan had thought on first sight, that the metal panel was a card reader of some sort, which was well within his usual remit to modify, but unfortunately on closer study it was far more advanced than he had anticipated.

After looking at it for a few minutes, he saw he was arousing interest from the two uniformed girls opposite, so decided that a manufactured sob story would work just as well and walked over to them.

"I'm so sorry to trouble you, my name is Alfie Springer, my sister Laura is in the competition and my mum, dad and sister are inside, but I can't remember what my seat number is, can you help me?"

He lied expertly, joining this with a worried frown that worked well on the smaller of the two girls, but not the taller.

"You're late, you were told to get here before the competition started," the tall girl looked at him suspiciously.

"Oh Emma, he probably got interested in one of the exhibits." The smaller girl smiled warmly at him "Hi, I'm Hannah!"

Not to be placated Emma demanded, "Where's your lily pad?"

"I put it down when I was looking at the rock stalls, and when I looked round it was gone. I'm sorry I didn't mean to misplace it, my dad will be really angry with me for losing it!" Tristan whimpered.

"See Emma, he lost all his information," she turned

back to Tristan, "don't you worry young man, we'll make sure you don't miss anything. What was your sister's name again?"

"Oh, thank you, thank you so much!" he said, and not daring to look at Emma, just in case she vetoed her friend's good intentions. "It's Laura Springer!"

"Laura Springer, here we are candidate number 75, reserved four seats. 821a- 821d in the Green Section."

"This is the Red Section!" Emma said smugly, "Green section is right the way round, on the other side. You better start walking!"

"Now, you look here Emma, just because the wonderful Neil, dumped you last night, you don't have to take it out on this kid!" The other girl added, "...... and to be honest it's a wonder to me why the poor soul stayed around as long as he did!"

"Hannah, that's a rotten thing to say!" Emma's mouth dropped in shock.

"It's true though isn't it? You have to bend a little my friend. It's 'give and take' in any relationship, not take and take!"

"'scuse me!" Tristan called out trying to intervene, but they didn't take any notice and so he spoke a little louder. "Excuse me!"

"I try, I really do try!" Emma wailed.

"Well, you will have to try harder!" Hannah took her hand, "That's if you want to get him back?"

"Ladies, Ladies, I need to get in here!" he pitched his voice even higher and shouted again even louder. "Now, ...remember!"

Both girls swung their heads round to look back at him.

"No problem Alfie!" Hannah smiled and became all efficient in a millisecond, "I'll get the door for you.

140

Now all you need to do is go right when you get inside. It will be a little dark, but just follow the foot light arrows until they change colour, to green. Then it's middle aisle halfway down."

Hitting a button on her rainbow coloured lily pad, she dismissed him to turn back to her friend and pulled her onto the chairs behind them.

Tristan said thanks, but neither of the girls was listening and without a backward glance he slipped into the auditorium before the door could close on him.

Hannah was right, it was pitch black, except for the footlights and as he came to his first clear aisle, he stared down towards the stage. He ignored the contestants already there, as their numbers were only in the low 60's and now knowing Laura was the 75th, was certainly a help.

His eyes roamed over the red coloured seats and by chance looked and watched fascinated by a few sparkling lights that floated, or as some were, darting around up in the air above him.

He had heard of little gems, who hadn't, but no one in his school actually had them, although he knew that a couple of families did have them who lived in Colchester, because they were sometimes in the local paper his mother read. He had never seen one in his lifetime and he was spellbound, especially as a golden brown coloured one, decided to flutter around him, before darting away across the auditorium and out of sight.

Channelling his mind he felt calmer than he had all day, he knew this was where he should be, for whatever reason, and snapped his head into gear, leisurely sauntering along enjoying the whole experience.

It took a full 20 minutes walking on the upper tier.

At first following the red arrows, then blue, followed by orange and he had to do some fancy talking to get him across the smaller glittering gold section which was designated for dignitaries only, and got him an armed escort to the yellow section.

Chapter 14

Rosie, Bert and Kristy

After the policeman had swiftly taken a few more details, he had asked both Ellie and the medic to go to the police station later to give a statement. Turning, he looked back down the street, but Rosie and Kristy were nowhere to be seen. He shook his head in disbelief and did a full circle, but they had vanished from view. The ambulance drew away and he back tracked his steps, annoyed with himself for taking his eye off them.

He swiftly moved towards a colleague, to ask if she had seen either of the girls and what direction they had taken. His associate denied knowledge of seeing anyone of their description even being there, as she was trying to keep the area clear for forensics, while struggling to get information from other members of the public and pointedly informed him to do the same. Shrugging his shoulders, he looked around one last time, smiled defeat at his co-worker and proceeded to help move the public on their way.

Back in the bookshop Pam had led them all, to her office at the back.

"What happened? Are you alright? Tea, anyone?" Picking up the kettle on the table behind her desk, "Does anyone want tea?"

"Pam, calm down girl, Rosie is good." He looked over to Kristy, who was still as white as a sheet, "Not sure about the other one though?"

"We can't stay! We cannot be involved with this! No one must find out who you are!" staring at Rosie, Kristy brushed her hand across her face, forgetting the hankie in her pocket, as she wiped the tears away that were still running unchecked down her cheeks.

Pam took in a deep breath to steady her nerves, as she looked at Kristy's face. Turning to Rosie's, she ran her eyes over the rest of her body and noticed her hand was smeared with blood, which prompted immediate action.

"Right, well, both of you two go and clean yourselves up. Go on, quickly now, skedaddle!" her firm tone of voice had Rosie running to the bathroom, with Kristy close behind.

"Now Bert, what the hell is going on?" Pam began to interrogate the old man.

"No idea, honest Pam! It all happened so fast. I'd only just got into the café when Rosie belted out of it when we heard the gun shots. She went straight over and started helping the man on the ground, until a young medic took over. Just before, that one," his head nodding in the bathroom's direction, "with her cousin, the shot man's wife, came up screaming. By then, the paramedic and ambulance crew came steaming up and the police were swarming around and telling all of us to stand to one side."

"Rosie was helping the shot man? Never! She can't stand the sight of blood!" Pam sat behind her desk, staring up at Bert. "Did they get the man with the gun?" her voice betraying her fear.

"No, he's long gone, I should imagine." Bert sat down in the chair facing her.

"Thank God for that!" Pam leant forward and lowered her voice "What is going on Bert, why is this girl so upset?"

"Well, as far as I can see. Her brother has just been

kidnapped and her cousin's husband is the one that's shot." He gave Pam a tongue in cheek smile, "I think I'd be a bit upset too, wouldn't you?"

"Oh Bert, you didn't tell me about the girl's brother being kidnapped." Pam pointed out.

"Oops sorry! You're right I didn't. Rosie said it was the lad she met here after her reading. The one she went to the coffee shop with." He added.

Pam was shocked. "Bloody hell! I let her go with him, but he seemed such a nice boy. He'd even sat the whole way through Rosie's reading, enthralled."

"I know you told me when you sent me to get her, remember Pam? Come on girl, you weren't to know! I found Rosie alone in the bistro when they took him." He voiced almost to himself. "Whoever they are?"

Before Pam could comment, Rosie and Kristy were back.

"We must leave, now! This minute, you promised!" Kristy was clean, but still had the haunted looked she had on arrival and raised her voice to screechy-loud, as she stood looking at Bert with an accusing air, "we have to save Rosie this instant, old man!"

Bert agreed, there was something in the way the girl spoke which sent a chill down his spine. His Buddy was in danger, from what though, he had no idea, but he knew deep inside that it was so.

"You're right, come on you two. Pam don't you worry. I'll take care of Rosie and call you later. Whatever you do don't phone Lisa!"

Turning to the girls he asked. "Got everything?"

Kristy picked up her makeup case and Rosie did the same with her bag, then with a reflex action, picked up her folder on Pam's desk.

"Then let's get the hell out of here!" Bert went to

open the office door.

"Please don't speak to anyone about Rosie, deny all knowledge of her whereabouts and you hardly know her if anyone asks!" Kristy emphasised to Pam. "Because someone will come, not today maybe, but sometime in the near future to search her out. We all have to keep her safe."

Pam obligingly nodded, not understanding what the hell was being asked of her, but knowing it was important that she did as requested.

Just as they were leaving the office, a policewoman came through the shop door at the front. Automatically Pam nudged the girls to duck down onto the mezzanine stairs and went forward to head the woman off.

"Officer, what's all the commotion about, I heard screaming!" Pam deliberately got into a position that blocked the view further into the shop and Bert, Rosie and Kristy managed to keep low and get close to the back exit door without being seen. Luckily at that moment, the bell on the front door heralded the entrance of some tourists and while the policewoman's head was turned at the distraction. Rosie lifted the rear door's bell clanger so she, Kristy and Bert could slip silently out the back.

In the walkways between the shops there were several more policemen walking around and Rosie's heart was beating ten to the dozen. No one spoke as they could see police cordoning off the minor passageways leading out of Covent Garden and headed towards Drury Lane, but before they reached anywhere close, Kristy switched direction twice.

"I'm taking us to Maiden Lane" she whispered to them. It was a side street which ran parallel with the Strand. Without any obvious haste, they finally turned

146

again to come to the back entrance of the Venus theatre.

"Quickly, in here!" Kristy said. Pulling Rosie by the arm she knocked on the stage door, which was opened by a small man of indeterminate age, but with a broad smile of recognition.

"Hello Arthur, is Sole still here?" Kristy asked.

"Hi Kris, yes she's a bit behind today. Do you want to go up? She's in the kids' room. Thought you had a job today, you going to stay and help clean up the urchins?" he asked casually.

Standing back he invited them to come in and they were quickly swept into the back of the building and once the door was shut behind them, they all gave a shared sigh of relief.

"Me mum used to be a cleaner 'ere, years ago!" Bert suddenly blurted out, "when I was a nipper, of course!"

"Really? I didn't know that." Rosie was surprised at the information.

"Yeh!, I got to see every show they put on for all the 15 years she worked here," he smiled as he looked around the small foyer.

"Changed a bit since then, been revamped and modernised in the last few years!" Arthur informed him.

"Oh!" Bert looked surprised, "well, it's only to be expected." But he looked disappointed anyway.

Kristy and Rosie looked at each other and smiled, sharing a warm moment before Kristy turned to the stage doorman.

"All right, if I take these two with me, Arthur? We won't be any trouble just want to see Sole for a minute!"

"Course you can love. The old boy looks as if he could

do with a bit of time, must be bringing back some memories, eh mate?" Arthur invited a reply.

"Yeh it is! Look I'll stay down 'ere with Arthur, if that's ok?" he nodded in the stage doorman's direction. "Might even get a cup of tea if I play my cards right, and I'll be here, until it's time to leave!" he looked at them both and winked.

"Sure grandad!" Rosie nudged Kristy and they mutually agreed that staying put for a while was a good plan and she followed Kristy to the dressing rooms.

"Good idea of Bert's" Kristy whispered "I doubt the police have our descriptions, but better safe than sorry."

"Kristy, we had nothing to do with the shooting. Me!" pointing to herself, 'innocent bystander' who tried to help, that's all I was. They know you weren't there when it happened, because Ellie will tell them that."

"But it isn't only the police we have to worry about." She said candidly, as they reached the last door along the corridor.

"I know, the bloody, squirrel nickers and magpie savers, could find out about me too!" Rosie said in a deadpan voice.

Kristy came to a standstill in front of Rosie and broke into uncontrollable giggles, not loudly, and she had to hold her hand in front of her face trying desperately not to make too much noise.

Going along a short corridor they entered a room crowded with an amazing two dozen children dressed as urchins, with a small rotund lady, sitting at the end of the room in an apron which gave her the body of a thin young woman, clad in a red bikini. Coming forward she ushered them back out of the room and back along the corridor to a much smaller room and closed the door.

148

"Kristy, welcome, we have just finished the urchins," her face broke into a broad grin, "I thought you were on photo shoot, but I am complaining not. I'd appreciate any help today, as June phoned in sick this morning, something about bad prawns, and could do later with help." Her English grammar did its usual Spanish turnaround.

"Sorry Sole, I can't. I've just come in for your help actually!" Kristy admitted reluctantly, as she watched the disappointment cross her friend's face. Guiltily her face crumpled and Sole immediately crossed the room to where they were standing.

"So what is wrong?" she asked in a more noticeable Spanish accent "Your eyes are red with cryin', and don't you dare say okay, you are!"

"Tom has been stolen!" Kristy tried to sound matter of fact, but failed miserably.

"Kristy no!," She gave her a huge hug, almost stopping her from breathing. "When?"

"About 20 minutes ago in Covent Garden, but more importantly, this is Rosie. Tom went there to find her, but it seems a magpie was already there and Walt got shot." Her expression contorting at saying it out loud "... and he took Tom!"

"No!" Sole slumped into the nearest chair, "and where is Ellie? Is Walter 'ert badly?"

"I don't know! Ellie went with Walt to the hospital, but she says I have to take care of Rosie here!" she sat in the chair next to her.

Sole focused on Rosie for the first time, "Well, hola Rosie!"

"Hello! Are you Symm too?" Rosie automatically asked.

"No, little one, I am not on Kristy's pathway," smiling

at her as she said it, "I am just an 'onoured guest."

"Sole is a really good friend. She knows nothing of the Symm, apart from what I and the family have told her."

"We seem to be in a bit of a fix. The police could be looking for us, I think, but we dare not let them know Rosie is involved, in case the, nickers and savers, I mean Squirrels and Magpies, find her!" once again turning to face, Sole.

"Of course, that is what amigos are for!" Sole said, obviously knowing the significance of the names mentioned.

"I hoped you'd say that. Could you look around wardrobe and maybe find a couple of summer hats or wigs for us and a hat for Rosie's grandad. He's downstairs with Arthur. It's only to get us to the station, nothing major. We think the police might have our descriptions, hopefully not good ones, but there might be others looking for us, so I have to get Rosie to her home, to keep her safe." Her eyes brimmed with tears again and she swiped them with the back of her hand. Sole, seeing the action, handed her a box of tissues as she continued with her sentence "Ellie went to the hospital with Walt, he looked awful!"

"There, there, I'm sure I find something, that will do for you"

Turning to Rosie she told her to take off her leggings, because they were too noticeable and as Kristy was in tailored slacks and white t-shirt that were pretty ordinary for work and Sole handed her a blue jacket from the back of the door.

"I'll just pop down corridor a time and get rest."

Waiting for Sole to return, Rosie took off her leggings and rammed them into her shoulder bag, then sat down beside Kristy, who without conscious thought took her hand gently and folded it between her own.

"I can feel a tingling when you touch me." Rosie looked round at her. "Can you do that with me too?"

"Yes, but tell me how you would describe it?" Kristy asked softly.

"I don't know what I could call this sensation, it's kind of strange, as if we are linked, I feel it more with you. It was just a shiver sensation with Tom."

"That's good. So what did you talk about with Tom? She asked.

Rosie blushed and admitted. "He was a bit lame at first, could hardly speak at all!"

"Tom? Really?" Kristy's expression puzzled. "That would be a first!"

"It would? Well, I must admit after we had a bit to eat and once he realised I didn't know anything about the Symm, he kind of, became a bit better."

"A bit better, at what?" Kristy was enjoying the information.

"At talking - silly! But he was really nice to me at the café and tried to explain things a little about what the Symm was. Mainly, why I had to stop reading to the kids, or writing and absolutely not to get the books published. I promised him, I would, but to be honest I don't know if I can ever stop writing, I have been doing that all my life!"

"You don't have to stop, especially if that's the way the Symm is interpreted to you, but I agree with Tom, you cannot read to any children publically or get published, it would be disastrous for you."

"Yes I know. That's what he said too!"

"I never thought Tom would be lost for words, but if you are of 'The Symm' and you feel others who are too, we are used to the feeling, it's natural, but if must be strange for one of the Lost."

"Who are the Lost?" Rosie cocked her head to one side.

"You! By the sounds of it! It's someone who was in the Symm and for one reason or another isn't now and to be honest, I'm not quite sure even that description actually equates to you and I might have it all wrong!" she stated.

That was no better an explanation for Rosie.

They stopped talking immediately when Sole came back into the room. She had two jet black wigs in her hand, along with a thin white cardigan which would reach over Rosie's skirt and blouse.

"There that should cover the most of you." Handing the disguises over to the two of them and they quickly dressed.

"The show is starting in 10 minutes. Oh, and I found this for your grandfather!" Rosie was handed a checked cloth cap, reminiscent of a bygone era.

"Oh he'll love this!" she said, kissing Sole on the cheek.

"Thanks Sole, I'll text you any news when I know myself." Kristy also kissed her, but on both her cheeks. Then taking Rosie by the hand, heard Sole call "Vaya con Dios" as they left the room to go back to where Bert and Arthur were just finishing drinking a cup of tea in the office.

"Right Bert, another 10 minutes and the show starts. Follow me and I'll lead you through to the front of the house." Kristy was on familiar ground and felt much more confident in herself.

"Got some colour back I see girly!" Bert smiled at her, "Bye Arthur, thanks for the tea and the natter," handing his cup back to the other man, he turned to follow the girls along the corridor, "it seems I'm required elsewhere now."

"Any time Bert, always here on a Saturday if you want to pop in for a chat!" he called after them.

It took only a minute to reach a door which lead to the theatre stalls, and Kristy carefully opened it and all three of them slipped into the moving main stream of the audience who were making their way to the front of the theatre and they swiftly went towards the exit.

Reaching daylight and keeping their heads low, once they were in the Strand, they turned left on Bert's bidding and made their way towards Waterloo Bridge. He had thought Waterloo East station would be less likely to be covered by police or anyone else for that matter. It was a slow twenty minute walk (at Bert's pace) and across the River Thames, as opposed to turning right to Charing Cross station, just a five minute walk away, west along the Strand.

Chapter 15

Jaime and the little Gems

Placing the box in his pocket Jaime hurried from the room and back down the corridor to the stairs where he could be close to the contestants and more importantly, a concentrated quantity of little gems!

If he didn't catch a little gem today, especially one that was in the final violet area, his chances of getting a special gem, would be gone for another four years.

He reached the entrance to the staging area and no one had questioned his journey, he was in Rainbow House colours and although he was not officially on duty, he was known by enough backstage crew for him to wander unchallenged.

This was now the time and the place. He had to think of some trap he could set to collect his prize.

"Professor Hubbard!" A voice called his name and he suddenly felt like a schoolboy caught in some mischievous act. Which apart from the schoolboy bit, he was!

He turned to find Noelia, standing at the end of the stage, ostensibly watching a numbered group go through their paces.

She was a good looking girl, intelligent, had a wicked sense of humour and had always been well prepared for the classes in Advanced 'ABL/AAL' message taking, that he taught. He was sorry to lose her now she was leaving the Academy, he vaguely remembered hearing she had a placement, somewhere in middle America he thought, but couldn´t remember exactly what area or job she was given.

"Noelia, how is it going?" Jaime whispered. He had wandered over to her, as if he had every right to be there.

"Good thanks! There are already 35 participants in the violet area and we are only three quarters of the way through." Her smile lit her face and Jaime suddenly realised that she wasn't good looking, she was stunning.

"It seems to be going well then!" he suddenly felt tongue-tied and not knowing what to say to her, so that he could continue their conversation.

"Very well, I'm enjoying every minute of it. Especially as I get to see the little gems too, I haven't seen so many, ever!" Enthralled by watching a green gem as it swirled round the stage front and then disappear.

"Yes they are pleasant," not wanting to sound too interested, "how many of them are attached to the violet zone contestants, do you think?"

"Just over half have gems, I believe but none of them are allowed in the zone, so it's hard to know numbers, but I can tell you that there are a good number of quarter days amongst them. Do you think there is any connection?" she enquired.

"Quarter days? No, I don't think so. The gems are far more important than that!" he said dismissively.

Noelia caught the tone though, and looked at the professor a little askew.

"Anyone in particular standing out?" he continued.

Although he couldn't see into the violet zone from where they were standing, his eyes were certainly focusing on that section, as if he could.

"No not really, they obviously all did marvellously, otherwise they wouldn't be there!" Noelia was now becoming a little curious.

She had always liked Professor Hubbard, he was

younger than most of the other faculty, hardworking, funny, but she knew nothing about him socially, as he wasn't one to join in the general out of academy activities.

"Where do they go when they finish the last part of the competition?" he began scanning the exit away from the stage.

"They are escorted by their competition companion, either to me here if they pass, or to the waiting room where they are kept until the end of the competition."

"So they wait here do they?" he said. Perhaps a little too greedily to himself, as if looking around for successful candidates, although they wouldn´t have the final task for several hours yet.

"Professor, are you, OK?"

She turned her head around as he had, not sure what he was looking for, but she had caught his tone and was a little disturbed by it.

"I'm fine Noelia! It's the first time I have been able to attend a competition since I was a competitor myself a few years ago now, and I'm not up to scratch on how it is actually run."

"Well you know it takes three years to get it ready and ..... Oh here comes the next two who passed!"

Before he could actually catch a glimpse of them, Noelia had gone two steps forward and on her touch they all disappeared in front of him. Leaving the other dejected contestants to emerge with their competition companion and pass into a newly opened doorway, just behind him which he surmised was one of the unsuccessful contestant's waiting rooms.

Turning back to the stage, six more contestants materialised and were standing at the side of the stage with their own coloured competition companions and

Noelia magically appeared behind them directing their companions forward on to the stage.

"Busy girl" He sidled up to Noelia just as the last contestant walked forward to their coloured area.

"Yes, but it has been a lot of fun, it brings back memories of when I was a contestant four years ago." Her face glowed.

"For me too, 16 years, but it has changed a lot in that time, much more up to date now!"

He complimented, but he was getting nowhere standing there and now he knew the process, he would now have to wait until the violet area was full. Then be patient until the competition finished, if he wanted to try for a top flight gem.

"Thank you Noelia, it was kind of you to take the time for me." A delicate scent of gardenias wafted over to him. A pity she was so young, he thought.

"Not at all, Professor!" Without a backward glance, she centred her focus back on the new contestants.

Jaime swiftly left to find a quiet waiting room he could relax in, as it would be quite a while before the final.

Chapter 16

The Competitors

Amitola had caught up with Laura and was walking by her side, even though she was still ignoring him, as they reached the end of the corridor to join Juniper and Sun Ya. They all turned left as indicated and arrived at the door to Area A1, where they hovered outside until Thor and Kawiti caught up. Laura stepped forward to take the initiative and knock on the door, but Amitola slipped passed her and smiled teasingly as with his longer reach he knocked on the door ahead of her. It swung open silently, to reveal a sizeable anteroom in a soft relaxing green. The group hesitated on the threshold, but they could see a beautiful, tall girl with sparkling eyes and a confident smile, standing just inside who waved them in and indicated for them to sit on the chairs.

As they slowly walked through into the room, the door closed as silently, behind them, but not before their five little gems followed through the doorway and, settled together in a corner, knowing instinctively not to duck and dive at this point in time.

When the group were seated, the girl came round and stood in front of them.

The first thing the girls noticed was her waist length rainbow coloured hair and that her dress was as white as theirs were, but it flowed to the floor with individual panels, each defined on the edge by one of the seven different rainbow colours.

The boys in turn, just gawped at her incredible beauty.

"Hi, my name is Sarah, I have been asked to be your adviser/companion for the rest of your competition. Win or lose, I will be with you individually, at all times!" Her voice was soft and reassuring.

"How are you going to manage that?" Kawiti asked curiously.

She smiled indulgently at him and immediately spun round, leaving an imprint of her own self on every turn, until a further six Sarahs were standing before them. Each in a different single rainbow coloured dress, but unlike Sarah herself, none had any real substance and were more ghostlike, than solid.

"Wow, that's some party trick!" Sun Ya exclaimed.

"I know, isn't it fantastic!" Sarah laughed "I've been practicing for weeks!"

Her natural smile and enthusiasm seem to settle their nervousness a little, as one of the coloured Sarahs hovered before each of them.

Laura had Green Sarah. Amitola, Indigo Sarah, Kawiti, Blue Sarah, Juniper, Red Sarah, Sun Yan, Orange Sarah and finally Yellow Sarah floated in front of Thor. The original Sarah stayed where she was, while each of the others floated round behind their candidate's chair.

"Right, now this is what will happen next. When your group is called, you will accompany the Sarah who is standing behind you, to the coloured section that matches her dress. No one else will be able to see her, as she will blend into the arena's background and will wait there for the whole time, staying for each separate contestant in turn, as each of you move through the trials."

"They stay put, we move on" Amitola verified. He winked at Laura who he had deliberately sat next to and she sighed, but smiled nervously.

"Correct! Your Sarah will give you confidence, but won't be able to help in the manufacture or choice of your creations. You will have six minutes to provide the results you req....."

"Six minutes, it can't be done!" Thor roared, standing up and taking a step towards the real Sarah.

"Yes it can, Thor, because time is not relative within the Rainbow arena," she smiled at him as if she were five years older, rather than actually 19, as he was. "You know this, but have just forgotten. It's just nerves, take a deep breath," she ordered and looking round the room she further advised the others, "and all of you lot, too!"

Rapidly calmer, after a few deep breaths, Thor returned to his seat and everyone sitting did as was suggested and took deep breaths, leaving Sarah to continue.

"That's better! Now each section will allow you to fabricate, design or analyse in whatever time you require. Some of you will finish earlier or take longer. It will not make any difference to the circle or the audience, as they will only feel as if it has just been, six minutes, although it is actually only a couple of minutes, otherwise we would never finish the competition in time."

"That's better!" Juniper whispered to herself, only hearing half of what Sarah was saying, due to her nervousness.

"The only examination in real time will be the last test. This is for the candidates who have reached the final selection and if lucky enough, you will read either the northern or the southern lights." She grinned at them again.

"What do we ...." Kawiti tried to ask.

Sarah shook her head at him, to stop the interruption.

"I would like to remind you that there is no space for error, if you make a mistake on stage, it cannot be rectified. The contest only accepts P.I.P: Projection, Inspection, and Perfection. That's all that is expected of you!"

Stepping back she took a sip of water from a glass she lifted from the table behind her.

"As you know, for the last three months, you have all been given special permission allowing you to practice your projections and fabrications. Your natural gifts have not been affected, but specific abilities will not be returned, until after you have left the arena."

Looking deliberately at Juniper, who smiled nervously back at her.

"Now allow me to refresh your memory as to which colour, is for which fabrication. All of you have put forward a list of requirements, which you will need in each section. I will now confirm with you your checklist so these are provided, and you will find them on or around the staging area."

Several minutes later, after Sarah had explained all the technical details, especially for the manufacturing of certain creations, she relayed her last piece of information.

"Lastly, your little gems are not allowed to be with you on stage, they are here merely as observers, until you move on to the arena. They will be able to wait nearby and there is plenty of room in front of the stage for them, until you finish the competition."

Sarah watched as the faces before her told their own story of fear and apprehension, but smiled again to herself. She was pleased to be attached to such a dazzling group, she could feel a certain strength about them, but only time would tell whether it was strong enough.

She now turned back to look at Kawiti to allow him to speak, but it was he who shook his head, as she had already answered all of his questions.

"After you finish the last of your six tasks, I will come to you all, simultaneously through my other Sarahs. I hope to have the pleasure of taking you to our hostess, who will escort you to the Violet area where I will meet you in person or if unsuccessful, your last coloured Sarah will take you off stage to the waiting room, with the other competitors."

"So you will be with us all to the end?" Amitola asked, not even considering they would not get through.

"Oh yes, and I will be so proud to be there with you." Sarah smiled.

"Does your dress change colour?" Laura couldn't resist asking.

"Good guess! Yes it does, every one of you that passes fills a panel of my dress and," she whispered, "I'm allowed to take it home with me, as a gift!"

"So if all six of us get through, what happens to your seventh panel?" Sun Ya wanted to know.

"Ladies, Ladies, this is not a fashion show! Let's concentrate here!" Kawiti emphasised so seriously, that all the other twelve, see and no see, bodies in the room laughed at his reaction.

"Kawiti is right! We have only another ten seconds before you leave. Good luck all of you and enjoy the ride!" Sarah spun again, but this time disappeared.

"Ten seconds!" They all repeated and looked from one to another, when they suddenly found themselves with their Sarah on the side of the stage ready to be called into the corresponding coloured area.

Laura was leading the group with Green Sarah standing beside her, Amitola was just behind her and whispered gently in her ear.

"Good Luck Laura, I'll be thinking of you."

Laura wanted to turn and tell him to think of himself not her, but suddenly another voice called out blocking any thoughts of anyone but herself.

"Numbers 73, 74, 75, 76, 77 and 78", please step forward." Noelia directed all of them towards their first colour entrance, but they were too nervous to see her. They followed their corresponding coloured Sarah on to the stage and then into the amazingly large boundaries of their colour defined area.

All, in varying degrees, were nervous to say the least.

Chapter 17

The Contest

Laura stood to one side of the enormous staging area with Green Sarah.

"Don't worry you'll be fine," Sarah whispered to her.

"Glad someone knows that, because it certainly isn't me!" Laura took a couple of deep breaths whilst sternly warning her stomach, not to throw up in the middle of the stage, and then stepped forward into the limelight.

"Laura Springer, what is your first fabrication?" A raspy voice asked.

"An, English, rose." She stopped and stammered.

"Very well proceed."

Her selection was the first simple flower in the contest, but Laura didn't know that. She only knew she was producing a rose with a unique flower and together with a heady perfume, would hopefully win her this section.

Taking a deep breath she made her way over to the staging table and once there, she opened the seed pod, which she had requested on her materials list and placed it in the pot of compost she was allowed.

Within half a minute a tiny green stem began to rise out of the earth, Laura concentrated on every tiny detail of its structure as it grew regally upward and with the tiny leaves unfolding as the bud formed perfectly at the top. Majestically the bud began to unfold, a petal at a time, building from the outside petals of violet, indigo, blue, red, orange and the final

164

rainbow colour yellow, in the centre. Along with a subtle, but wonderfully concentrated rose perfume that wafted across the staging area.

She stood back, her head aching with the energy used, but she was pleased with the result and only hoped all her other selections came out as well.

The two judges Steven Baker and Margo Powell came to stand beside her and gravitated forward as their interest was understandably ablaze on smelling and then seeing, the remarkable flower.

Unfortunately as they made their way closer to the bloom, the petals each in turn, changed their colour to pure white.

The colours themselves had been a fantastic illusion, as Laura had used an intricate combination of hidden prisms, and generated a soft ray of sunlight over the light dusting of dew, attached to each of the petals.

The judges studied the now perfect white flower from every angle and finally walked back to their seats.

Laura was sure she saw a slight smile on their faces, or it could have been a grimace, she wasn't absolutely certain.

Her six minutes were up and she waved goodbye to the wall as she left Green Sarah and walked to the door of the Indigo area, waiting for Thor to finish, so she might enter.

AMITOLA

Indigo Sarah led Amitola to his place and disappeared into the background knowing intuitively he would not look once in her direction, as he was far too focused with his project. She smiled as he took deep breaths, calming himself, but chuckled as he jumped at his name being called.

"Amitola Sandoval, what is your first fabrication?" The voice asked.

"An Anna's hummingbird." He replied, to the direction of the sound.

"Initiating a low level force field," it came back, "very well proceed."

Amitola walked to the table and reached for the length of a branch which was supporting a large nest built of small twigs and moss, bound together with what looked like spider silk. He stood calmly concentrating entirely on the nest's opening and within seconds a tiny bird flew from the nest, so small it was hardly visible, until it landed on his shoulder.

One minute later the bird was fully grown with his natural colours of bronze-green back, pale grey chest and belly and had a crimson-red crown and throat. His bill was long, straight and slender, and he touched it to Amitola's cheek with affection.

Another minute saw him taking off from his vantage point and flying to a group of wild flowers that suddenly appeared on the table and after feeding from their nectar, slowly began flying backwards and forwards from the table to his nest. This was obviously just to show off his new accomplishments and then flying a little further away each time, he crossed the stage.

Finally, he headed up above Amitola's head and rose almost to the arena's ceiling, before diving towards his creator at 50 mph and a sudden loud squeaking sound came from his tail-feathers. This made Amitola smile as the little bird came over to him and hovered there before again flying to the wild flowers to feed. When he finished, he became aware that he was not the only

166

bird on the stage as he could sense another. Looking at the branch Amitola was still holding, he noticed a lady hummingbird with a green crown and some red markings on a grey chest and a dark rounded tail, sitting on one of the other smaller branches.

Flying back and settling on a higher branch, his voice could be heard around the staging area, singing his thin reedy song to his new girlfriend, who quickly joined him. Amitola had not moved in all this time, but when he saw they were there, he looked purposefully at the nest and they realised they were in the wrong place and together they flew around Amitola's head, almost as a fly past and returned into the nest, then popped their heads out together.

Carefully laying down the branch Amitola stood back and noted his judges, Ang Dickinson and John Webb for the first time, as they had been sitting at the side of his working area with their white lily pads.

They nodded in unison and indigo Sarah came beside him. "Well done! Now off you go to the next one!" she said softly and waved him off the stage.

KAWITI

At the same time as the other two, Kawiti was marching onto his staging area and kept nervously repeating to himself, "I will be fine, I will be great!" As if he could conjure up some magical phrase that would calm him.

Blue Sarah stood as close as she could, before blending into the background.

"Kawiti just go and do your best, it is all that you need to do!"

Her voice was comforting and he stopped shaking his

head as if to clear it and smiled back at her.

"You know you are incredible!" she added.

"Of course I am!" he beamed back at her.

"Kawiti Teira, what is your fabrication?" The same uniform voice asked.

"A single cell thunderstorm!" he replied confidently.

"We have initiated a high level force field. Proceed!" The voice came back.

With this, Kawiti crossed the stage to where a jug of water was ready for him on the table. Lifting it, he deliberately poured the contents over the grey cloud marked out on the stage floor. He then restored the empty jug back where he found it.

Returning to the wet patch, he stood silently looking at the pool of water and within seconds a soft steam rose up from it. A minute later a small fluffy cloud formed in front of him, which grew larger as it levitated still higher in the confines of the given area. Within another minute the warm air cloud was buffeted by the higher cold air mass around and above it. This contoured the cloud into its common anvil shape, before huge droplets of rain froze and returned to the stage as small lumps of hail.

This indicator of updraft and downdraft air producing changes in the wind speed, it was allowing the cloud to suddenly manifest a small lightning bolt that lit up the stage. This was followed immediately by the sound of thunder and gained a shocked gasp from the audience.

Within yet another minute, the wind above dropped completely and the cloud began to dissipate, letting the hail stop slowly and then just a light shower of rain was left as the cloud disappeared completely, leaving behind a faint impression of a rainbow arc reflected in the puddle on the stage.

The judges James Modlock and Wendy Harvey stared at the rainbow and actually turned and smiled at Kawiti as blue Sarah proudly hovered in the background.

"You may leave now Kawiti." Sarah whispered to him.

"Of course I can!" he grinned back, now confident that his next assignment would also be, just as exceptional.

JUNIPER

Red Sarah was very aware of Juniper's talents, as a strong aura was surrounding her, but unusually it almost felt as if it would devour her, rather than support her. "You are very talented Juniper, dig deep and find that tranquil space in yourself."

"I'll try Sarah, I really will!" she sounded like the little girl she was, but as soon as she approached the mark on stage near the table, she rapidly became calmer and wiping her hands on her tunic, she knew she was ready.

"Juniper Lakota?" The disembodied voice asked.

"Yes!" Juniper automatically answered.

"On the table in front of you, there are 16 crystal rocks, four each of beryllium and carbon, eight of alumina. Each crystal was taken from a different area of our world. We would like you to organize and place the gems into the boxed sections, which have the named place of origin for every individual example. Once a piece is placed inside, you cannot retrieve it, so choose carefully."

Juniper gave a self-satisfied smiled, it was her favourite assignment.

"Do you understand your task?" The voice asked.

"Yes, I understand!" she answered back.

"Very well, proceed," the voice came again.

Juniper stared down at the box, then at the pieces of rough rock which were left haphazardly in small piles around it. It had labels in alphabetical order with all of the 16 names in 'could be' places, which were in more than one of the four gem categories. She realised she would have to examine each rock very carefully, before placing it within its moss lined cubby hole.

"Now where do I start? One of each type would be best," she thought, "and it will keep my mind active."

She rummaged in the first pile easily placing a beautiful clear blue sapphire into the box named USA, the box automatically sealed and she continued by dropping a substantial sized diamond into Botswana, the third was a ruby from an ice shelf off Greenland and the final emerald was from Austria.

Starting again she went with a sapphire from Tanzania, then a diamond from South Africa, a raspberry ruby from Macedonia and an emerald from Zambia.

Next, she sorted through the pile at the far corner of the table, the rock she chose was difficult, but focusing, she suddenly saw what she was looking for, a really tiny diamond from Australia. The pile closest to her revealed an emerald from Canada, a ruby which looked as if it was from Madagascar, but somehow she wasn't sure of this one, but the next rock was definitely a sapphire of Kashmir.

Her final four were an easily recognised diamond from South Africa and a Brazilian emerald, then a pigeon's blood ruby that she knew definitely, was from Burma so she was able to quickly place the Madagascar ruby in its rightful location that left the final sapphire to be dropped into the box marked Sri Lanka.

"Thank you, you may leave now."

Eileen Read and Eric Shields made their way over to the now full boxes.

"Oh well done, Juniper, I love the girls choices,!" Red Sarah laughed. "The boys are boring, only silica, carbon, uranium and iron."

SUN YA

Orange Sarah almost had to push, the visibly shaking Sun Ya onto the stage.

"You have nothing to worry about your configuration will be perfect."

"It won't, 'cause I can't remember what it's going to be," she whispered back.

"Yes you do, now go, you'll be fine!" Sarah laughed, taking a step behind her.

"Sun Ya Sham, what will you be creating?" The raspy voice dragged her forward into the limelight.

"I don't ... know!" she stuttered, "I mean, ... a Tricolour Beagle."

"Very well, you may proceed."

Sun Ya walked forward on her shaking legs, to the table which held only a small triangular shaped dog bed and suddenly a new baby beagle pup, poked his head through the opening and even though his eyes were closed, he looked to all intents and purposes, to see his mistress and scrambled out in her direction.

"Lyka, how are you, my baby boy?" Sun Ya crooned as she scooped him up in her hand and gently setting him down on the blanket, below the table.

Curling up beside him, she seriously concentrated on

getting him to grow into the yearling he had to be, for the next section of the competition.

Within a couple of minutes she had him grown to his full height of 15 inches and his lovely hazel eyes never wavered from hers, as she worked towards her goal. The moment she finished, his front legs were straight, his tail relaxed down behind the muscular pair at the rear of his tricoloured body.

His mind focused on Sun Ya, in what was a little beagle's way and followed her merrily to the other side of the stage, found a dish and lapped up some water, then a small amount of food which had been placed there also. When finished he stood to attention next to her.

The course had recently had the scent of Sun Ya purposely dragged across the floor, through and over 20 obstacles that were set out across and around, the staging area.

Sun Ya dropped to her haunches to speak to him.

"Lyka Sham, just do your very best and come right back to me." She stroked his noble head affectionately.

"Are you ready Sun Ya Sham?" The disembodied voice asked.

"Yes." She stood up, looked down at Lyka, who was already sniffing the floor for her scent and called, "Go!"

Head down Lyka flew to the first object and did not hesitate round any of the set route and following all the natural instincts Sun Ya had provided him with, he was already crossing a stream and picking up the scent on the other bank. Charging next through a small group of bushes and coming back on himself, to pick up the scent that piloted him to a burrow and scurried through.

172

All this was done within the time allowed, he had gone over under and around every obstacle that was set for him.

"Yes!" Sun Ya jumped for joy, as he flew back to her and stood proudly next to her leg, while she slyly bobbed down to give him a doggy treat and stroked his ear. "Lyka, well done!"

"Your task is finished" the voice rang out. "Please leave the stage. Your dog will be cared for."

Reluctantly Sun Ya moved next to Sarah and as she left, Lyka tried to follow, but for some reason he couldn't move and no one, but her Sarah, saw the tears in both sets of their eyes.

THORLIEF

Yellow Sarah followed Thor, but unobtrusively slid into her position at his back, knowing that he was positive and prepared for his time on stage.

"Prince Thorlief Vinter, what is your first fabrication to be?" The voice asked.

"A Komodo dragon!" he answered confidently, and smiled to himself as he heard Yellow Sarah gasp at his choice.

"We have activated a high risk force field. You may now proceed." The voice came back.

Going up to the table, Thor found the megapode's nest that would have his dragon egg inside. Picking it up he listened to see if there was any movement and smiled as he heard, the baby dragon using its egg tooth, to escape by making a hole for himself inside. Putting down the nest he quickly took a seed from a dish nearby and planted it in an enormous composted pot beside the table. Using his mind he concentrated on getting the tree to mature before the tiny dragon came out of its nest and mere seconds after the tree was fully grown, the tiny greenish dragon had escaped his birthplace to come toddling along the table, to look at Thor, who quietly welcomed the newcomer.

"Hello Grumpy9! Eat lunch before you start," he told him.

He placed a few small grubs in front of the little animal, who found them immediately and ate them up in just a few gulps. Once the food was gone, he instinctively advanced straight for the tree branch which had grown over the table and began climbing up to the safety of its elevated limbs.

Unfortunately as he struggled to get higher Grumpy9 began to grow and before he reached the uppermost branches, both Thor and the dragon rapidly become conscious, that his weight was not conducive to the lack of strength in the thinner twigs. Without any hesitation, he turned round and made his way back down to the shelter of the wide lower branches and the earth below.

Before he reached the ground however, Thor placed a huge plate of carrion meat, between them on the stage, just to satisfy his now much larger charge's appetite. It was a precaution, just in case Grumpy9, being a neonate carnivore, the dragon might classify Thor as a member of his food chain.

Grumpy9 jumped from the pot, to the ground and using his tongue to detect the food, he sauntered over to the carrion, swishing his long tail behind him. With big quick bites he swallowed the meal, which almost weighed as much as he did himself, in a couple of minutes.

Thor smiled when he saw Grumpy9 had finished his

meal, and he quickly produced a small area of the arena floor to be flooded with sunlight, just on the far side of the tree.

The dragon turned towards Thor, but his overwhelming instinct was to lie down in the warmth of the sun and more importantly, to wait until he had digested his meal in peace.

Everything was going to plan, and the young dragon lazed for a time until he regurgitated several large white deposits inside the sun circle. Standing up quite suddenly, he began to grow at a much faster rate than any of the Grumpy's between 1 and 8, had achieved in practice.

Thor was astonished and mentally fighting for control of Grumpy9, when suddenly the now full grown 180lb dragon came running towards him. Thor stood his ground immediately realising that this newborn was just being friendly, and not aggressive, so went down on his haunches as the young charge came to a stop at his feet.

"Good boy Grumpy9, good boy," Thor called to him.

"Prince Thorlief leave the area now, we will eliminate the dragon once you are clear." Chris Corbett's voice rang out.

"Eliminate Grumpy9! No!" Thor was fuming. "Under no circumstances will you destroy him. He is to be returned to Komodo Island to be with his brothers and sisters."

"We will deal with him, now please leave the staging area!" Dawn Dunsford added, but her words shook in fear.

"No, I will not leave the staging area. Sarah, sort this out! Grumpy9 is not to be 'dealt with'. He is a living creature and he will be returned to his natural habitat.

Is that understood?" Sounding, much like his father, he stood his ground and Grumpy9 lay down at his feet not moving, almost as if he knew what was being said.

Yellow Sarah came up behind him.

"Thor, I understand your predicament, and I promise I will make sure that nothing happens to Grumpy9. Leave him with me, I will shadow a seventh Sarah, so she can be with him, until he is put with the other animal creations, which are being sent back to their own homelands."

He could feel her hand on his shoulder.

"Now go, they have to clear up the stage before Laura can come into the area to do her fabrication. Apologise and go, I'll sort it all out!"

"Thank you Sarah. Of course!" Thor turned to where he could see Chris and Dawn on the other side of the force field.

"I'm sorry judges, I didn't intend to cause a disruption, and I apologise profusely for my interruption of the competition."

Leaving the stage Thorlief glanced back at Grumpy9, who looked at him reproachfully at leaving him behind, but snuggled nearer to Yellow Sarah and then he noticed another Sarah was also there as she glistened in a very fine sheen of silver light and was standing close to Grumpy9 on his other side.

"I bet the last couple of minutes won't be transmitted for the population to see!" Thorlief thought to himself and smiled.

Chapter 18

Rosie, Kristy and Bert
****
Ellie

Catching the Dartford train to Welling at Waterloo East station, Kristy was taking her new position of guardian to heart, by only allowing them to sit in a carriage which was virtually empty and watching to see no other passenger boarded with them.

Once seated, a universal sigh seemed to roll off them all and Rosie couldn't help but notice how Bert seemed suddenly to look exhausted, as he sat facing both girls.

"Are you alright, grandad?" Rosie asked softly.

"A bit tired, darling girl," and he settled back into his seat, "not used to all this gallivanting around at my age!"

"Yeh, not our usual every other Saturday, I'll admit! But we are safe now!" she smiled at him, her voice more hopeful than sure. "How about I phone Dad and get him to pick us up from the station?"

"Not a good idea Rosie! Unless this is what you usually do!" Kristy immediately put in. "If it isn't, you would have to explain why you needed to, and you don't want to worry them unnecessarily!"

The final ' yet' was not said, but certainly intended.

"She's right Buddy, better to leave it until we are face to face. I'll just have a nap until we get there!" Closing his eyes and leaning back on his seat.

"He sounded shattered?" Kristy said in a hushed tone, as she could see how worried Rosie was.

"He's fine. He has the constitution of an ox and can sleep for England!" she smiled indulgently, "my Nan's favourite saying was that he could sleep on a clothesline, and she was right, listen!"

Gentle snoring from the old man, had Kristy doing a double take.

"But, he's just closed his eyes!" she chuckled.

"Told ya!" Rosie laughed at her new friend's expression of disbelief.

"OMG!" Kristy smiled back and watched as the old man snuggled down a little more for comfort, at the sound she made.

The train journey had them pass old and new businesses along the trackside and they silently watched out of the window, until Rosie saw Southwark Cathedral. She pointed it out to Kristy, then explained that it had been the venue of her cousin Julie's recent wedding and that they were riding over the ancient Borough market, one of the largest and oldest food markets in London and told her that her mum's brother, John had toiled for most of his working life there.

On approaching London Bridge station, she further explained that most of her grandparent's family were born in the area and Guy's hospital which towered over the station was where her brother Mike was born.

Kristy was glad of the brief history lesson, as it took their minds off of their own predicament for a few minutes and by mutual agreement, decided to wait until they had examined every person that came into the carriage at London Bridge Station, before having any kind of conversation about the events of the morning.

Luckily once they arrived at the platform, their carriage stopped exactly where five adults and two children stood. Rosie recognised a couple of late,

178

Charlton home football supporters, obviously waiting for the Greenwich line train, together with a family who had clearly just arrived from an airport, if the mountain of luggage and sunburn, were anything to go by but none of them replaced the one passenger who had alighted from their own coach.

That left only a young courting couple who had noticeably been shopping in the West End, having an array of named carrier bags, and a mum with two children, who were chatting away about all the sights they had seen in the city, especially a number of Toy Stores.

Once the doors had closed, the relief was tangible for both of them and they relaxed enough to begin the question and answer session that was now a foregone conclusion, just to clarify both their thoughts.

"OK! Where do we start?" Rosie said "Tom tried to tell me a bit about the Symm, but I just couldn't get my head around anything he was saying at first, it was so unexpected and it just didn't make any sense to me!"

"I'm not surprised. I still can't believe what has happened! Especially, the fact that you really are one of the Lost!" Kristy turned away and had a far off look aand her eyes never left Rosie's as they headed south. "Although it is exciting finding you, unfortunately, the cost was harrowing!"

"Yes, and I am sorry I caused so much heartache!" Rosie's voice was saddened by the events.

"That wasn't your fault! What happened to Tom could have happened at any time, believe me!" Kristy swallowed hard, as she voiced the truth of the matter. "Tom and Walt knew the dangers! For the last six years they have been saving kids who have been taken from their families by both squirrels and magpies. So far, they have saved quite a few from slavery and in some cases worse."

"What's worse than slavery?" Rosie questioned not really understanding the position, even now.

"Worse, can in some cases be a forced marriage or even death." Kristy replied, truthfully, "These men are predators of the first order, they will do anything to make money, and the Stolen are forced to work for them."

"You are kidding right?" Rosie's face drained of colour.

"Unfortunately, no I'm not! I don't mean to scare you, but you have to understand this part of Symm family life and you recognize now how it can happen." Knowing she had said enough and was frightening Rosie, Kristy changed the course of the conversation. "Look let me try to explain the Symm a bit more, shall I?" Our history is quite interesting!"

"Yes, please. Tom didn't really have time to explain much, just about the 'nickers' and savers', so go ahead!" She leaned back against the window turning her pale face to see Kristy's full on. Maybe she would get a better understanding once she had a clearer picture of this Symm thing.

"Well, we originated years ago to help Mother Nature with redressing the balance of her world and ours. When people were starting out, the balance was easy for her, she made enough food for everyone and we co-existed with the land and sea in harmony, but she didn't expect us, as people, to propagate quite so well."

"Too many, too soon." Rosie nodded.

"Yeh, and our intelligence was very much of a surprise to her too, even though she invented us, she certainly didn't realise we would excel there either.

That said, she managed for thousands and thousands of years alone, then a few thousand years ago, things got too much for her. The people were spreading like wildfire over the planet and to help her, she decided to give some families gifts that would serve all, and redress any imbalances, within their own part of the world." Kristy paused and Rosie nodded for her to continue.

"At first she gifted six families, who were attached to basically the six continents as we know them, and this worked well, except she only gave the gift to the firstborn male in families. As you know yourself, children in those times died, due to starvation, illness and accidents, but even if they grew, men tend to fight, for one reason or another and it became almost impossible for her to keep her charges out of the wars or major incidents that they seemed to get involved in. Of course this sanctioned many firstborns to die before they could pass on their genes. So about a thousand years ago she added women into the balance. How am I doing so far?"

Rosie gave her the thumbs up mesmerised by what she was hearing.

"Firstborns have their gift on birth, but before they mature at the age of 20, they themselves must pass this gene onto their own first born. Siblings of the same family also have gifts, but not as defined as the eldest. Firstborns marry or not nowadays, but they still have to pass on the gene before they reach the last day of being 19, if they don't, they won't pass that particular gene to their progeny. Does that make sense to you?"

"Yes, I think so!" she mumbled. It was a lot to take in.

"Good, now this is the best bit, only a certain mix of the Symm heritages are allowed and therefore only particular firstborn's have the gift of seeing into Mother Nature's world!" she looked at Rosie's incredulous face, "and they see it through their gems in their sleep, like you do!"

Kristy stopped speaking immediately as the tannoy told them they had reached Lewisham station, and they again called a temporary halt to their conversation until the mother and children left the carriage and a small group of cub scouts entered with an Arkala, with a couple of parents in tow.

When that group were settled at the far end of the carriage, Kristy resumed her history lesson.

"The gems belong to either gender but only Majestet firstborns, as far as I am aware. These are made up at different levels of Symm, Tom is Majestet and a Fin, so can see through the window."

"Am I one of the Majestet, and a Fin?" Rosie raised the questions.

"To be honest Rosie, I don't know, but I would assume so. Tom would I think know instinctively what arm of the Symm you are. Fortunately for me my own gift is to feel the balance, not the individual. I am aware of weather changes and temperature differentials." she smiled at Rose's facial expressions as she tried to visualise what that actually entailed. "Lately though I've been able to see little gems flying around in my sleep. Tom said it's only because there is a high concentration in England for the competition, but I think it is something more than that." She said almost to herself.

"Honestly Kristy, I don't actually feel anything particularly." Rosie shrugged her shoulders and screwed up her face. "I just see and hear what the little gems are doing!"

"Wow, you hear through your little gem? That's brilliant. Tom can only see, but not hear with his, although he has a real understanding of what was being said or going on around his charge especially and certainly more than our Dad ever did with his."

"Oh, I didn't know that. I only knew that Tom is sentinel to Thor, Prince of Winter, but yes I can hear everything."

"Who do you look after, Rosie?" Curiosity made Kristy ask.

"I suppose I'm sentinel to the whole Springer family, they are very ordinary, and it's Laura, Maddison and Alfie, who I'm with mainly!"

"Never! A whole family how do you manage, I've never heard of anyone being sentinel to a family before." Kristy was really impressed.

"That's what Tom said, and that I was very special. I think he said something about a Primera, I wasn't listening much by then!"

"No, you're kidding me, honestly, wow!?" Kristy was shocked. "A Primera ..... Really, Wow!"

"OK, stop with the wows! Just tell me what it means?" Rosie smiled at her in earnest.

"We are now approaching Blackheath station." The Tannoy announced.

"I think we are safe now, let's take these wigs off. All I want to do is scratch my head." Kristy changed the subject.

Both girls pulled them off and Kristy put them carefully into her makeup box along with Rosie's cardigan ready to return to Sole.

Rosie checked on her grandad who was still sleeping

and then looked out of the window at the back of the lovely old buildings they were passing.

At Blackheath station, the group of young cubs left the carriage and a couple of girls of about Kristy's age came on talking on their mobiles. They pocketed the phones and sat further down the carriage and began chatting with each other about meeting their boyfriends at Dartford, so they could go shopping.

When the train moved on again Kristy answered Rosie's question.

"It means your family over the centuries has never left the Symm, you are one of the six original Symm families and there has never been anything, but Fin in the heritage line, for thousands of years."

"The original, six families! How on earth can that be?" This was beyond weird for Rosie. "Come to think of it, how do you know there were six?"

Kristy moved forward and taking her hand in her own, began to explain.

"In any Symm family, one member inherits the history gene and the historian make's sure that we are told of our heritage. Our family's historian is my Aunt Georgie, my dad's sister and she is Ellie and Francesca's mum."

"When we met, Tom told me Ellie and Francesca were young children, not grown-up's!" she smiled at the thought.

"No really, I can't wait to tell Ellie that!" Kristy snickered, imagining what that conversation would be like. She let go of Rosie's hand then, as the Symm was flowing between them and clouding her thoughts..

"Ellie's actually a year older than Tom, and Frankie is the same age as me," she continued. "My Aunt Georgie married Uncle Trevor when they were both 17 years old. For them it was love at first sight, but as Uncle Trev is Majestet and Fin, his family told him, he wasn't allowed to marry a Majestet child, who was only second, born.

The lovebirds finally ran away together, it was supposed to have been, ever so romantic at the time, but caused a great deal of grief though, as his family have never spoken to him since."

"That's sad for him."

"But reasonable in the circumstances as Uncle Trevor's family lost their heritage when this happened, you see. It must have been really distressing for them all. Their family status was lost, because Uncle Trev married below his line."

"Bit archaic isn't it, in this day and age?" Rosie stated.

"Rosie, you have to remember our lineage is the oldest in existence as we know it, and we can trace our roots to the original six families, most not directly of course, but even by association, some can still feel what line they are in. I know it would hurt Mum and Dad if Tom was to marry out of line. Anyway that isn't going to happen now is it?"

Rosie felt immediately guilty at being the cause of Kristy's pain.

"But hey! You however are of the direct line, a Primera and one of the Lost too!. I can't get over it!" Kristy leaned back in her seat, "I bet Tom was over the moon at meeting you, I know I am!"

Rosie felt a little out of depth with all the information Kristy had imparted to her and she sat back in her seat staring over at her grandad, with unfocused eyes. Where was he in all this? Where were any of the family, for that matter?

185

All this information would have been interesting, if it was about someone else, unfortunately it wasn't and she was fighting her inner-self trying to fully comprehend what was relevant to her. Too much information at once was making her feel physically sick and she leant back in her seat, closed her eyes and actually felt her head trying to fill in all the gaps and it hurt like hell!

They stopped at Kidbrooke, Eltham, Falconwood stations without speaking another word, as both girls were trying to work out the issues it conjured up, from so many different angles herself.

"Welling station! Next stop Welling station." The train tannoy called out loudly.

****

Ellie was sitting with Lucas, in Dr Bush's office listening to him reiterate the course of Walt's operation in detail, as to what had taken place, and then its results.

"So you see, Ellie, everything is fine here, but you need to get back home to your parents and then go to Rosie and Kristy with Luc." He stated in his self-assured way and his voice emphatic. "You both know the main objective is getting Tom back, your cousin is vital to the Symm, as is Rosie, at this moment in time!"

"I understand, but I can't leave Walt!" she pleaded, "I want to be with him and I need to be with him!"

"Walt will be fine Ellie, I'm looking after him remember!" Pointing his finger from one to the other, "It is you, as well as Luc, who have a mission and you both need to be there with Kristy. Luc can communicate with me any time or place and I him." He smiled at her and deliberately let his eyes drop to her abdomen, " ..... and the little one needs to know his mother has done her duty."

"A little one? What little one?" Questioned Ellie and followed his eyes down to her tummy. She vaulted up out of the chair and twisted round in confusion, only to sit back down again. "Little one! As in a baby?" she cried out in total shock.

Dr Bush folded his arms in front of him and leaned back in his chair, looking to all intents and purposes like the proud father himself.

"I'd say about six weeks gone," he smiled indulgently, "a beautiful baby boy!"

"Pregnant? I'm pregnant?" Ellie looked at him, her eyes surprisingly wide.

"Yes and quite safe for the next week or so while you help co-ordinate Tom's rescue."

"Oh how do you know all this?" She asked. Then squeezed her eyes shut, trying to control her feelings of joy and worry all at once.

"Don't ask, 'cause I've tried to ply it from him for years," Luc laughed. "Just accept what he says as true. He never lies.... ever!"

"Luc is right Ellie, I cannot lie, which is unfortunate sometimes in my line of work!" He got up and came round and sat on the edge of the desk. "But, I must admit, I have learnt to be an accomplished diplomat when it comes to replying to a woman's age old question of; Do I look good in this outfit?"

All three laughed at this, and both men watched with little surprise that when Ellie stopped, her hand rested gently on her stomach.

"A baby boy!" she whispered.

"Yes, but not for seven or so months, so bring

yourself back to this moment in time!" Dr Bush was now focused totally on them both. "Rosie is an exceptionally gifted child, well Primera's usually are, in addition to the fact I have not felt one like her in the Symm for a very long time, and she is absorbing her new status extremely well."

"What Primera? Did you say Primera?" both Luc and Ellie looked equally shocked.

"Yes, I said Primera! They still exist you know!" he grinned at his own joke and went back to his seat behind the desk. "You are each mediators, having to be the level headed ones now. You are both heading into unknown territory where families do not remember the Symm and an interwoven group of families that do. You will have, not one jewel, but four need to be returned home to their rightful families and they can only do it with your help."

"You're talking in riddles, Uncle Doc!" Luc stated flatly.

"You are probably right, Luc, but it will become evidently clearer as you go along," he smiled at them both, "and before Walter's operation I arranged for Rosie's brother to be at the train station, as they needed a lift home. They will all be safely in the house when you get there."

"No pressure then!" Luc exclaimed, looking at Ellie and smiling grimly.

****

When the train stopped at Welling station, Bert woke instantaneously, was the first one up, encouraging the girls to hurry along as they needed to get back to the house, and in his old eyes, to what he felt was a safe haven.

Off the train, they moved quickly down the platform

188

and out of the station exit and were about to turn left to get to the main road, when suddenly Rosie heard a familiar whistle and turned her head to see Mike leaning on Bluebell, four cars up from the entrance, waving for them to go to him.

"Mike what are you doing here?" Rosie ran up to him and gave him a big kiss and hug.

"Well this is a better welcome than I visualised. I had all sorts of scenarios running through my head and none of them like this. I had a phone call at work from some bloke called Dr Bush, to ask if I could meet you. How the hell he did he know I was free to go? How he knew Jimmy, the late orderly, had come in early by mistake. I don´t know?

With that he opened the door and pulled the seat forward, still rambling on to her.

"He gave me the arrival time, then said you might need me at home when you got back, while we wait for someone called Ellie, and not to ask why?" he turned back so Rosie could enter, then added, "I didn't understand any of it."

"Oh that's fantastic Mike," she took his hand, "I'll tell you all about it when we get home."

Kristy, who was right behind Rosie, smiled at his bemused, but quite handsome face.

"My name's Kristy Osmundsen, Ellie's my cousin by the way and thanks for doing this. You don't know how much we all appreciate it!" she scrambled into the back of the car with Rosie and putting her makeup case between them on the seat.

"Not at all!" he mumbled then turning round to Bert who had slowly ambled along behind the girls. "Grandad, are you all right?"

"Just take us to your Mum and Dad's place, Mike,

please!" Bert slowly got into the car. "Long story" was all Mike heard before the old man slammed the door shut.

"Fine!. Will do! I always wanted to be a chauffeur, anyway!" Grumbling to no one in particular, "Why on earth do I need to be a doctor? I have a batty family that I could spend a lifetime analysing!"

No one spoke in the five minute journey and there was thankfully no welcoming committee at the front of the house. Although as Rosie opened the front door, they could hear Dave, Lisa and Vicki laughing hysterically in the kitchen.

They entered the kitchen diner, from the hall and all four stopped in their tracks as they watched Dave tossing a pancake across the breakfast bar for Vicki to catch in the crepe pan she was holding. Lisa was trying to cook another on the stove and they were all belly laughing at what they were doing.

"What the blazes is going on here? Pull yourself together Dave! For goodness's sake grow up man. We have a crisis here!" Bert yelled at his son.

Everyone went dead quiet as Bert swung round and sat in his favourite chair, and then all hell let loose.

Dave threw down his own crepe pan loudly on the stove. Lisa switched off all the burners and Vicky ran over to Rosie, still with her own pancake pan in hand before realising it, then running back to the island and returning to her friend again, empty handed.

"What the hell is the matter Dad?" Dave yelled.

"Bert, are you alright?" Lisa called from the kitchen, remembering to turn the electric kettle on, ready for the inevitable cup of tea, she would no doubt need.

Jack had heard the commotion from upstairs and came running down to see what was wrong, nudging his older brother out of the way so he could see into the room. "What's going on?"

"No idea! But it looks as if the gang's all here!" Mike leaned on the door jamb, listening while the entire group were talking at once and no one really getting any answers. Placing two fingers in his mouth, he gave a loud shrill whistle which made everyone in the room hold their hands over their ears, and before anyone could make any further noise, Mike yelled at them.

"Sit down all of you, I don't know what the hell is going on here, but Grandad says it's a long story, and I think we would be best advised to listen to what he has to say. Dad, Mum all of you, it's important. Now sit!" he commanded and all dropped onto the nearest seat, chair or footstool. Mike sat on the edge of one of the dining room chair's nearest the door. "Right, so let's hear this long story shall we?" he turned deliberately towards his grandfather and nodded for him to start.

"Mike, don't you speak to ...." Lisa began.

"No one says a word until we know what's going on" Mike called out, "Grandad! The floor is yours!"

"Can't help you, Mike! It's not my story to tell" He looked intentionally at the two girls who were sitting together on the three seater sofa, with Vicki.

"It's my story!" Rosie stood. "Well for the most part, but Kristy will have to fill in the blanks. I hope I can explain it properly, it's really confusing and I don't understand all of it myself." She turned to Kristy, who nodded for her to start.

"OK, well when I'd finished reading to the kids at the book shop today, and I was talking to Pam while we tidied up and this really good looking guy came up to me, to .....!"

"Did he hurt you, are you alright?" Dave went to get

up.

"Dad, I told you to be quiet, don't jump to conclusions and let Rosie continue." Mike nodded to Rosie to continue.

Dave glared at his eldest son, but settled back in his chair and Lisa captured his hand in hers and gave it a reassuring squeeze.

****

Ellie and Luc were expected at Trevor and Georgie Kalms, Pimlico house, as she had spoken to her parents several times from the hospital, and they took a taxi back again across the Thames at Vauxhall Bridge. Reaching her old home, Ellie let Luc in with her own door key and entered the hallway, as he was merrily chatting away behind her on how nice the house was and could she explain what a mews was again.

"Mum, Dad?" she called out and almost immediately her mum Georgie came running from the kitchen and her dad Trevor stood at his study door while both women hugged fiercely.

Luc hung back, but while the women began to chat, both men gravitated towards each other and met midway in the spacious hall.

"Luc, welcome!" Trevor held out his hand and Lucas shrugged off his back pack, and leaving it on the entry hall floor, joined the man to take his hand.

"Mr Kalms I really wish it were under better circumstances.   Ellie and I will get Tom back, I promise." Luc replied.

"Call me Trev, everybody does! I don't doubt you will succeed, and it appears your uncle agrees with you. Come let's go in to the kitchen, you must be hungry after your long journey?" Catching up to both women, who then stopped in front of them.

192

"Dad, you just said the magic words." Ellie turned on hearing this. "You must have read his mind!"

"Hey, I don't think about food all of the time." Luc responded defensively.

"Liar!" she whispered jokingly and took his arm to lead him into the kitchen. Both parents joined hands, sighed with relief and followed them.

While they were eating the authentic Thai dishes Georgie had prepared for them, the dialogue continued.

"I rang Norway after your first call with the news. Teddy was all for coming over, but Julie agreed with us, there is nothing they can do here. He can coordinate a rescue from there if necessary, and for a start his wheelchair won't fit through any of our doors. Plus we don't have a disabled bathroom" he explained.

"Oh!" Luc didn't know what else to say.

"It's his legs, he was on a rescue a few years ago where he got crushed in a boating accident and since then his mobility has deteriorated greatly, although he still insists it has been enhanced by the motorised chair." Looking then at Ellie "They send their love to you, by the way."

"That's kind under the circumstances, but I still don't have any news of Tom for them!"

"But *I* do!" her father stated.

"How? When?" Luc and Ellie voiced together.

"Terry brought back the car to us over an hour ago from Covent Garden and he'd been in touch with his partner Connor who, it appears, followed the man with the gun. He described to him, how the shooter met up with Whitet, Tom, and another man outside Covent Garden Tube Station. Connor said they all got in a car which was waiting for them, but he was able to get a taxi and followed them to London City Airport, unfortunately he lost them in traffic for a few minutes, so they got through the concourse before him. There was only one plane departing and he just missed the closing gate for Venice, which he assumed was their destination." Trevor relayed.

"That's great news! Not far to follow them to, at least!" Luc commented.

"I thought that too, so I rang Ricardo Biocca in Rome and got him to fly up to Marco Polo Airport and wait for Whitet's plane so he can follow them, as I'm pretty sure Italy, will not be their final destination!"

"Dad. Ricky doesn't know what Tom does for a living!" Ellie blurted out.

"So what, he is Symm has eyes, ears, lives in Italy knows Tom well enough to recognise him. Who could be better under the circumstances?" Trevor replied, "and he is one of your mother's best friend's sons!"

"Sorry, of course, silly of me!" Ellie admitted defeat at the logic.

"I should think so too" Trev smiled at her.

"I know! Have you heard from him yet?" Ellie looked expectantly at him, but he shook his head.

The conversation became general after that and gravitated to the lounge, where they had their coffee.

Only having just gotten seated and as if by magic, the telephone rang beside Trevor, making them all jump. He answered after the first ring and seeing who it was on caller ID, he put Ricki on speaker.

"Ciao, Trev. Tom arrived 30 minutes ago here, and he wasn't resisting the man with white hair who was holding his arm, but apart from that, he looked good!" Ellie smiled to herself, she had forgotten how wonderfully familiar his Scottish/Italian accented English was, as they hadn't spoken since her wedding

194

last year and then, only briefly.

"Where are they going?" Luc called.

"In the terminal when they passed me, the white haired man said something about getting the transport at, what sounded like Sibenik or it could have been Split though, I'm not sure as it was noisy. All four of them got into a car outside the terminal and I'm now in the hire car you arranged for me, following them. It does seem they are heading for the Croatian border. I'll ring back when I know more, addio!" He took a breath and abruptly rang off.

"Good call, Trev, this Ricardo seems on top of the situation." Luc praised.

"Certainly seems to be!" he replied, nodding his head in agreement.

"Dad, Oh, I´ve just remembered, Dr Bush told us that Rosie is Primera!" Ellie informed them.

A shocked "wow!" was expressed from each parent in turn.

"Primera! That's not what I expected!" Trev said, and as if thinking out loud he continued, "thank goodness Whitet only got Tom, he obviously wasn't privy to this fact." Warily, he turned to look at his wife at this tactless remark.

"I honestly think Tom was always his target, love." Georgie stated softly.

"Croatia, why there?" Lucas asked, still trying to understand what was going on.

"Islands, hundreds of small islands off the coast, perfect cover!" Trevor said. "Whitet loves an island. He lived on one just off Denmark in the North Sea and Tom and Walt got the Lokkint Blue from him there about five years ago. He moved pretty quickly after that, to a remote part of Crete, but still Teddy found him and Tom and Walt were able to get the Enever Emerald, but he's been off of the radar since then."

"Finish your coffee, you two, and then you'd better make a move down to Welling!" Georgie instructed.

"Where is Welling?" Luc asked, his coffee gone in one gulp.

"South London/North Kent border, I'd say about an hour, in the car from here." Trev turned to his daughter, "Ellie, I've asked Terry to chauffeur you both, just in case you need to bring anyone back. Luckily he actually knows where Welling is, without satnav" He picked up the phone, "I'll get him back here, asap!"

Both of them stood and followed as Georgie made to leave the room.

"Take Luc up to the spare room, both of you can get washed and changed, before you leave. There are still a whole load of clothes in your old room darling." Georgie advised.

"Thanks Mum! I have some news ......" Ellie started to say, but Trev interrupted, he'd finished his call and had followed them into the hall.

"I'd have come with you sweetheart, but someone has to prepare for the next Stolen. I had news an hour ago from Gill in Sydney, that a package is due from Oz tomorrow morning and now Tom and Walt are out of the picture, I'll need a plan." He came up behind them both, and then wandered off into his study.

"I'll help you Trev." Georgie said, leaving Ellie at the bottom of the stairs and followed her husband into the room.

"I know you will sweetheart. I know you will!" Trev replied.

Ellie shrugged her shoulders and escorted Luc up to

the next floor and in truth, this was probably not the best time to tell her parents her baby news anyway. It might colour their judgement as to what she could, or couldn't do at this moment in time, and nothing was going to stop her finding Tom, nothing at all.

****

In Welling, the lounge was eerily silent as Rosie explained, as best she could, her conversation with Tom and the awful shooting of Walter.

Kristy then gave details of how she got there, their trip to the theatre and finally the arrival at their home.

When finished, the interrogation came from all directions, but with so many questions all at once and being asked over and over again, the girls were repeating themselves, until Mike finally called a halt to proceedings.

"Right that's enough! Leave them both alone!" his voice bellowed over the chaos.

"Mike's right. The dinner that Vicky and I prepared is in the oven. Can't say how much of it is left, as we haven't been paying attention to it, but Dave, you get the table expander. Jack, Mike you get the table sorted. Leave grandad to sleep, I'll do his favourite egg on toast later. Lisa smiled as she acknowledged Bert, who had left the confrontation to others and headed for sleep mode, yet again, with no one noticing. "Girls you come with me."

None objecting to their given jobs, they all moved in unison.

"Vicky, cooking?" A surprised Mike, whispered to Jack, as they got the cutlery and place mats for the table.

"Yeh, she comes in every other Saturday afternoon. Mum's teaching her the basics, so she won't starve or have to live on takeaways, when she leaves home!"

"Clever girl!" Mike smiled, following Vicki with his eyes, as she went back into the kitchen.

Dinner was chicken casserole and actually benefited from the delay in eating it, as Lisa had unconsciously turned the oven down and not off. Vegetables from the garden were in abundance and after a shot in the microwave were able to fill their plates to make up for the smaller than usual portions of meat.

When they had taken their seats, Mike ordered them to talk about anything other than what had happened. At least until they finished their meal, so everyone could follow the story, and not the gist of it.

Half an hour later, their main meal gone, and no one ever said no to Lisa's signature dessert of Raspberry Pavlova, even Bert who had woken up half way through dinner, insisted on eating his egg on toast off a tray in his armchair, but still had a small portion.

With a concerted effort by everyone, the table was cleared and the dish washer stacked, as Lisa and Rosie prepared the coffee, tea and water so they could listen more comfortably when they returned to their seats in the living room.

The first question when they were finally settled was asked by Mike, but was obviously on everyone's mind and was aimed directly at Kristy.

"So explain this again to us Kristy, the hierarchy thing, Tallys and Flints and things!" The scientist in Mike was curious.

"I'll do better than that, I'll draw it for you and it'll be easier to see!"

She reached for a napkin and Mike handed her his biro.

"I'll start with Primera, they are the first chosen families, then -

Pimera, + Others = Tally

Tally + Tally = Horizon

Tally + Horizon = Talzon

Horizon + Horizon = Flint

Horizon + Flint = Flinzon

Flint and Flint = Fin

"That sounds complex Kristy? By looking at it, you can have Tally's marrying Flinzons and Horizons." Mike asked, seeing that Kristy had not put anything of this in her table.

"That's true and it does make the gene pool bigger, but also gives it constraints too!" she looked straight at him. "Almost half the world has some level of Symm in them and you'll find those people are the ones who care for the environment." She didn't have to say that the ones, who had none, were not.

"So where does Rosie come into this?" Lisa asked.

"Well Tom is Fin, this is the highest ranking in the process and he can feel other Fins, Flinzons and Flints, because these are the only level he is able to marry into. He says Rosie is Primera, which means she is Fin too, but has come directly from Primera – Tally – Horizon - Flint to Fin without any mixing of the lines and she would have been born from only Fin, the whole of her lineage, over hundreds, if not thousands of years."

Just at that moment the doorbell rang, Dave made to rise, but Mike being closest indicated him to sit back down.

"Hold that thought, no one speaks until I get back, I

do not want to miss a thing!" he ordered and left the room. Reaching the door in seconds, he didn't fling it wide as he would normally do, but opened it just a couple of inches and stared out onto the porch.

"Is this the Norton's residence?" A young woman asked him, "we're looking for Kristy and Rosie?"

"Yes, it is, hello!" he smiled at the trio in front of him, and opened the door wider to let them all enter. "You must be Ellie, we've been expecting you!"

Ellie's face was a picture, but Lucas pushed her forward into the hall in front of him and Terry followed up behind.

"Dad, Jack, bring in some more dining chairs we have company." Mike called into the room, ushering the three visitors forward.

Kristy rushed to hug her cousin, as Ellie entered the living room, leaving Mike in no doubt he had guessed right and steered the two men to the seats in front of the unlit fire, which Jack had just placed there.

After the introductions and information as to who Lucas and Terry were, Ellie sat with the girls on the sofa.

"How's Walt and is there any news of Tom?" Kristy was longing to hear any news, which Ellie was able to give. She explained everything to everyone, from when she left them to go in the ambulance until Terry drove them to the front door here in Welling.

"The thing I can't get over is if Rosie is this Primera thingy, how comes as a family we aren't included?" Jack asked.

"That is what my Mum was trying to get straight in her head too!" Ellie was sitting holding Kristy's hand on the sofa."She can't follow the gene through any families and couldn't confirm Tom's evaluation at all."

200

"Tom asked if I was adopted, as that was his first thought!" Rosie said softly.

Lisa laughed out loud, "Come here my darling, what on earth was he thinking. Of course you aren't adopted!" Lisa pulled her from her seat on the sofa and into her lap on the armchair next to her and hugging her close. "Tell her Dave, we can give a blow by blow account of you and your brother coming into this world, can't we love?"

Dave stood up and moved nervously behind his chair. His face now pale and suddenly wringing his hands, then putting them in his pockets then immediately pulling them free again. No one had noticed his anxiety at any point since Rosie had began her story, but it was certainly showing now.

"Dave, what's wrong? Why aren't you agreeing with me?" Lisa's voice was slightly accusing.

"Because I can't love, I can't agree with you!" he admitted softly.

The whole room went silent.

"I don't understand, Jack and Rosie are ours, they were born at Edd's house..........!"

"Please Lisa!" Dave pleaded. "Please, let me tell this in my own way. I have wanted to say something for 16 years. Let me tell you how it really was!"

The room suddenly dropped in temperature and Dave's eyes shone with misty tears, as he looked at all the conflicting emotional expressions of his wonderful family and also in the sea of new faces in front of him.

Lisa looked deeply into his eyes and said one name, "Ailleen?"

"Yes love. Ailleen!" Dave nodded, as if the name was the catalyst to end the long ago nightmare, he was finally sharing.

Chapter 19

Tristan and the Families

As Tristan left the golden glittery VIP section, he turned and gave the backs of his armed escorts, a cheeky farewell wave. Then twisted round ready to cross through the yellow section, and was just going on to the green, when he heard the name 'Laura Springer' come from a voice on the stage of the auditorium.

He looked over the shoulders of a Chinese family sitting in the back row following the six contestants on stage. He did not know what Laura looked like, so as there was an empty seat at the end of the row, he slipped into it.

"Hello son, you lost?" the Chinese man asked him.

"Yes, I went to the loo and can't remember which number seat I'm supposed to be in. Is it okay to sit here for a little while?" Lying skilfully, he smiled back. "I'm sure I'll remember where it is, at some point!"

"Of course you can, no one has taken the seat since our arrival, so you are welcome to stay. What's your name?" but as soon as he said it, he promptly returned to look back at the stage before Tristan could reply. "I am Kwok Sham and our daughter is Sun Ya Sham. There she is now!" he pointed, as Sun Ya finished her task of placing minerals in the boxes on the stage, turned and beamed a brilliant smile towards the audience.

The camera was focused on her face and she mouthed, "Thank you, so much papa," as she stood waiting for her move to the next coloured area,

"My kind and wonderful daughter!" his obvious pride shining through, but from out of nowhere began to sob like a baby, as her words had obviously touched him deeply.

"Are you all right, Sir?" Tristan asked politely.

He had never seen a man cry before, well not that he could remember. His mum inevitably cried when his dad left to go away for tours of duty in the army, but then he didn't blame her. The separations were sometimes as long as a year and when he was younger, Tris remembered he had even cried in that time too.

"Yes, yes of course!" he smiled, gulping in lots of air, whilst he wiped his face with a handkerchief his wife had slipped into his hand, "We have worked together on this section for some time, as it was the only one that I could help her with. The rest are totally natural gifts and hours of study, with lots of concentration!" Mr Sham sniffed, proudly.

"I'm Tristan Kane, Mr Sham. Nice to meet you!" Introducing himself, he could see Sun Ya was still waiting for her next section to become free.

"So Tristan, do you have family here?" Mr Sham settled back in his seat, a satisfied smile now on his dry face.

"No, but I do have a friend's sister competing," he admitted, "I think I may have missed her though!"

"What's her name and I'll bring her up on my pad, you can get repeats of all the contestants!" his hand hovered over the keys, waiting for Tristan to reply.

"Laura Springer!" Tris didn't hesitate.

"Really! What luck, she is in my daughter's group!" The older man began putting Laura's name into the lily pad he was holding. "Quick press the blue button in front of you and you can catch the last four fabrications she made, she is fantastic. I must admit they all are, but then I think I'm biased as my Sun Ya is with them!"

Within seconds Sun Ya had moved to the next section and Mr Sham's focus was again on his daughter and didn't hear Tristan as he thanked him for his help.

Pressing the button as directed, the screen activated immediately on the back of the seat in front of him. It showed Laura at her best and she looked a lot like Maddison, he thought. The time flew by as he watched all four sections and even jumped from one to another of the other members of her group. He was really glad he managed to get to see how fantastic the competition played out and was now enjoying every second of it.

Finally after the six members of Laura's set had finished their respective criterion efforts, the next group of competitors arrived. On screen, it gave close-up pictures of group numbers 78,79,80,81,82 and 83, with information on their backgrounds. Tristan wished he had managed to get the same, for the six he had just attentively watched, merely to know a bit more about them, as he was now fascinated by them all.

"Well, I think our six are the best group so far, don't you? Not one made a mistake that I can tell," Mr Sham spoke quietly to Tristan. "Now they have finished, it will be another couple of hours before the final test in the Violet zone. I wish they would tell us how they have all done, but I suppose the suspense will keep all of the audience here to watch. Though I would stay, even if I knew Sun Ya did not finish her trials."

"You would, really?" Tristan said "Why?"

"Well of course, because the final selection is fascinating to see, I was once given the chance to participate in Hawaii, many years ago," grinning broadly, "I too made it to the final, but unfortunately my ABL was not up to standard as I could not read all of the lights!"

"I bet you were pissed off!" Tristan said, then screwed up his face, after voicing the vernacular term, realising at once it was not quite a word he should have used to a stranger. "Oh, I'm sorry!"

"A better phrase Tristan I could not have found myself. Yes, I was royally ´pissed off´ that they did not want me. Fortunately, as it turned out, I was picked up by a corporation that zeroed in on my many other skills and offered me a job in Malaysia. I have had a very prosperous life since." He grinned back at Tristan, "but I was sorely pissed at the time!"

"So let me get this straight, Rainbow House, pick the best of the contenders, but other companies also get a look at the finest runners up, that is so cool" Tristan had never thought beyond today. Well actually he had never thought of Rainbow House in any way, except when his Dad would tell him to work hard, otherwise he would never get into it and which up until today, he had no wish to be in it anyway.

"Only the older years, 17 and over are considered, the younger ones normally go back to their schools and colleges to sharpen up their skills, but are kept in the loop for some time after the contest. It is a good platform for the talented to be on show!"

At which point, Mrs Sham nudged her husband and said something that Tristan did not understand and Mr Sham replied nodding agreement, at what his wife had said.

"My beautiful wife has advised me that we should continue our conversation over dinner Tristan Kane, would you care to join us as our guest please? We have a table booked in the Spanish Restaurant, "Las Cañas" in the upper green level, I'm sure we could fit you in."

He smiled broadly at Tristan, who nodded in stunned acceptance.

"Unless you want to see the rest of the competition that is?" he added blithely.

"No, I mean, yes, thank you, I'd love to come Mr Sham. The no, was for seeing the rest of the competition. I only came to see Laura anyway!" Along with Maddison, of course, he thought.

His home life in Essex did not consist of much eating out, especially in a restaurant. His father hardly left the house when he was home, and his mother would go nowhere without him. The closest he had ever been allowed to go to, was to the local pizza or burger bars and even then that was rare. No way, was he missing an opportunity to actually eat in a real restaurant, especially as his favourite meal was paella, which his father, when around, would cook for them.

"Good, I will introduce you to the rest of my family as we go along." He started to rise.

Seeing the movement Tristan got up immediately and stepped into the aisle letting the family out of the row. Mr Sham straight away put his arm across Tristan's shoulders and drew him along with them.

By the time they reached the restaurant, which was situated on the top level of the auditorium, Tristan had been introduced to Mrs Moi Sham and their younger children, Su Ling and Kwok Junior, who informed Tristan in no uncertain terms, that he liked very much to be called Steve.

On reaching the entrance to the restaurant he actually felt a little guilty at that juncture and wishing fervently that he hadn't lied to Mr Sham when they had met for the first time.

Entering the busy and wonderfully traditionally Spanish decorated restaurant, Tristan stood for a second to just take in the ambience of his surroundings, only stepping forward on hearing Mr Sham's voice call his name. The family had followed the maître d', who was manoeuvring them round the circular and square tables and showing them straight to the largest two, set with magnificent centre pieces and an array of crockery, cutlery and glasses, on the far side of the restaurant where the windows faced out over London's picturesque skyline.

"Tristan?" Suddenly the sound of his name, said as it was, by a familiar soft voice behind him, sent a shiver up his spine. "What are you doing here?" Maddison was right on his shoulder, leading what looked like her own family, towards the same tables that Mr Sham was about to sit at.

"Maddison! Hi, I never expected to see you!" he cringed visibly as he spoke. 'and I wish you hadn't found me here,' he thought abstractly.

"I bet?" she gave him a crooked smile "Are you following me?"

"As I see it, that's exactly what you are doing, to me!" he smiled cheekily at her. "Isn't it?"

"In your dreams! Mr Kane!" she threw back at him and whispered. "No seriously, what are you doing here. I thought you said you didn't have a ticket?"

He slanted a shy covert glance at Mr Sham and chewed on the inside of this cheek as he thought of a convincing reply. They were almost at the table, but he stopped in mid stride as he thought a bit longer, about how to present his next answer. He really wanted to be a part of this evening and decided to come clean. Taking a deep breath he answered quietly.

"I managed to sneak in, and sat with Mr Sham, when I was looking for you, and he invited me to dinner with his family." He admitted shyly, and was a very un-Tristan like, move for him.

Maddison eyed him thoughtfully and hesitated, as if constructing her response, then murmured.

"Good! I thought for a moment there, you were going to fib to me!"

Well, she'd judged him pretty close and he rushed on to answer.

"I almost did!" he admitted freely, "although I did tell him I was a friend of Laura's sister!"

"Well, at least that wasn't much of a lie!" she crinkled her face with pleasure. There was something about Tristan that she liked. Liked very much!

"Hi, Tristan, I'm Alfie, Maddison's brother!" he came from behind Maddison, making them both jump, "She told me all about meeting you, NOT!" Glaring round at his sister.

The two protagonists looked at each other and started to laugh out loud, Alfie must have heard every word they said.

"Hi Alfie!" Tristan shrugged his shoulders in defeat, turned again to Maddison and pulled her forward, "Wow, what a fantastic view!" Only speaking to cover his embarrassment, but he didn't drop her hand as he escorted her over to introduce her to Mr Sham's family.

"Mr Sham this is Maddison, Laura's sister." he mumbled.

"Hello, Mr Sham nice to meet you at .....!" Maddison's voice was silenced as her father came up behind them.

"Kwok? How are you, old friend?" Stan called.

Maddison, Tristan and Alfie all turned and stepped

back, as he barged passed them and gave the other man a hug.

"These are our friends, Ron and Janis Ray, their son Paul, is also in the competition!" Stan began to introduce everyone new to everyone else.

Maddison smiled at being in the centre of the hand shaking and kisses, as Tristan just stood staring, dumb struck at all the new faces around him.

"Hey, don't forget me!" A soft, warm harmonious voice came from around the back of the Springer's and when stepping into the circle it obviously belonged to a impeccably dressed and beautiful Native American woman.

"Star, how lovely to .... " Kwok began.

"And, what about us?" Another two voices joined in, as Stargazer was followed by the high profiled King Nicolas and Queen Sophie of the Northern Winter (along with the obligatory two massive body guards, of course) and King Lenny Lakota of the Southern Autumn family with his two wives, (and three equally burly uniformed body guards in tow).

Slowly approaching from the rear, Tristan saw a colossal Maori man with his wife who was holding the hand of a petite little girl who would, he realised, have been the image of Kawiti Teira, if she'd worn glasses and was another two years older.

Out of the blue King Lakota's voice boomed across the room over all their heads. "Quiet everyone. As it could be no other restaurant than Las Cañas tonight, I am choosing the wine and paying the bill!"

"Hey, Lenny you did that last time!" Stargazer called. "In India, at the conference last year, remember?"

"No I didn't!" King Lakota replied, "Did I?"

"It's my turn, anyway, Lenny!" Freddie Teira yelled

above the general greetings and ensuing discussions of whose turn it was to pay. Then out of nowhere, he suddenly turned and changed his stance to face the children with a traditional Maori 'Haka' face. This had the little ones screaming and Tristan for some unaccountable reason, deliberately stepping bodily in front of Maddison and Alfie.

"Ah, hah! Just like your father, the fearless protector!" Freddie nodded sagely, and then returned immediately to talking with the rest of his cohorts, without a backward glance.

Kawiti's little sister stepped around her father. "He does that all the time, he thinks he is so funny. My name is Nyree, and you must be Tristan Kane."

With no time to rationalise either of the comments, Tristan was chivvied to one side along with Alfie, Maddison and Nyree by the maitre d'.

"You lot!" Pointing deliberately to the adults. "Behave! Now sit down all of you. Adults to the left and the youngsters, you go to the right. Now!" he yelled at them, moving forward and trying to clear a path.

"And you, appendages!" Yelling and pointing to the entourage, then directing them on to a table set for five. "Go sit at that table. The one that leads to this area, now move it!"

This order had Tristan, Maddison, Alfie, with the Sham children and Kawiti's sister, all rushing to sit at the table set for six and the adults who numbered 14, slowly gravitated to theirs.

"Raul, you haven't changed a bit, you old reprobate how are you doing?" Freddie swallowed up the maitre d' in a bear hug, "I hope Juan is cooking tonight and not you!" Naming his friend's, world renowned, elder son and chef for the evening.

210

"I think if you let me breath Froggie, I might just feel better," gasping loudly and Freddie released him, "and no, I don't cook any more. I just can't compete with Juan, far too good!" he admitted generously.

"I should think not! He's brilliant, brilliant! Deserves, every single one of the stars, he's won!" With this, he sat down on the largest chair, obviously put there for his convenience, without a backward glance.

"Now will the rest of you please sit!" Raul's final call was in desperation, to everyone around him.

"But Raul, I haven't got to speak to you yet!" Queen Sophie had come up behind him and as he turned she gave him a kiss on both cheeks in welcome.

A flustered Raul smiled back up into Sophie's eyes.

"I'll sit with you once you have eaten and I've served the brandy!" his voice cracking as he spoke, and admitting to himself, she hadn't changed a bit since he had last seen her.

"Perfect!" Returning his smile, she glided as only Sophie could, and quickly followed her husband to their own chairs at the table.

"I've always thought so!" he thought, as he made to leave the floor, but couldn't resist tracking her with his eyes, as she took her seat.

At the table, Maddison could not stop looking at Tristan's, 'cat caught in the headlights' eyes either. He was obviously trying to take in some of the conversations around him and then realised that she was actually doing the same thing herself. Although, she at least had an advantage over him, as part of what was happening had been disclosed to her the previous evening by her father, before going to bed.

He had explained to her, that all the participants of his own Rainbow House competition group of 20 years ago in Hawaii, had met up with each other every year by having dinners in a country of convenience and then once every four years meeting up at the competition.

When unbelievably this year, all of their children had got through to the final competition, a couple of them, (not naming names of course), pulled strings so that all their offspring were together in the same group.

They all thought it was a huge joke, as the only two children who knew one another were friends Thorlief and Amitola, (their mothers were good friends), but they weren't aware of the rest of them and would not associate any of their names with the actual parents. More importantly they had never met each other.

Her father had been right! Thinking back, Maddison could remember her mother talking of places all over the world, and the names Kwok and Moi, Stargazer, Freddie and Sue, Lenny in Africa who had lots of wives, the only one she recalled was Jewel. Sophie and Nick who lived in Norway and even Raul in Spain entering the conversations occasionally, but really never taking it in at the time, as she had never met any of them herself.

This was because, if any of the group came to England, her parents had accepted dinner invitations to see them in town, alone. She now realised when they went on a holiday to some distant part of the globe, alone on honeymoon again, but was obviously to see their friends.

Suddenly Lenny's voice boomed out, bringing everyone to attention.

"Welcome, welcome, to the fourth anniversary party of Rainbow House – Hawaii 1 competition. I bow to the seven best of the best *losers,* and of course raise a glass to our star competitor and the only one of the glorious eight who actually made it to the Seasons

Academy, Billy Kane, who unfortunately could not make it tonight, but sent us his son Tristan, in his place!"

The tables erupted with applause and even the children raised their glasses of water to Tristan, who was now even more confused and could not compute this new information at all.

His father went to the Seasons Academy, he was chosen and these obviously very influential, rich people did not, what the hell happened? Shell shocked could not have described Tristan better as he sat still at the table and looked at Maddison, as if in a trance.

"This is not happening!" he thought.

"Right, now we eat. Raul, bring on the fatted goat!" Lenny's voice boomed out.

"Goat!" The younger children screwed up their faces, as Raul clapped his hands and the food began to arrive, carried in, by numerous waiters weighed down with different choices, and had been waiting eagerly for the signal. The rich aroma of the best Spanish tapas in London, came wafting to the tables before the food was placed on the table in front of them.

"Come on Tristan, you must be starving, eat" Maddison encouraged. "You can talk to everyone when we finish, they are really happy that you came!"

"Dad planned this? He is hardly around for me and he arranges this, I don't understand?" he murmured to himself.

Stargazer was sitting behind Tristan and heard his plea, so turned half way round and laid her small hand gently on his shoulder as she spoke to him.

"All will be revealed when we finish our meal, Tristan!" she smiled at him "It is good news, now eat young man, you are getting thinner by the second."

Something in her tone was calming and settled over

Tristan like a warm blanket and within a minute he was digging into his favourite meal of seafood paella, which had miraculously been placed in front of him, and the questions he thought he wanted answered, were now nowhere to be found.

The meal was loud with laughter and good with food, all the children spoke to each other about the exhibition and what they liked best. Alfie and Tristan talked about the London multi-sports season which was about to start in the autumn.

Maddison didn't say much, she was just glad to be sitting next to Tristan for no other reason than she liked to hear his voice, very much!

Dinner finished, dessert came as often as the younger table wanted it, and equally as often as the coffees, followed by brandy or liqueurs did for the adults. Raul at that point pulled a chair over between Lenny and Kwok to once again enjoy harking back to the last time they had met up. This had been two years previously and in the Maldives at Lenny's last wedding to wife number four, who along with wife number three, were both now too heavily pregnant to make the trip to England this year.

The younger children, including Alfie, finished their meal and promptly buried themselves in their lily pads and the wondrous array of games it possessed.

Not interested in games, Tristan and Maddison wandered over to the window to look out on the view of the London's night sky, and then sat down on the window seat.

"You really don't know why you are here, do you?" Maddison smiled at him.

"Not the foggiest idea, I honestly thought I got here completely on my own. A little unorthodox in the journey, but not really thinking it through too deeply, as to the whys and wherefores, of what would happen at journey's end!".

"Well, you will find out soon enough. Not long to go! I can see Mr Ray looking at the clock, we have been here a while and the final is due soon!" Maddison pointed to Paul's dad, so Tristan knew who she was talking about.

"Is it really ni.." she stopped abruptly.

A knife tapping the side of a crystal glass, had everyone's head turn to King Nicolas, who was standing at the table.

"Attention, settle down. Now both tables turn your chairs towards each other so you can follow the conversation!" he called.

Maddison and Tristan rushed back to their allotted seats and as the scrapping of chairs on the wooden floor quickly settled. Tristan could feel the atmosphere tingle around him.

"Now officially, Tristan Kane, Ron and Janis Ray we would like firstly to welcome you all into our small circle of friends," he bowed formally in their direction "and I hope all of our offspring forgive us for keeping our friendships secret all these years!"

"Here, here! Welcome!" Came loudly from all the adults and also from the children.

"Now Tristan. Billy has told us to tell you what we know of him, as once he was accepted into Rainbow House, he was not allowed to tell anyone what type of career, they had actually chosen for him."

"He is in the army and disappears off the face of the earth for months. Then comes back a different person every time. I hardly ever see him any other way." Tristan stated forcefully.

"Good, that is exactly how it should be!" Kwok said.

"If he can fool his own son, then he really is a master of his craft!"

"You are losing me here!" Tristan said "What craft?"

"He is our 'peepel' hunter in the world of little gems!" Stargazer turned to tell him softly.

"Little gems, you mean those little lights that fly around your heads all the time," Tristan pointed up at a couple, one hazel and one blue. "They have a world?"

"They most certainly do, and are highly intelligent. Raul, ask your little gem a question!" The amused voice of Queen Sophie called, watching as the hazel gem was flying around the maitre d's head.

"This is not a parlour trick, Sophie!" Raul insisted.

"Oh, go on, you know you are the most fluent in gem talk" Sophie flashed her wonderful smile at him, "Nick hardly gets one, out of three words together translated in a sentence, with ours."

"Gem talk?" Tristan's eyes went even wider if that were possible, along with the rest of the children at the table.

Maddison was singularly excited and watched the hazel gem settle close to the tip of Raul's nose. It was something her own gem did sometimes, when she was talking to it.

"Are you enjoying the contest?" Raul spoke easily.

The gem fluttered quickly and flew round his nose coming back to its original position leaving no doubt he understood the enquiry.

"He said it was very good!" Raul smiled at the group, "I wasn't going to ask, but can't resist." Looking round at his friends, who realised just what the question was and nodded in agreement.

"Are they in the final?" he asked.

The whole group waited with baited breath as to

what the answer would be, and the gem disappeared for only a few seconds, before coming back again to settle on his nose. Fluttering in bursts of energy until Raul jumped in the air, filled with incredible pride and an ocean of relief.

"Yes! Yes! Noelia confirms that they are all through to the violet area!" he yelled.

Mayhem ensued, and with it Raul called for Juan to provide champagne, as all the parents were jumping up and down, with the children running round cheering.

Tristan, who had no one to cheer for, stood to one side looking at all the happy faces, especially Maddison's.

"Join in son. This could be about you in four years time!" A very familiar voice came from behind him.

"Dad?" Tristan turned to see his father holding his mother's hand and both were grinning from ear to ear. "Mum?"

"Sorry we're late, we were hoping to get here before now!" his mother, Jan said and hugged him to her, "We are so proud you made it here too!"

Chapter 20

Dave's truth at last!

16 years earlier on 21st June

Cambridge was such a beautiful county usually, but not today, as all that previous night and into this afternoon, it had been raining heavily. It was as if the clouds were like a bathtub and overflowing on to the earth, straight down, in bucket loads.

"Dave we have to stop, I really do need to pee!" Lisa's urgent request came over the thunderous downpour.

"Again!" he sighed.

"Yes again, it's all this water. I saw a sign down the road and it said the next garage is about a quarter of a mile ahead of us. Please look out for it this time." She pleaded.

"I didn't mean to drive past the last one. I just couldn't see the exit!" he tried not to sound too put out by her request.

"I know love, and I should have been looking out for it too!" her hand was gently squeezing his knee.

So, as a man on a mission Dave leant forward, his chin almost resting on the steering wheel and the windscreen wipers were going hammer and tongs, to clear the rain. In this road, he could barely see the bonnet in front of him, let alone the road's tarmac, and within seconds a sign gave the exit as being only a few feet away.

"Turn left now!" Lisa called out to him.

The car did a swift left turn, luckily the road was good and he didn't skid even a little in the large puddle at its mouth. The country lane it led to, was bumpy and Lisa felt every bounce as the cars suspension didn't soften any of them.

Dave didn't even register the rising high water in the ford they crossed, as he was concentrating so hard on reaching his final destination.

Lisa raised her eyes to heaven and thanked God a few times, when the lights of Edd's Garage and Mini Mart came into view.

Dave swung into the forecourt, slammed on the brakes, released his seatbelt and got out of the driver's side, running. Reaching the other side of the car and opening the door, as Lisa had just managed to unbuckle her own seatbelt and Dave held out his hands to help her exit the car.

"Get the umbrella out the back, you silly sod, you're getting soaked." She could hardly see him for the rain, but he took no notice.

"I know, but I need to help you out first, and I could do with two hands for that." He reached in and made sure the seatbelt was out of the way,

"That's true, me and the barrage balloon, do seem to get stuck in the seat every time," she gasped.

"36 weeks pregnant with twins, you're allowed!"

He took her outstretched hand and pulled her gently out of the car seat, but only once her legs were out of the vehicle itself. He got her on her feet, then dived into the back and grabbed the umbrella. One touch and it was covering them both, as he slammed the door with his foot then helped his wife up to the small garage shop. Quickly through the door, they both scanned the bright interior.

"Where's the Ladies?" Lisa barked at the young shop assistant behind the counter and the girl's eyes almost popped out of her head as she pointed to the back of the store.

Dave lowered the umbrella and closed it up, watching as his wife waddled as quickly as her legs would carry her to the toilet.

"She's enormous!"

"Nothing gets past you does it, Scarlett?" An old man was sitting at the end of the counter, with a broad smile on his face. "You all right son?"

"Yeh! We seem to have found every loo from Melton Mowbray and the rain bucketing down all day doesn't help!"

"Where you headed?" he swivelled round to face Dave.

"London, got an appointment with the midwife and her consultant tomorrow, so we have to get back."

Placing the dripping umbrella in the plastic bowl by the door, he moved forward to stand with the old man at the counter.

"She looked a bit exhausted mate! Have a seat; you looked as tired as she does. Couldn't you rest up tonight and leave in the morning?"

"I don't think she would entertain that idea!" he gave a feeble smile, as a jumble of words tumbled out to explain their predicament. "She's just spent ten days with her mother. Anyone would look tired after that! Lisa just wants to go home to our eldest, Michael, she misses him and I don't think she trusts my mum. Not that she should, I mean, she only brought up three kids herself, but what does she know. We should never have come, but her mother insisted. The old girl broke her bloody leg, and wanted waiting on, and Lisa in her condition too. Selfish old moo!"

A voice came from the end of the room. "You talking

about me mum again, Dave?"

"Not specifically. Just in general" He mumbled and she smiled back, as she waddled towards both men.

"Em, I can tell!" she reached him and hooked her arm through his. "I think we should get a move on. If we're lucky we should reach home in a few hours, three at the most in this weather.

"You sure Lisa, you look really washed out." Dave going down the old man's route, she did look very pale.

"I'm sure love, I just don't like being out in this weather is all. I'm fine, honest!" Squeezing his arm, lovingly.

"Well you two take care. There've been a few flood warning alerts on the radio and TV, for most of the day. So be extra careful and keep the local radio station tuned in while you drive, as they give the road conditions in the area too." He advised.

Just then the door swung open and all four heads turned round to see a young girl in her late teens come through the door, her hooded raincoat was soaking, and she was heavily pregnant too.

"Gald blimey. Another one!" Scarlett gasped.

"Here lass, come and take a seat, you okay?" The old man came forward.

"Need the loo!" her words came out in a rush.

"Back of the shop darling," Lisa said, pointing to the door she had not long closed.

"Oh thank you, I'm desperate!"

She disappeared, down the aisle only slightly quicker than Lisa had herself.

"Know that feeling! Oh, look love, they have Fruit Salad sweets, I haven't seen them for a while, and old fashioned cough candy too, be a love and get me some for the journey."

Dave smiled and nodded to Scarlett to give his wife whatever she requested, but noticed that she was more interested in the door at the back of the shop, than the sweets she was ordering.

Within a few minutes the girl was back out again, the hood on her coat now lowered, revealing a pale pretty face with long blond hair, and quickly giving a wave as she too waddled up to the counter.

"Hi, Scarlett!" Her voice was soft and sweet, with an accent none of them could place, "I haven't seen you in a while."

Scarlett stopped what she was doing in total shock, as the blond turned and spoke to the old man.

"River's just broken its banks, Mr Edd. It wasn't too high and I thought I could get across the ford, but the car stalled. The ford is deep water already, above my wheels anyway and it's running really fast."

The girl sat on the old man's seat and pulled down the zip of her coat. Lisa rested against the counter watching and with her mothering instinct, on high alert. She hadn't liked the fact that the teenager was out of breath, and splattered with mud which had found its way into some of her hair that was plastered to her face with the rain.

Dave thought the same thing, but there was something in her eyes, something more than stalling the car in the river that had him worried.

"Good grief girl, what you doing here? I thought your dad said you were studying in Bristol." Edd returned.

"Oh, so that's what the story was, was it?" She looked exhausted. "No, just got myself, knocked up and I was hidden away." A lifeless smile held a meaningful quality.

"I'm sorry sweetheart!" Edd put an arm round her

back and hugged her tightly.

"Me too!" and promptly began to cry.

Lisa stepped forward and gently took her hand.

"Hey, my mum didn't talk to me for a month after I told her I was pregnant the first time and I was married and all! Had a good job, she felt I was too young and giving up my future! Families, eh!"

"Yeh, pain in the backside aren't they?" She sniffed and wiped her tears with the back of her hand and tried to smile, but it didn't reach her eyes.

"If the River Wousen broke its banks, we are in big trouble, we're on an ox bow here, and if it's risen that much, you won't be able to get over either ford, even in a 4x4, which we don't have." He shook his shoulders and stared out of the window.

"You mean we're stranded! Is there any high ground?" Dave asked, trying not to panic.

"You're on it mate! Luckily my house is at the back of the garage. The river has never reached us, even in the 1970 floods and they were the worst in this area in living memory, so we should be fine!"

He turned again to the girl behind the counter. "Scarlett, you ring your mum and let her know what's happening, and tell her not to let your dad try to get over to us, even in his tractor. We are not exactly low on food and I've got plenty of beds in the house, gas fire and a wood burning Aga, so we won't get cold if the electric central heating goes off. Snug as a bug in a rug, we'll be!"

"Cool, no problem!" The girl replied as if a whole lot of weight had been lifted from her young shoulders.

"But we can't stay, I have to get home to Mike!" Lisa cried out.

"How old is he?" Edd asked gently

"He's three."

"And he's been spoilt by his grandma for near on a couple of weeks, I bet! Another day isn't going to do him any harm love, and I'm sure he would want his mum and dad back safe, now wouldn't he?" Edd sweet-talked.

"I suppose!" But it was said reluctantly.

"Well that's that settled then!"

Dave sighed in relief and turning to the old man asked. "Can I use your phone to ring my mum too, we told her we were leaving hours ago and she'll be worried sick if we don't turn up. I want to keep my mobile battery topped up, just in case the phone lines go down for any reason."

"Good thinking lad. Call me Edd, everyone does by the way, and of course you can use the phone. Scarlett's finished, you go right ahead and I'll take the ladies back up to house. I've already locked up the garage for lunch. I was a bit late today."

"Thanks Edd!" Dave grabbed the old man's hand and shook it vigorously.

"Now both of you come with me! I'll take you to the house, it's only a short walk round this building. It will be better than here, as I can put on the central heating and make us all a nice cup of tea!"

Opening the door, he turned back to Scarlett and Dave, "You two can bring what fresh produce you can carry, and anything else we might need that we have here in the shop, then you Scarlett, can lock up and come up to the house."

With a resigned sigh, both girls followed the old man out into the rain. Dave had given Lisa his umbrella in passing, and Lisa held it over the now hooded younger girl.

Within minutes they were in Edd's hallway, stripping

224

off their outdoor clothes as he pointed the way to the living room, and carried on straight into the kitchen to make some tea, switching on the central heating as he passed the timer in the hall.

"Come on I'll get the fire on, it's a gas one like Dave and I, had when we first got married and living in our flat in South London." They were both shivering a bit, with being wet and cold.

Lisa ungainly kneeling down on the floor was true to her word and had the fire on in no time. After a giggly struggle to rise, and only with the girl's help, both were sat on the settee in front of it warming their hands.

"What a rotten day, eh!" Lisa managed to toe her wet shoes off and pointed them at the fire.

The girl looked into the glow, not caring to answer.

"What on earth made you come out in this?" Lisa tried again. "Do you need to use the phone?" Pointing to the device, as it sat on the table next to the television. "Why don't you ring your family and let them know where you are!"

"I rang them on my mobile, when I stalled the car. I explained that the river was high and they told me to come here and wait until the rain stops," the girl's resigned voice replied, "they knew Edd would look after me!"

"Oh right, of course they would!"

Not another word was said until Edd came into the room carrying two mugs of tea.

"You two look washed out, so I put sugar in both, even if you don't like it, it will do you good!"

He handed them each a mug and went down on his knees and turned the fire up, so it threw out more heat.

"I've been listening to the radio, it looks like it could

225

stop tonight and the forecast is good for tomorrow!

"You look like a drowned rat, Lis." Dave came into the room holding his own mug of tea! "Scarlett's in the kitchen starting dinner, Edd. She said she could do with a bit of help though!"

"She'll have to wait a minute, I've got to make sure the beds are done, but there is plenty of hot water girls, and lots of towels in the airing cupboard. This used to be a proper B&B, when my wife was alive, but not so much these days. Times have gotten a bit hard lately, but you never know when the wandering stranger will put in an appearance, so I keep the beds aired with new sheets on and so you have plenty of everything, but I'm just going to make sure!" Edd explained before turning to leave the room.

Lisa was the first to take up the offer of a wash and getting her hair dry, would be a plus.

"Hold on a minute Edd. I'd love to clean up!" Taking a gulp of tea, she handed Dave her mug and struggled out of the sofa.

"Do you want me to come up with you?" Dave asked as he helped her on with her shoes.

"No thanks love, Edd can show me the way." She smiled at the old man and taking his arm they left the room together.

Dave sat down in the armchair opposite the girl and looked at her over the top of his mug.

"You've run away haven't you?" he spoke unexpectedly and made her jump.

"No, I haven't!" she gamely snapped back.

"Really, then why the hell were you out in this unforgiving weather? No one in their right mind travels voluntarily, well unless you have a wife that is desperate to get home, or you are someone who is running from home!" he leaned back in the chair and watched her wrestle as to whether or not to tell him the truth or lie some more!

"How did you know? She plumped for the truth and Dave sighed.

"You have the look!" he smiled. "I was a porter in one of the big London hospitals, when I was first married. A&E mostly and we would get a lot of homeless kids in, especially in the early hours on a winter's morning."

"I can't go back you know and there is no way I could let this baby have the life I'm having. It isn't right," she blurted out, "I mean, isn't it wrong to willingly do that, knowing what will happen and let it go through what I went through?" She was crying now.

"What do you mean what you went through? Did your family hurt you?" he bristled, his family was his life, and no child should ever live in fear.

"Look, I can't tell you, please I just can't. You wouldn't understand. No one would understand!" she said between lesser sniffles.

"Well, I could give it a go." He took, the now empty mug, from her hand. "When you're ready, I'm listening!"

"No, that isn't our way!" she mumbled.

"What way?" Dave tilted his head to one side "Are you mixed up in some kind of cult?"

"No! It is a precious way of life, not in a bad way, as in a cult," She looked up at him and smiled through the tears.

"Then I don't understand how this affects you! Please explain, maybe I can help!" he took her hand in his own and a slight tingling went up his arm as he rubbed gently to help the circulation. "What's your name sweetheart?"

"Ailleen," She answered stroking her tummy lovingly

"....and this is Buddy. We both have a special gift, in our way of life."

Dave was even more puzzled by the information.

"Okay!, and this is bad how?"

"I was stolen, er I mean, kidnapped, when I was 13, by a Magpie!" she unexpectedly grinned at Dave's shocked expression, as she continued to explain. "This is what we call a man, who can use my gift for his own purposes and become very rich. I was stubborn though and he realised he could not control me, quite as he expected or wanted to. After a few years, he bought a Danish boy from a Squirrel, just so that we could make a baby for him."

"Gifts, magpies and squirrels?" It sounded like a fantasy, but looking at her face he realised, she was not exaggerating.

The girl continued to smile at his confusion.

"Why?" Dave could hardly believe his ears, "this is England for goodness sake, and that's barbaric!"

"Actually it wasn't so bad, I was lucky and Viggo and I fell in love, but although he will still be under the Magpie's influence until he reaches 20. I think I actually lose my gift as soon as the baby is born, which is quite good for me. It stops him manipulating me for gain, but I'm not sure about that part. It may only be wishful thinking!"

"What gain?"

"Let's say, he became very rich on what little he can force from me."

"But your baby will have this gift."

"Yes, and he can manipulate it from a very early age. He is also able to send me away, but keep the child, but only after it reaches five years old, though. In his world my little one will not have life's lessons to fall back on and stand up for itself, like I can!"

"How old are you?" Dave asked, she looked so very young, but sounded extremely old.

"17 today, and my boyfriend is 16." Aileen looked coyly up at him with a broad smile.

"A toy boy eh!" Dave made her laugh out loud at his words.

"Yes, it is easier for squirrels and magpies to catch a younger child. He was 15 when he came and was very obstinate. I think, from what the servants said, even worse than me and he never lost his will to escape. The Magpie's plan was to join us as soon as he could, but my body would not oblige and it was not until I turned 16 that I had my first period. No one had told me what to expect and stupidly, I told them immediately of it arriving. Well, I thought I was bleeding to death. How was I to know it was normal?" Looking down at her hands and not at Dave, she continued.

"Cunningly by then he had turned into a kind and giving man. I was thrown into my boyfriend's company, but even then, he tried to keep a distance between us. That said, I was lonely, but he was more worldly-wise than I was and one day when we sneaked away from the servants, he was able to tell me a little about what really was happening to us."

"It never stopped you? You know!" It embarrassed him to say the words.

"Sex, hey I was young, immature and he is gorgeous." She laughed, then suddenly grimaced "Ouch, stop that Buddy!"

"Funny name, for a baby!" Dave smiled.

"Her name will be Rosetta after my great grandmother and as she is my little rose bud, I decided that I would call her Buddy, until she gets here and the name doesn't let the Magpie know exactly what gender she is. I'm the only one to know, it seems mothers can always tell."

"My Lisa did that too!" said Mike, "She said our eldest was a boy, the whole way through her pregnancy. I must say this one has been a bit different, she says she can only see one boy, although the doctor says both the children are healthy, they can't see one properly in the pictures, as it is fitted across ways."

"Ouch!! That hurt!" The girl let out a deep moan.

"You alright, little one?" Dave was concerned, he knew that ouch from Mike's arrival, and asked "How far apart are your contractions?"

She shook her head. "Not very close yet. My waters broke while I was in the loo." She chuckled at Dave's expression of fear. "Hey, don't worry. I think I've read every book on childbirth ever written. I can handle this and there is no way, I'm letting him get Buddy." She assured him.

Dave's heart went into his mouth and he admitted to himself that he was worse than useless. She could have the baby now, with only a young girl and old man to help. He had even had to give up the job at the hospital, because he couldn't stand the sight of all the blood and anyone in pain made his stomach flip, when they were near him.

"They got sloppy about guarding me," she continued, "I put on a big act of really enjoying the pregnancy and making a big deal about walking in the grounds to stay healthy. I had a few pains earlier today, that's why I made a break for it. My boyfriend didn't want me to go, but he helped me get the car out of the garage and out of the estate! He couldn't come with me, because he was due to read this morning and he could say I was resting, which would give me more time to get away."

"Well you are safe enough here for the time being, especially with the weather so bad" he agreed.

"Maybe I could find my real family again, if they will take me back and ...."

"One thing at a time darling girl!" he smiled at her, "Let's get Buddy up and running first."

They both laughed out loud.

"Yeh, and it will be nice having people around when I have Buddy. You won't say anything will you Dave, please! I want this time to be special, I'm not afraid of the pain, and I know I am perfectly healthy. A midwife has been keeping an eye on me from six months, she just didn't get the dates right. Well, I suppose I did help with that just a bit, as they think I still have over a month to go!"

"Crafty!" Dave smiled.

"Needs be, as needs must!" she smiled cheekily back at him.

"Right well, why don't you go upstairs find yourself a room you like, dry yourself off and tidy yourself up a bit."

"Dave!" Lisa screamed from the floor above and had Dave shooting out of the room and running up the stairs two at a time. The girl, he now realised, was the least of his problems.

Lisa was standing in the middle of the landing still holding a hand towel, her legs wide apart, a puddle of water on the floor.

"Me waters, broke! I'm not bloody due for weeks, what the hell was that doctor thinking and saying I could go up to me mum's," she shriek, "I've just started me contractions!"

"Don't panic, sweetheart!" Dave said, as he was

panicking for both of them.

Edd came along the corridor to see what was happening.

"I've just changed the big double bed at the front, go back and dry off in the bathroom. I've already put the fire on in there, with a couple of hot water bottles. It will only be a short while before its real cosy. Dave can bring up your suitcase for you."

"I'll help Lisa." Came a laboured voice halfway up the stairs. It was Ailleen and she must have followed him out of the room, "Edd have you got a rubber sheet?"

"No, but I do have a plastic tablecloth, will that help?" the old man offered.

"Perfect," she smiled up at him, "and I need some clean towels, string, scissors and a few other things, I'm sure to think of later."

"Well don't just stand there you big lump, I need me nightie and things, go on, go and get em!" Lisa ordered.

Dave ran down the stairs, as the girl went up to help, her face showing that her own contractions were coming at a regular pace themselves.

Within five minutes Dave was back, the donated plastic blue chequered tablecloth in one hand and their suitcase in the other. Finding the bedroom, he took over getting Lisa dressed and into bed.

"God, Dave it's too early and miles from anywhere what if anything goes wrong?" Lisa cried. She was now on the tablecloth which covered the bottom of the bed, in her nightdress and with a duvet draped over her legs.

"Second births are easier than the first, I've been told, Lisa." Ailleen chipped in. Coming into the room she sat down in the chair by the bed. She'd had a quick wash and put a brush through her now dry hair. "There

232

isn't a thing I don't know about deliveries and I've read every book they've printed on the subject over the last six months, don't worry, Nurse Know-it-all is here to help." Her smile was calming and with a firm and knowledgeable voice, she continued. "I'm it Lisa, there is no way, we, either of us, is going to have a chance, unless we work together, right?"

"Your right love!" Lisa agreed reluctantly. "Dave, you go and boil water or whatever it is blokes do. We'll call if we need you."

Gratefully Dave left the room, listening to the girls talking, with the occasional grunt from Lisa. The little girl didn't make a sound, although he knew she must be in as much pain as his wife.

"Well this is a turn up for the books. Did the doctor say her delivery would be straight forward?" Edd said as Dave came back into the living room.

"Think so. Lisa doesn't say much, she knows my stomach can't take the gory details." Dave admitted and sat on the edge of the sofa.

"We can hear them from here, Scarlett is finishing off dinner, her mum's a real good cook and so is she, when she puts her mind to it!"

"The girl told me that she was kidnapped, when she was younger and brought to live with the man she lives with?" Dave whispered to his new found friend.

"Really, although I can't say I'm surprised. Weird and strange crowd that lot up at the Manor. Lived there for about two years now, but they came from somewhere up north and they certainly don't mix with any of the locals. I only know him, because he gets his petrol from me and from when he had to drive the girl to school, after they first arrived. It seems the council got wind of her not being at school, when they first moved here and he couldn't find a home school teacher. That's where the two girls met, they were in the same class for a while, Scarlett told me, but she said the girl wasn't there for more than four months and hardly spoke when she was. I saw her a few times after that though, she liked coming to get her sweets on a Saturday, with another young girl, but they were always with the teacher and they never said a lot. Then last year I didn't see any of them at all, that's when his lordship told me she had moved on to Bristol."

"Do you think it's true then, that she could have been kidnapped?" he asked.

"Could be, doesn't look anything like him, that's for sure!" Edd didn't hesitate on that point, "Oh, I forgot to tell you, I've already rung the emergency services and they said they will get here as soon as they can, because there are two prenatal babies involved."

"Dave, the babies are coming," Ailleen called down the stairs.

"Oh, my God!" Dave went straight into panic mode. "What do I do?"

"Don't look at me mate! You've been through this before, not me!"

"I only drove the car to the hospital and sat in the waiting room. Then I held her hand, I don't remember what else!"

"Well you've done the first two already today. Now you have to finish off the last job!" Edd couldn't help, but smile, "I'll call the emergency services again and tell them the good news. They might try and get someone out who can help, somehow."

"Yeh right, will do, hold her hand. That's right, hold her hand" Before running upstairs he turned back to Edd "Oh and by the way the girl has contractions too, think we may need help sooner, rather than later."

Leaving Edd gob smacked, Dave charged up the stairs.

"I'm here Lisa, my darling!," He called from the doorway, not wanting to venture any further in.

"About ruddy time, where the 'ell were you?" Lisa gritted her teeth as a contraction hit her.

"Lisa, you have to push, I can see the head," but taking a deep breath suddenly let out a fearful cry, "Oh my god, I need to push too."

"No you don't little lady, you are delivering mine, before you get a chance to do yours!" Dave's face told her, by now he was in full panic mode.

"I don't think I have a choice in this Dave, now shut the door" Crawling up the bed to Lisa's side, she lay down beside her and they both produced their children. Dave watched in wonder as both babies appeared exactly at the same moment in time.

Taking a longer deep breath, Ailleen was on point, almost immediately.

Lisa however, was not really focused, as she was still in great pain with the next baby.

"Oh what do I do? What do I do?" Dave looked at Ailleen for guidance.

Ailleen struggled to sit up and smiled at him.

"Well for a start go over to the dresser, I left all the stuff you need over there. Bring it onto the bed, then follow my instructions and cut the umbilical cords on both babies." Dave was all butter fingers, but followed what she told him to do, to the letter.

He gave Ailleen, her daughter to hold, while he cleaned up his son, and within ten minutes they had both babies washed and wrapped up in towels. Both parents were smiling their faces off.

Lisa however seemed not to have noticed anything that had happened around her, she had her eyes closed and was moaning softly beside Ailleen.

"Take the little beauties down to Edd and Scarlett, so they can look after the new kids on the block and I can get to help Lisa with your next one." She whispered to Dave.

Dave nodded, opened the bedroom door and gingerly took first one up in his arms and then the other. The proud dad carefully carried them down to Edd and Scarlett, who were hovering in the hallway waiting for news.

Handing the two babies over to their shocked minders, he only had time to tell them that the next one was on its way and ran back upstairs immediately as Lisa gave out a cry, but this time the contractions, although close together, were not it seemed producing any results.

Ailleen was getting worried. It was taking a long time, a very long time. But luckily Dave's aversion to blood and pain appeared to have gone by the wayside, as he held Lisa's hand.

"Oh Dave, it's not coming out, I........" she took a deep breath as another contraction hit her, "What are we going to doooooooooo!" Again the pain was immediate, and hardly a minute, between them.

Ailleen wiped Lisa's face with a cool cloth, looking at Dave with a worried frown.

"Lisa, it won't be long, just try and get your breath between the pains. The baby will be fine, it's normal as some second twin's come out really slowly compared to the first.

She looked at Dave, who mouthed. "Really?".

She shrugged her shoulders and her head shook,

236

telling him she was not exactly telling the truth at that moment in time. She did however, manage to get Dave to leave the room while she cleaned herself up after her placenta finally arrived and he popped down to get them both a cup of tea and peak at the newborns.

By the time he got back to the bed, Lisa was straining to get the new baby out and within seconds, he arrived. But not like his brother, there was no cry and he was half the size of the bruiser he had just handed back to Edd, downstairs.

Ailleen quickly cut the cord and took him in her arms, rubbing him vigorously with a hand towel, she had ready for him.

"Dave, you have to help Lisa with the placenta."

Dave's face blanched and he shook his head.

"You'll be fine, it's nothing to worry about. Just massage her tummy for her. I'll go in the room next door and try and get his circulation and breathing going," She began rubbing the baby's back vigorously, but she wasn't getting any response he could see that, and she turned back when she opened the door..

"Just one thing, Dave, my placenta is over there, in that plastic box. We have to get rid of both of them, before the ambulance arrives."

"Why?" he stood shocked that there was even one already.

"Not sure, just know we have to."

She skirted passed him and left the room, still rubbing the baby's back.

Dave turned doggedly back to Lisa who was not really responding in any coherent way either, she was crying hysterically and he went back to calming her down. Soothing her and not mentioning the new boy at all, just in case the worse did happen.

Just then Dave could hear voices from downstairs and thinking it was the ambulance men, got up and opened the door to come face to face with a white haired stranger in a very expensive suit and weirdly a pair of sunglasses.

"Where is my daughter?" his deep baritone voice, was filled with a fierceness that Dave was sure would shake the building. The man was almost forcing past him, trying to look inside the room and see behind Dave.

"What the devil do you think you're doing? My wife has just had our babies, get the hell out of our room." Dave didn't even have to put on a stern voice, the man in front of him gave him the willies and he was protecting everything around him.

"But I was told my daughter was here!" The man was taller than average and bulky, but this didn't scare Dave in the least.

"She was, and ever so cheerful and very brave she was too. My wife having her two little ones, while she was having her own!." Dave could have kicked himself at the slip.

"She's had her child, wonderful, wonderful" The man's mean face lit up like a beacon, and Dave cringed at the thought of what the poor girl was going back to.

A voice from the end of the corridor, brought both men to turn their heads round, "You're too late Dad. The child I had isn't breathing." Holding the baby to her, she walked towards them. "Thank your wife for her help with my baby, I will always remember you both and tell her, I quite like naming babies after their grandparents, they are lovely names for her two little ones." She must have heard them talking and was already dressed back in her wet coat, trousers and shoes.

238

When she reached both men, Dave gave her a gentle hug, catching a glimpse of his silent son, "I am truly sorry for your loss," and took a deep breath.

"And I am so happy for your gain" she whispered.

"Get down those stairs, you stupid little mare," the man ordered, "I'll get the baby to hospital, I don't care how much it costs, we'll get *it* breathing." No word of comfort to the girl as a tear dropped onto Dave's hand and she was prodded downstairs, passing Edd in the hall as they left.

Dave immediately went to follow them, as his conscience suddenly kicked in. He could not allow this man to take his little son, no matter what, but suddenly heard Lisa yelling to him from the bedroom. He could do no more than turn back to his wife, as Edd came up the stairs towards him.

"I called the police when he stormed in, so they should be able to stop him on the road, if they can get across the ford." He looked up into Dave's distraught face, "and the ambulance service came back and said they will be here in a matter of minutes."

"Only it's too late now Edd. I can only hope she can get help for herself."

"Me too! Dave, me too!"

Dave returned to Lisa as she pulled herself up into a sitting position.

"Dave, what happened, where are the babies? Are they all right?" She was trying to get herself up on the pillow. Her placenta was now there, and Dave quickly put it with Ailleen´s in the plastic box. His fear of blood and guts had definitely disappeared without a trace as he gently placed the box under the bed, ready to dispose of it a little later.

"They are both fine darling, a gorgeous boy and a

beautiful girl, just what you wanted," he didn't hesitate, "Scarlett has them downstairs, until we can clean you up a bit. Edd managed to get through to the ambulance and get them to come to the house. They said they will be here anytime now"

"I had a girl and a boy, oh Dave, I have a little girl and two boys now" Lisa was ecstatic "What about Ailleen, where is she?"

"She isn't here love. Her dad came and took her away with her baby boy. He didn´t make it."

"Oh she must be devastated, poor little love. Oh Dave, she was so wonderful with me, I would never have made it without her."

"Yes, I know my lovely!" Little did she know just how much. "Lisa as we have a little girl, if you don't mind I'd like to call her Rosetta and I'll let you choose the boy's name, that's fair, isn't it sweetheart" He had his fingers crossed behind his back, that she agreed.

"Well now, where the hell did that name come from, but you know what, I like it! So yes Dave, more than fair. I'm so happy, but it ain't half painful having two, no more eh!"

"You know we couldn't afford any more anyway love!" he said, his heart beating faster than ever.

It was about ten more minutes before the ambulance arrived, but they had pulled out all the stops to get to the babies in case they were needed. When Edd asked about passing a car, they said they hadn't seen a car going towards the hospital, and had only just got over the ford themselves coming this way, because the rain had stopped and it was receding enough to allow them across.

****

In the living room back in Welling, Dave continued the story.

"I took it that they hadn't bothered to go to the hospital with our little boy, because they couldn't revive him." His face crumpled and tears were freely falling down his cheeks. "I kept in touch with Edd for years after. Just in case he had heard of anything about Ailleen, but from the beginning he told me that the family had moved away, that same day. Within a week the house was boarded up and within a year sold on, he always said if he heard anything on the local grapevine, he would let me know, but he never did."

Chapter 21

The Final Task

The six contestants were all sitting with Sarah in their allotted part of the Violet section. A table covered with a wonderful array of their favourite foods, but unfortunately was only being picked at, by the nervous group.

"How long do we have to wait Sarah?" Laura asked again.

"Laura, I told you, this is not real time, it will feel only about 15 minutes here, and then you go out and read the lights.

"But we don't have any of the Sarah's there?" Sun Ya was shaking again.

"That's because you don't need any. This is the final remember and you have each other. That's certainly better than a lot of the contestants. Some of them were the only ones, to finish out of their six. I am allowed to watch from the side with the other companions" she boasted shyly. "I think I may be the only one that will have their dress full of colours."

"Hi, you lot!" Came from behind them in a stage whisper, as Paul Ray's face, came round the corner of the violet curtain.

"Paul, you got through!" Laura jumped up and gave him a hug.

"Paul, how many made it through?" Kawiti called.

"No, idea," raising his eyes up at the question, "but I think it must be in the 50's as I've had to go round almost all the sections trying to find you. They have six names printed to the curtain outside each of the rooms and it takes time to read them all. I knew some of you would get through, but I'm really glad it was all of you!"

"Thanks Paul," Amitola answered, as a chiming rang out from the stage area.

"Damn! The last section has just finished. I have to get back to my Holly, as I told her I was only going to the loo!" Promptly retracting his head round the curtain and disappearing from sight.

With no warning, before they could even talk about seeing Paul, a mere ten seconds later, Thor, Laura, Sun Ya and Amitola were suddenly sitting on one half of a segmented stage. They were side on, to the audience and sitting at a table that was facing a gargantuan screen which was showing a replay of all the Northern Hemisphere contestants who had won their place in the final, including Paul.

Facing the same screen on the other side, were Juniper and Kawiti and they were also sitting with, albeit a much smaller Southern Hemisphere contingent of other winners and watching their own screen.

"Now ladies and gentlemen, I would like to introduce you to your judges for this section," Noelia had appeared, standing between the two sandwiched screens, and facing the audience. She indicated to her left and called "Carolyn Saxby", then turning to her right, "and Fred Burgess."

Again the audience clapped excitedly on hearing the names of their favourite judges, on this the final challenge.

Noelia raised her hand for silence as the two judges stood in their places, just on the edge of each section.

"We will activate a soundproof shield around the contestants and judges. So you parents out there, please, don't go yelling the answers. I can vouch that they won't hear you!" Noelia said light-heartedly.

The parents themselves returned with 'Shame!' and back in the same tone. All knew the rules and it smoothed the process a little, when Noelia once again spoke.

"This is, as you know, real time, the contestants are allowed only ten minutes to complete their reading, which if correct, they will be removed and placed back in the violet area. If unfortunately, they do not pass this final hurdle, they will automatically be escorted by their contest companion, back to their waiting areas with the other failed contestants."

Laura became hot, then immediately cold, as she sat in her seat and it was only when Amitola, who was by coincidence, sitting next to her, hooked his little finger with hers, that she suddenly felt calmer. She only acknowledged his touch with a gentle closing movement of her finger to his, and smiled dumbly at the screen in front of her, as if nothing had happened.

But they both knew it had.

****

King Lenny and King Nick had arranged for all the families to be accommodated in a booth above the gold section, so they could see the whole of the last task, together.

The Rainbow House lecturers had vacated the room reluctantly, half an hour before, so it could be cleaned ready for its VIP ensemble, giving them the best view in the house for the final part of the competition.

Raul and Juan, managed to join them just as Noelia had introduced the judges and settled back to enjoy this part of the contest with them.

244

The youngsters had their noses squashed to the window in anticipation of the results and Tristan sat with Maddison on one side and his parents on the other.

"Dad, why didn't you tell me about the little gems?"

"I couldn't son. Top Secret until today and I wanted you to see how intuitive you were in getting to the contest on your own."

"Why?"

"Because, there may be a possibility of us travelling together to the world of little gems, very soon."

"Cool!"

Chapter 22

Jack

When Dave finished his monologue, he waited anxiously for the ruckus to begin, but to his surprise no one made one derogatory remark. Well, for a start they were all far too stunned at his disclosure, to utter a word.

Jack couldn't take it in, abruptly he moved to slide open the patio doors and disappeared out into the garden. The revelation was disturbing, but also strangely comforting to him. He had once had another brother, but then Rosie wasn't his biological sister, that news above all, made him feel physically sick.

Vicki was the only one to notice Jack leaving, and moved over to the window as the others began to ask all the relevant questions of Dave and which any family needed to clarify. She stood at first in the open doorway, watching his obvious despair, as his whole body was racked with sobs. It was only when he started to run down the garden, did she follow him.

"You alright, Jack?" She asked, after she had raced after him, she'd stopped a few feet behind, but waited until he halted and his breathing was less laboured. "Out here all on your own!"

"I'm never alone!" his voice choked up, as he spoke and when he turned round, his cheeks were flushed as well as being a bit wet.

Vicki hesitantly ventured forward and handed him a clean scrunched up tissue from her pocket.

"All these years, I've hated you, you know that!" Wiping his face roughly, the tissue immediately disintegrating with the force he was using.

Vicki took a stunned step back.

"Yeh, well hated is such a harsh word. Maybe you just didn't like me much!" her expression questioning.

"Oh no, I really do hate you!" his eyes were drying, but grinned back at her all the same.

"Why? For goodness sake, I never did anything to you, did I?" she queried. Her mind raced trying to think of something she had done in the past, to cause this accusation.

"No, not a thing," he shrugged his shoulders, "except you were Rosie's friend and her confidante!"

They began walking to the bottom of the garden across the lawn. Luckily it was edged with solar lights now glowing along the pathway, which was helpful in finding their way.

"You were jealous?" she whispered totally in amazement. It never entered her head, and she was sure Rosie had not realized it either. They had never intentionally left Jack on his own. He was a boy, and he did different things, didn't he?

"No, not in the way you may think. I was lonely, I only had an imaginary friend you see, and he was always with me." Opening up, for the very first time in his life. This part of who he was frightened him and at 16 he thought he should not be showing his weaknesses to anyone, especially Vicki.

"Wow, you did!" There was absolutely no sarcasm in her comment. "For how long exactly?"

They were at the end of the lawn and Jack sat down on a driftwood bench that Dave and Lisa had placed at the side of the garden. Its long brass plate engraved with a poem Jack had written, having pride of place, and one she had read many times with Rosie.

'In memory of Nanny Vi, who loved it here to sit,
to watch the different kinds of sky,
and all the birds in it,
but wouldn't she just fly, if she saw a foxy git.
Not once did she ask us why? So never did admit,
until finally our hearts did cry,
as she was forced this world, to quit.
She is now up high, in the sky, and she can fly,
knowing why. Whilst smiling just a bit.

From Rosie, Jack, Mike, Lisa, Dave,
and Bert, who misses his lovely chit. x´.

An eloquent memoir, for it was one of Jack's favourite places, which he shared with his grandmother who was the only person, he felt seemed to understand him and he missed her very much.

Vicki plonked herself beside him and both of them looked up at the stars. Jack propped his feet on the edge of a stone planter before replying to Vicki's question.

"Forever!" he grimaced, at having to say the word.

"Forever, as in you still have him around?" Vicki turned towards him, a thought suddenly forming in her mind.

"You actually believe me?" he looked at her somewhat bemused and admitted candidly. "I can't sleep, because I keep thinking, I'm going barmy!"

"Of course I believe you! Does this friend have a name?" her voice was pleading for an answer.

"Dali! He's called Dali. Strange first name I know, but I never thought so when he told me. He's been part of me since I can remember, although even though I knew he was here, I didn't really take much notice of him until about a year, maybe 18 months ago. That was when it became really weird!"

"Rosie told me today, that you talk on your mobile all the time in your room?" Vicki broached.

"So!" Jack said defensively and took his feet off the planter, bending forward and holding his head in his hands.

"Well, I saw your mobile recharging on the breakfast bar with Rosie's, before I left this morning, but I still heard you talking in the night. So I wonder now, that if you weren't on the phone, maybe you were, just, talking to Dali?" she put forward kindly.

"So! Your point is?" he said again.

"Well I just had a thought, maybe, just maybe, your twin didn't die at birth, like your dad thought and it's actually your brother who is communicating with you!" she declared, and half turned away from Jack, her arms crossed under her small breasts and waited for him to get his bearings back and come up with some pithy zinger, which would effectively put her in her place.

Except, instead of levelling his steely gaze on her, she turned to see, only to find he was actually considering what she had put forward.

"You mean telepathically?" Jack asked. Suddenly the idea was actually appealing to him, but he shook his head, "Nah, that's not exactly what we do!"

"Well, whatever it is, I don't know!" Vicki tried to put her thoughts into words. "It's only that I saw a programme on identical twins a few months ago and they had some mental abilities, it's a gift." She looked intently into his eyes.

Jack shook his head in confusion.

"This could help your mum as well, knowing her other

son could be alive, somewhere!" continued Vicki.

"Won't she be blaming Dad for giving him away in the first place and keeping Buddy?" This in itself was a painful thought for him to accept himself.

"No, I don't think she will. He did it for Rosie's sake and as far as he knew, your brother had died. What choice did he have? Imagine knowing Rosie was going to become a slave or whatever it is. Jack! Think about it, it must have been a horrible dilemma for him at the time and he's the one who has had to live with it all these years!"

"I suppose! And I really do like having two good looking chicks in the house, most of the time", He smiled at her.

Vicki thumped his shoulder in retaliation.

"Now tell me, do you know anything about Dali? Where he lives, who he lives with, that kind of thing?"

"Kind of!" he answered vaguely, but seeing her expression, tried to think clearly. "Look, I have never believed what I heard. Alright!" he blustered, "I was frightened that I really was just hearing voices and everyone would think, I had lost the plot!"

"Well!" she glanced at his now earnest face, her heart pumping twice as fast as was usual, "now is the time to admit it to all the family, because you know this could be the clue they need to get Tom, and maybe even save Dali and his mum and dad. I mean Rosie's mum and dad!"

"Oh, so now I'm useful?" But smiled when he said it, "and you think Dali is my twin and the white magpie Whitet, who took Ailleen, was the same one who took Tom? A bit of a coincidence though don't you think? It all sounds hard to believe!" he shrugged his shoulders, and stood up facing the house.

"But, I believe you, Jack!" her voice rang with its usual honesty and she got up to join him on the path.

"Well then, what are we standing here for, let's see if anyone else believes this fairy tale!" he grabbed hold of her arm and pulled her along down the path.

"Jack!" Vicki jerked back at his arm so he had to stop, before they were halfway to the patio, "I just have to ask, before we light up the sky with fireworks!" she smiled at her depiction of what might happen inside the house. "What is that smell, coming from your room?"

"I'll tell you, as long as you don't laugh!" he grinned shyly.

Vicki nodded vigorously "Of course, I won't laugh."

"Ok then, I burn candles. You know, in all sorts of scents, just to help me sleep. I know it's girly, but it really helps, especially when you think you are going round the bend!"

"Cor, I'll have to try that. I never want to sleep until the early hours, myself!"

"Ah, you're not just saying that?"

"As if I would, Norton, as if I would!" said with a smile, she put her arm through his and they both walked back to the house.

Going back through the patio doors into the house, they returned to the lounge, which was disturbingly quiet. The only sound was of Rosie and Lisa crying in each other's arms, and very low conversations between the others.

On seeing them both standing in the doorway, Dave went straight over and gave Jack a hug.

"You all right son, I'm sorry, so sorry I didn't tell you sooner!"

"Dad, you did what you thought was the best thing,

for all of us!"

He disentangled himself from his dad, going straight over to Lisa and Rosie and gave them both a brief hug, which only prompted more tears from Lisa again.

Jack stood beside them looking a little lost and not knowing what to do next. Looking over to Vicki, who was by then sitting on the edge of Mike's armchair, she tilted her head towards Kristy, Ellie, Lucas, and Terry. With a nod of acceptance, he went and stood over by the fireplace and cleared his throat, directing his voice at them.

"Look I don't know how to put this, because I don't believe it myself!"

Dave stepped forward, but Jack stopped him in his tracks.

"No, sit down Dad, I believe you, I just can't believe what I am going to tell the rest of you."

He stopped talking and turned back to Vicki, who mouthed "Go on!"

"All my life I have heard voices! Although I knew about Rosie being able to see and hear her stories in her sleep, with me it's more just disjointed voices and I'm bloody well awake when I hear them. I thought I was going barmy, especially lately as over the last few months, one voice has become clearer and more distinct."

He caught Lucas and Terry smiling at each other, as they sat in front of him.

"What?" Jack demanded petulantly at both their expressions, "What have I said that's so bloody amusing?"

"Jack! This is part of the Symm. My uncle, Dr Bush has audio ability too and I myself am lucky to have it in a lesser capacity!" Luc said with a broad grin, which he

252

seemed to permanently have across his face anyway.

"Lucky! It's been a ruddy nightmare!" Jack vented.

"Yeh, it does get a bit noisy sometimes, doesn't it?" Luc agreed.

"And I thought you meant you were telephoned, in New Zealand!" Ellie sighed "but what you actually said was, you were literally 'called' by Dr Bush?"

"Yep, certainly was! My dear Uncle Doc said jump, but I just didn't realise how high it is to England!" Laughing at his own joke.

"So, why me? I'm not like you!" Jack objected fiercely.

At that point Lisa stood up wiping her eyes, she joined Jack in the middle of the room and put her arm around him. Managing hesitantly, to come into the conversation.

"Ironically, I think we may be!"

"How?" Jack shook her arm off and faced her square on.

"The how's and wherefore's, are a bit difficult to describe, I just know for the last few months I've noticed a difference in the way I see things. I kept remembering my mum's last words to me before she died."

Lisa hesitated, but Dave went up and stood close.

"She said "It is our Symm to carry the balance of the world!" Then my mum laughed, a really weird laugh and took my hand "Didn't do us any favours though, did it Lisa, your Nanny Gert said we were royalty. Lied about that too!"

"You never said a word to us." Mike said, "Mum, why not?"

"I was scared. I didn't know what it meant, but from that day to this, I started to feel things. Nothing tangible, but even more so, when I was with Rosie!"

"Now I understand!" Ellie voiced reflectively. "I wondered why Rosie's mum would attach to someone who was not of the Symm, she was probably drawn to you that day, Lisa. In her predicament she could have had two choices, one dark and one light, your road was the light for her."

The two women smiled at each other across the room.

"You've lost me?" Bert said, ".... and I thought I was following all this new information, quite well up to now!"

This broke the ice and everybody started to laugh at the comment, until Vicki got up and yelled.

"Quiet, all of you, Jack hasn't finished, so listen up, please, it's really important for you to hear what he says!"

Mike took her hand and brought her back down on to the arm of his chair, and wrapped his arm round her waist to keep her there. Vicki relaxed immediately as she rested her head on his shoulder.

"Go ahead son." Dave said, taking Lisa back to the sofa and they sat next to Rosie.

"Look, I never listened to the voices much. I thought I was going crazy if you want to know the truth, and so I didn't pay much attention. The only voice I liked anyway was Dali's. He would talk to me and tell me things that didn't make sense at first, but he was fun sometimes and gave me descriptions of all the scenery around where he lived. He likes the countryside a lot, birds especially, and it seems a lot of them breed where he lives on an island in the middle of the Mediterranean Sea somewhere, anyway I think that's where it is. It's the impression he gave me and he lives with his mum and dad. His mum is called Ailli and his dad, I think his name is Fig, and he works for a man whose voice, I really can't stand. I think it is Whit it, but I could be wrong!"

There was stunned silence, before all hell let loose.

Lucas rushed over and picked him up to swung him round the room. He probably would have thrown him in the air, if the ceiling wasn't so low.

"You little beauty!" he cried.

"Put me down you big galah!" Jack yelled. He had heard the Australian expression on TV and thought it was a good call for Lucas at this moment.

Without preamble, Vicki stood back up and joined Jack, as Luc dropped him back on his feet.

"Shut up the lot of you!" she looked sternly round the room and everyone returned to their seats.

"Things have been changing here over the last few months. Things I think as an outsider, I notice more than the family does. When I was talking to Jack outside, I thought of an idea." Then turning to Kristy and Ellie, asked. "Do you think it might be a twin thing? I remember you saying earlier that twins don't happen in families of the Symm. Well this family has three sets that I know of, including Dave's brother and sister. Maybe, because the gift was lost years ago, this could be the reason they have so much stimulus now. Maybe Rosie gave a boost to Jack, as they were born within seconds of one another and also being brought up together."

"Well that kind of makes sense, in an odd sort of way." Terry said.

"So let's try to get Jack and Rosie to visualise a bit, maybe she might see something? Vicki suggested.

"I don't see anything in this world, Vicki, you know that, I've never seen anything, but the Springer's world." Rosie spoke for the first time.

"Ah, ah! Oh yes you have, I know it might have only been once or twice, but do you remember last Christmas, we both wanted that copy of a Prada handbag so badly in the market. A few mornings later, at school you were in a foul mood, because you dreamed I'd got a real one and you got the copy."

"Which I did, I was so envious of you." She smiled sideways at her mum. "Sorry mum, I would have been happier if Vicki had got a copy too, instead of the real thing!"

Vicki laughed, "Anyway it happened and you saw it happen right. I know Jack knew it was going to happen too, because that same day in school, he said something to me that didn't make sense at the time. 'Here she comes, the posh handbag girl with a mother with more money, than sense'. She screwed her face up at Jack and smiled. "I brushed it off then, but you must have sensed what Rosie said to me. There was no way you heard us speaking as she had whispered it in gym class, with no one else around." She grinned at the discomfort the words brought Jack, as he remembered what he had said.

Vicky turned to Rosie. "Because neither you, nor Jack understood what was happening. It was from about then that you started arguing a lot, so there was no way of knowing that you each had gifts that were compatible. Maybe it is, maybe it isn't, but you could give it a try, if it doesn't work, so be it!"

"Give what a try?" Rosie said.

"Contact Ailli through Dali, because I think he is the key to all this and is Jack's little twin brother. I think they are identical, there is a thing called twin to twin transfusion syndrome, it's where one twin gets bigger than the other. In this case I think Ailleen must have rushed Dali to hospital after he was born and made sure that he lived."

"That sounds like a thing, she would have done." Dave agreed.

"That could also be the reason she said to get rid of the placenta. Identical twins share only one, so the hospital would have seen that Rosie and Jack weren't brother and sister."

"Clever girl" Mike came over to hold her hand. "Vicki's right, this is so off kilter with what we know or don't know in the Symm as in our case. We have to find out what is happening and they may be able to help."

"It might be too much of a coincidence that it's Whitet who has Tom too, but maybe the Symm has brought us all together" Terry asked. "Can you both try?"

"Well Buddy shall we give it a go?" Jack asked boldly of his sister.

"You bet ya!" Rosie chuckled as she crossed the room and high fived her brother's hand, to seal the pact.

"Hold on a minute" Vicki yelled, "Doesn't that mean that if Jack has a gift, Mike as he is the oldest, would have one too!"

"Yeh, I suppose that logically that's correct." Ellie agreed.

All the room turned as one to stare at Mike.

"Don't look at me, I don't have a bloody thing, sorry!" Mike shook his head, "I am yours, aren't I mum?" he teased.

"17 ruddy hours in Guy's Hospital, worth of eyes wide open labour, that's what you are!" she smiled back at him.

Chapter 23

The Little Gem

Suddenly out of nowhere, the outer rim of a tornado hit and Jaime was knocked off his feet immediately, but flung miraculously unharmed through the opening that led to the corridors which accommodated the majority of the failed contestants waiting areas.

Intuitively knowing what was happening, and as much as his greed was paramount, his training of 16 years at Rainbow House would not allow him to see anyone hurt unnecessarily.

He started by getting up from the floor and yelling at the screaming participants, who poured from the rooms off the corridors, to head for the bathrooms and then even shepherded a small mixed group close to him inside the girls' toilet himself.

Telling them loudly to hold on to the toilets as quickly as they could, knowing plumbing was their safest anchor, he managed to get them to sit on the floor in the partitioned areas tightly packed together. Even though some feet were sticking out and obviously most were crying, he was able to get them to cover their heads with their arms and huddle as close as they could to each other.

He then sat on the floor of the entrance, bracing his back to the door, hearing the other noises that accompanied the terror outside, and bemoaning the fact that his one chance of getting rich, was now taken forever.

Or was it?

A little gem, as grey as the North Sea in a storm,

suddenly appeared and was obviously looking for its owner, he raised his eyes to follow it dashing to one area and another. Not realising he was doing it, he pulled out the box from his pocket and held it out in front of him in the palm of his hand.

Without preamble the box opened automatically and a strange green light came from within, homing directly at the gem. In the few seconds that followed he could see the struggle for power between the two, as the gem was forced, metaphorically kicking and screaming towards the box.

The pleasure he felt in capturing the gem was short lived however, as the door behind him suddenly began to vibrate violently. The last thing Jaime saw was the box snapping shut, just before the door folded and flew open, smashing into his head and knocking him semi-conscious.

Although he still had the box in his grasp, the force of the turbulent wind moved his body across the floor slamming him against the farthest wall and wrenching the box reluctantly out of his hand to fly up into the current of air above him and then out of sight.

"Bye gem," he mumbled, philosophical, before losing consciousness

Chapter 24

The Escape

"Is everyone all right?" Thorlief was dusting himself down, even though his white tabard was just that, pristine and untainted, with not a micro-speck of dust to be seen. At another time, this would have been laughable, as every face he examined belonging to someone who was upright, was streaked with dirt.

Looking over heads, he could see several casualties and noted that Juniper, Sun Ya and Laura were gravitating towards the injured. Sarah and a couple of other companions were trying to calm down a group, who although uninjured, looked justifiably distressed.

"What the hell happened?" Amitola called to him, his jet black hair now covered in a grey mist of dust as he came up beside Thor.

"Rogue tornado!" A familiar voice came from behind them and turning they saw Paul appear from around some rubble. "It materialized from outside the staging area and it's not one of the competitor's tasks. I can only think it must have come from the main floor, because it materialised in front of us, and not the side. Oh and thanks for the push, by the way," he acknowledge to Thorlief, "it was the last thing I remember as a piece of wood headed in my direction." He smiled, thankful that had Thor knocked him through one of several opened trapdoors and on to the canvas slide that led to safety under the stage.

"You're welcome, but as you saw more than I did, exactly where ......"

"Paul, are you alright?" Laura's voice came out of the

blue, as she ran up and whilst doing what the tornado couldn't do, almost knocking Amitola off his feet, but at least said sorry to him, as she hung on to Paul.

"Hey, Lau, get a grip, I'm fine," he tried to free himself from her iron grasp.

"Do you think the families got out OK?" she asked.

"To be honest, I think we better think about ourselves first." Thor said, but at Laura's stormy look, he took a step back, but gamely carried on. "We have to find a way of getting out of here, it isn't safe!" Glancing deliberately back to the floor above them, which groaned appropriately.

Finally out of Laura's hold, Paul and then Amitola followed his glance upwards.

"Thor's right Laura, this is hardly the best place to be now. There is a ton of scenery above us, ready to fall down any minute," Turning to Thor, Amitola asked "So what's next?"

"Well, the trapdoors are definitely not a way out, I barely got ours shut before the rest of the stage set was about to try to follow me. So how many of us are there here?"

"73, including all of our group, 14 companions, with Sarah and three judges, but two of them didn't look too good though." Kawiti came up to them and pointed in their direction. "I think one banged her head as they tried to get her down here, and the other one definitely twisted his ankle while he helped a couple of the others get out of the way!.

"That's a lot!" Thor commented to himself.

"I've already checked the under stage exit over there," Kawiti stood beside Amitola and pointing behind again, "unfortunately that way's blocked!"

"Great!, Well we have to do something, I'm not sure

how much weight the stage can hold, but I don't like the sound of the creaking above us."

On those words the thud of more scenery falling on to the stage made them all jump, and a few of the contestants screamed at the noise.

"Right, Kawiti, do you think you could get some of the guys and try and clear the blocked exit, we need to get away from this area pretty quick!"

"I'll help!" said Amitola and Paul, at the same time.

"Good, I'll go and ask the judges if they know any other ways out. Laura, can you manage the other injured?" Glancing hopefully, in her direction

"I don't know. It's the open wounds that are the problem!" she admitted.

"I think if you tear your dress it actually grows again, so you could use it for bandages!" Kawiti shouted as he headed in the opposite direction, followed by his two associates.

"How does he know these things?" Laura looked at Thor and laughed.

"Beats me, but I'm glad he's here with us!" he admitted quietly.

"Me too!" she smiled back at him and Thor watched as she walked towards Sun Ya. A huge smile forming as she pulled at her skirt, ripping off a length of it as she staggered across the debris.

Turning in the opposite direction he headed to see Fred and Carolyn, noting as he drew closer, that both did seem the worse for wear.

"Majesty" Fred tried to rise from his place on the floor as Thorlief came towards him.

"Fred, sit right back down again, I need your help. Is there another way out of here?" he went down on his haunches to be at his elder's level.

"Not that I know of, it's the first time I have been to London." he acknowledged.

"I saw a map on the side of the stage, but I didn't take much notice. I seem to remember there were a couple of tunnels leading out of here." A girl's voice beside Fred said, she was holding Carolyn in her arms and Thor couldn't see her face for a mop of curls, but she shook her head, seemingly to clear her thoughts.

"A couple, well that sounds promising, I expect one was the exit we are trying to clear, and the other is probably for props, which would be great, because it might be bigger and I really think we might need to move quickly. Can you remember if they were close or apart?" Thor stepped forward just as the girl looked up at him, and he took in a sharp breath.

"Noelia, is that you?" he was stunned at seeing the sister of his childhood friend, Juan. "Are you ok? I didn't know you were one of the judges?"

"I'm not! Fred and Carolyn are. I was Rainbow's hostess for the competition. The exits are directly across from each other, Thor! One was stage left the other stage right" she informed him.

"Kawiti, Paul, Amitola!" he yelled over "Quick, we might have an exit opposite the one you're working on. The rest of you guys, keep at that one, just in case it isn't."

All three of them headed towards the wall opposite and then quickly tearing away a small amount of debris they found across a narrow doorway. Unfortunately it was not the larger exit Thor was hoping for, but it easily opened on to a narrow passageway. Paul and Amitola came straight back to tell Thor.

"There's a corridor" Amitola told him, "Kawiti's going down there now, let's get the rest heading in that

263

direction, because I don't think this stage is going to last much longer!"

Thor agreed, the floor was definitely groaning loudly above them again, and putting on an imitation of his father's deep voice, he yelled out.

"Right everyone, we have to get out of here. *Now!* Anyone standing that can help someone else who isn't please do so. Move as quickly as you can over there!" Thor pointed towards the new exit.

Without further ado, Amitola immediately scooped Carolyn into his arms and headed for the opening, yelling at everyone he passed, to follow him, then handing the elderly lady to another one of the older boys, to take her on through the passageway, before turning to go back for someone else.

"First time in a long while I've had such a gaggle of good looking males pick me up!" Carolyn smiled at her new rescuer. "What's your name son, just so when I wake up, I'll remember who you are?"

Her head rested on his shoulder as he strode away through to the doorway, a smile on his face directed at the old lady, but she had fallen unconscious in his arms, before he had time to answer.

As if the stage heard Thor's request, another loud crash from above and sent everyone scurrying towards the exit. He bent down and helped Fred up as Noelia was pulled to her feet by Paul, who gamely put his arm round her waist to steady her.

Laura and Juniper were leading a girl with a broken arm and a boy with a bad gash on his forehead, both of which were dressed with part of Laura's dress, which unfortunately wasn´t growing back to its original length, as quickly as she had hoped.

Within a couple of minutes they were all in the

tunnel, just as they heard the sound of the stage giving up the ghost and crashing down behind them. Luckily Amitola was last in line and in time to slam the door shut and stop the inevitable dust bowl travelling up the corridor after them.

"Go, go, go!" he yelled, prompting the others to rush along as fast as they could down the corridor, luckily lit, although sporadically, by emergency lighting.

Further down the passageway they came to a fork that seemed to be sloping upwards. Without warning, the ceiling started to crumble in the corridor they were in, dropping chunks of ceiling on top of them.

Kawiti yelled encouragement as he got them to split up and go down either of the forked aisles, as the main one itself was obviously becoming unsafe to stay in for any length of time.

"Go, go, either one will get you out, come on move quickly." He was shouting above the throaty rumble groaning above their heads.

Even the injured seem to jump at his words and headed for the left hand fork which had more lighting, and Thor's group, going down the one on the right.

Amitola anxiously looked behind as the main corridor began to crumble with cracks appearing in lightning strikes across the ceiling. He visualised their location as being still under the enormous stage and certainly not out of danger yet, so imitating Thor's bellow, he encouraged them all to go faster. After a while their passageway obviously passed out of the staging area and was at least not falling to pieces above their heads. From then on it continued to twist and turn, with Thor trying to open every passing door on their journey, but all were securely shut with no visible handle to open them with, and each having the unyielding metal swipe plate on the side.

Sun Ya and Juniper were leading the group, but were dragging their feet tiredly, until they came to an abrupt halt, having been stopped by two narrow metal doors. One had the word EX and the other IT written in gigantic letters, but the girls waited until Paul got there before they voiced their fear that there was still no way to get out.

"They say that the door won't open!" Thor heard, Paul call back and he with Amitola left Kawiti, to weave their way forward, passing Sarah and Laura, whose dress, Amitola noticed, was back to the same length as all the other girls. They couldn't reach Paul however as the corridor was packed.

"Which way does it open?" Thor called to the front as he wasn't able to see from his angle.

"Inwards to us, by the looks of it, but still no handle or anything to pull it forward, so makes it a bit of a pain!" his voice called back and began thumping the solid mass in front of him.

"Not for me!" A disembodied voice, yelled at them from the other side of the door. "Stand back, I'll have it open in a tick!"

The line shuffled back just in time, as within a matter of maybe three or even four ticks, the door flew open, to find Tristan standing at the entrance, not much cleaner than the motley crew from the passageway. He was holding an old fashioned knife, which he had obviously used to pry open the metal plate on his side of the door and again to short circuit the connections inside.

On seeing the group, he immediately handed the dove handled knife back to Alfie, and helped Juniper who was the first person through the doorway to get across the fallen debris on his side. Maddison standing across from him, helped Sun Ya.

"Maddison?" Paul almost let go of Noelia at seeing her, when he reached the opening, he was so surprised.

"Is Laura with you, Paul?" Alfie asked standing on tiptoes to try to see round him.

"Alfie, Maddison, is that you?" Laura shrieked from inside, just as Amitola was stepping out and she pushed him to one side, so she could see her brother and sister, peering in through the doorway.

"It's them Laura, they're both here!" Paul called back to her, his eyes not leaving Maddison once, as he stepped into the dusky night air.

"Where is here by the way?" Amitola asked Tristan.

"The back of the auditorium, not many people here, but at least there is lighting, so we can see what we are doing" he answered.

They both stared at their surroundings and Amitola took Laura's hand, determined to help her across the damaged wall and she smiled at him weakly at his touch.

"Sorry I've been a grouch," she admitted, coming to the conclusion, that he really was nice after all.

"Yeh, you have, but I'll get used to it!" he chuckled.

She shook her head smiling, as finally she was out in the open, and threw herself at her two siblings.

There were some blocks that had fallen from the peripheral wall around them, and all the 25 who came through the door, either sat where they could find a space on the small wall, or found a flat surface to stand on.

"How did you find us?" Laura asked while embracing Alfie tightly. Paul was already hugging Maddison, after Noelia was safely settled on the low wall by the side of the entrance.

"We didn't, they did!" Tristan pointed up above Laura's head at the cluster of little gems flying around in all directions, almost dancing in excitement and blinking on and off.

Thor smiled a broad gleaming smile recognising the five that belonged to his group and turning, sat down next to Noelia. "I believe I recognise the honey brown one dancing round the others."

"Thought you might! I bet Juan will be here any minute now, you watch!" she smiled back, "but who does the emerald green one, belong to? I have never seen that colour before." She asked Tristan.

"Don't look at me! I have no idea who any of them belong to." Tristan admitted. "Out of all of them, Maddison could only recognise her own gem, but they all seemed to converge on us and wouldn't leave us alone until we followed them. We left a blue one behind, that belonged to King Nicolas, with all the families."

"The gems found us a safe way off the upper floor and kept buzzing for us to follow them, until it became clear we had to go all the way down here." Maddison continued the story,

"So the parents are coming?" Thor's head had swung round at the name of his father and felt ashamed he had not thought of his own parents, until Tristan had mentioned them.

At that point Sarah, who had been tending some of the wounded, came over to where they were standing and yelled out.

"Peapod!" The gem came straight to her and flew around and around her head, and landed on her nose.

"Well that's good, we all appear to be here!" Juniper said smiling broadly.

Chapter 25

Rosie, Jack and Dali

Everyone went quiet, whilst Rosie and Jack went over to the dining table so they could face one another. Closing their eyes, a strange feeling immediately clicked between them and both minds went instantly rushing down a long dark tunnel, only to stop abruptly in a black void.

"Jack, are you here?" Rosie sounded scared, as a sudden sense of claustrophobia surrounded her like a cloud of unpleasant gas.

"Yeh, I'm with you, I still can't see anything, can you?" Not understanding how deeply her fear was affecting her.

"Who's there?" another voice cheerfully asked, "Is that you Jack?"

"Hi Dali, I brought my sister Rosie to meet you." Jack answered back immediately.

"Really, is she pretty, like Lizzie?" Dali asked.

"Yes, she's prettier than any girl I know!"

Squeezing her hand gently, his reassuring touch immediately cleared the cloud from around her and she felt less fearful.

"Hi Dali, how are you?" Rosie asked hesitantly.

"I've got a bit of a cold and I'm in bed, I like to laze in." he answered smugly.

"That's a shame, Dali!" Rosie jumped as a sudden bright light opened up before her and with the obvious sitting up action, she realised immediately that she was seeing a small bedroom in a foreign villa, "Oh, you have opened your eyes. Is this your room Dali?"

"Yeh, it isn't as big as Lizzie's, but mine faces the beach. Mum knows I like to hear the birds in the mornings. Here, look through the window?" he knelt then, having automatically accepted that Rosie could see what he saw, with absolutely no qualms at all.

They were looking over a patchy scrub of land to a wide expanse of sandy beach and blue sea. It was certainly not in the British Isles that was for sure.

"Oh, it's beautiful, where is your mum?" Rosie felt her heart beating so loud, she could hear it in her ears.

"She's in the garden, the other side of the house. She's really good at growing things." He said proudly.

"Me too!" Rosie whispered.

"Do you want to see her?" he added eagerly.

"Oh, yes please, Dali, I'd love to see her," he jumped up out of bed then, and ran barefoot through the small villa.

"Can you see anything yet, Jack?" Rosie asked softly.

"No, not a ruddy thing! I think I only get the radio, when you get the TV!" he laughed.

"Yeh, I like telly," Dali said, as he stopped at an open doorway to put on his flip flops.

"Dali hasn't much electricity in his house, it's all solar. I remember him telling me that," Jack added. "He only gets to watch TV in the big house occasionally."

"We might get our own this year, Dad says, they have a new gem coming to stay in the house with Lizzie. Whit might let us have the dish at our villa too!"

Rosie froze and she felt a small surge of strength coming from Jack as he placed his hands back on hers at Dali's words, just to help her keep her focused.

"Oh, isn't it a lovely flower garden. Is that your mum, Dali?" They were out of the house now and he was

270

walking towards the dry stone wall. Rosie could see a woman tending the flowers she was bending down and Rosie couldn't see her face. It was scary and she almost lost the plot, as she looked down at the woman. Her mum!

"Mum, I've got Rosie in my head. She says you have a lovely flower garden." Dali told her.

"That's nice darling and what does she think of the veggie patch?" she asked him distractedly and still bending over whilst dead heading some roses.

"Dali, tell her, Rosetta thinks the veggie patch could do with a bit more water." Rosie responded. Her voice was cracking at the thought of speaking to her biological mother.

"Rosetta says you could do with a bit more water on the veggie patch," he grinned at his mum.

"Sorry love. What did you say?" Ailleen came up from the ground and turned to look at her son. It was a shock, for although she was looking at Dali, he had lost his eye colour and it was replaced with an exact match of her own muted blue.

"Hello, Ailleen, my twin brother Jack is here with me and we need your help." Was all Rosie could think of to say as she stared at this woman. It was like looking at an older version of herself, just a little bit thinner with a very tanned face, but she was still young and quite beautiful.

"Rosie says hello mum, she and my friend Jack are here, but they need your help."

"Oh my goodness, Buddy, you're here, how? Oh, this is wonderful. How are Lisa and Dave? Tell them I took care of Dali for them, it was touch and go at first, but it all worked out!"

Dali stared at his Mum in shock. Jack was repeating

everything to the room behind him and heard his parents gasp at what he told them.

"Mum, have you gone mad?" Dali asked.

"Yes I believe I have!" she threw down her trowel and rubbed her own grubby hands on her skirt. "Let's go in and have some fruit cake and milk."

"But it isn't Saturday Mum, it's Sunday and I haven't even had breakfast yet?"

"You have Rosie in your head and that calls for a celebration." Ailleen took Dali's hand as if he were ten rather than the gangly 16 year old he was.

"And remember I've got Jack too!" he smiled beguilingly at her, "but he only has the radio and Rosie has the telly"

"Jack too! Well then, that sounds like a double celebration." She pulled him on.

"Two slices of cake and two glasses of milk for them, but what about me?"

"Don't get greedy Dali" Rosie impulsively put in.

"Rosie says, I mustn't get greedy!" he laughed at the expression on his mother's face.

"Got a good head on your shoulders Rosetta. That's my girl!" Ailleen's eyes welled up with tears, tightening her grip of Dali's hand.

Suddenly before reaching the back door, she caught sight of a figure of a man coming towards them across the hill, behind the villa. Ailleen stopped them to watch his progress, then when she thought he was within hearing distance, she spoke to Dali.

"Oh look, Dad's finally home at last." She waved her arm and with an urgent edge to her voice, called to him, "Vig, please hurry up!"

Within a seconds Viggo vaulted the dry wall and ran to where they were standing outside the villa and hugged them both, as if he hadn't seen them for years, let alone a mere two weeks.

"Dad, I've got Rosie in my head and we are having cake to celebrate." Dali just couldn't contain his excitement.

"What, did you say? I didn't hear you." Viggo asked his son.

"Viggo, Rosetta has found a way of coming through to us!" Ailleen took her husband's hand and squeezed it tightly.

"She's in my head, Dad!" Dali said proudly and quite happy that his mother had relinquished his own hand, "and Jack too, he's my best friend."

Jack shuddered realising in all this time, Dali really did have only one friend, apart from Lizzie! It was him. He wanted to look seriously at himself, but that would have to wait, he had too much going on now and had to be there for Buddy, at this moment in time.

Viggo looked over at his son, noticing for the first time that his son's eyes were not their usual amber, but the lovely blue that matched his wife's.

"Rosetta?" he questioned.

"Hello Viggo, you look tired" The words out of Dali's mouth came quickly and as he relayed them to his father, Viggo turned, staring open mouthed at Ailleen, as he returned the pressure back to her hand.

"Oh it is her. Ailleen, it's our little girl!" Then suddenly looking furtively around him, he hustled them into the villa and closed the door firmly behind them.

Ailleen smiled indulgently at the two men in her life and immediately went over to the kitchen worktop and began to get the cake, milk and put the kettle on for tea.

"Rosie says 'hi' Dad, she doesn't know how much time

they have left, but they are looking for Tom Osmundsen, is he with us? They need to find him and bring him home."

Viggo was struck dumb as the words sank in, but sent a shiver down his spine.

"Oh Rosetta you can't come here, it's too dangerous." Viggo panicked.

"She says she must find him" Dali said between bites of a huge slice of fruit cake

"Then she must do it without our help!" Viggo said, emphatically, he was pacing up and down the kitchen.

"Viggo, what is wrong with you? You have moaned about us living here for ages. Why the suddenly change of mind?"

Viggo went quiet, too quiet, and Ailleen shot him a glacial glance, before he turned away from Dali to face his wife.

"I shot a man in London!" he whispered, his face was pale with remorse, "Whitet told me that if I didn't do as I was told, he would make sure, you and Dali weren't here when I got back!"

"Oh Viggo!" Ailleen sat down on the nearest chair, as her legs could not support her.

There was silence in the room, but Jack came back into the conversation and immediately spoke to Dali. "Tell your dad that he wasn't that good a shot and the man was only wounded. His name is Walter Treleavan and his wife Ellie is here with us now and he is out of danger. She is Tom's cousin."

"No, you didn't kill him Dad, he was only wounded." Still looking puzzled at Viggo's admission.

"He's alive, Really! I knew I'd aimed away from his vital organs, but Whitet told me, he was dead." Viggo began to shake.

274

"Of course he would, he needed you to think that, so he had you under his control, forever." Ailleen got up again, and strode back over to the dresser, getting two glasses and the brandy bottle from the dresser and returning to the table, put the glasses down gently, but slammed down the bottle in front of him. She was none too pleased with what she had just heard.

"Rosie says we have to tell them where we are, it's crucial to the Symm, and Jack agrees with her!" Dali continued.

"What do you mean crucial, Rosetta?" Ailleen asked as she poured brandy into both glasses.

Back in the Norton's lounge, Terry had moved over to the table as soon as the conversation had begun and was sitting strategically next to Rosie and asked her to repeat what he saying to her.

"Something is building in the Symm which needs to have Tom involved. He will be 20 in about four months, so it's important we get him out soon." Rosie related. "We need to know where he is so we can organise a rescue."

"Oh my goodness. Lizzie!" Ailleen murmured out loud "They are both Majestet and she is also Fin!"

"But she is only a child!" Viggo held his half-filled glass and downed the brandy in an angry gulp.

"I like Lizzie, she's pretty." Dali added to no one in particular, "but Jack says she's not as pretty as Rosie!"

"Who is Lizzie?" Rosie asked.

"She is another Stolen, a Majestet Fin and just turned 16". Ailleen informed her.

With this news the adrenalin that was keeping Rosie going began to wane, and Jack could feel its loss. Not being really aware of what he was doing, he refocused and let her take some more of his strength, to keep in contact with her parents. He conveyed Ailleen's news to Terry, without Rosie having to repeat it herself.

"I don't have much time and I don't know when I can get back. I'm getting really tired."

"Buddy, don't go. Viggo, you tell her our location, this minute. I want to see our daughter again and if it's possible I would like to leave this so-called paradise forever." Ailleen demanded.

"I honestly don't know the exact location, we came back by helicopter from the mainland and it took about 30 minutes to get here. You must listen carefully Rosetta, for what I tell you will be the difference between life and death, if and when, you find the island!" Viggo whispered.

Relaying the information was getting harder as time went on, and Rosie could feel she was losing her concentration, as she and Jack constantly passed on the instructions which were going backwards from Terry and forward from Viggo.

"Sorry, guys I have to go, I feel shattered."

"Buddy, we love you!" Ailleen was devastated and Rosie felt the same.

"I know, I think I've always known, but just found out today!"

"Bye Rosie, can Jack come back tomorrow, I can still talk to him, can't I?" Dali asked.

"I'm sure he'll try Dali, but can you do me just one more favour?

"No problem!" he said with no hesitation.

"Look in the mirror, so I can see what you look like."

Dali moved over to the large mirror over the open fireplace and stared into it, except he did not see himself. He was able to see Rosie's reflection clearly and smiling broadly as they simultaneously connected.

"Oh Dali, you look exactly like Jack, but I think you're better looking," she teased.

"Gee, thanks a lot sis!" Jack said.

"Oh, just one more thing, ask mum why you are called Dali?" Rosie asked quickly.

"Why did you call me Dali, Mum?"

"I used the first two letters of Dave and Lisa's names. That was all I had of them" Ailleen supplied, "I wanted you to have a bit of them with you always!"

"Oh Mum, how sweet!" Rosie said, as her head hit the table and she lost consciousness, totally exhausted. A chorus calling either 'Rosie' or 'Buddy' sprang from everyone's lips.

"Jack, are you still in touch with Dali?" Terry asked.

"No, I think it took too much out of him too! Bet he did exactly what Rosie's did! Wow, that was so weird, but really awesome!"

Luc immediately crossed the room and swept Rosie up in his arms as Dave directed him up the stairs to the third bedroom and she was gently placed her on the bottom bunk.

Mike followed closely, checked her vital signs, and came to the conclusion that she was just exhausted with the mental link and went down to do the same check on Jack.

"I'll stay with her" Lisa said, sitting on Rosie's typing chair, the only seat in the room. "She's still my baby!"

"She is a very brave girl Lisa. She should sleep until morning, exhausted, but for the first time in her life, dreamless, I think!" Luc patted her gently on the shoulder. "She has adapted extremely well, considering she had no prior knowledge of the Symm."

"She has, hasn't she?" She looked up at him "Luc I think I can feel the Symm flowing through me, seeing you all and hearing Ailleen tonight has made a big difference to me!"

"It's called cascading, it means your family is in the tributary of the Symm and little by little you will all be brought up to speed as to what is needed of you," he smiled. "Perhaps that is why I am here, to help smooth the way!"

"I understand, Rangatira imi!" her head dipped in respect.

"Lisa, now I'm flabbergasted. You recognised my origin and status line, got the pronunciation a bit off kilter, but good enough!" he sank down on the floor, which was a feat on its own, in such a small room. "Lisa do you think your family are Majestet?"

"I honestly don't know Luc, but if I am, the line was lost two generations ago and they are all now gone. My grandmother was a child, when her parents and her four brothers were lost to the war, but I know I am the last female in heritage terms, and now you have said the word Majestet, it sounds familiar."

"This is wonderful news, this family is truly Symm, and with it Mike, Jack and Dali should also be Majestet, incredible!"

"Does Mike have a gift too?" She asked.

"Some gifts are not quite what you might expect, Lisa, although this is an area I have no real knowledge of. Especially in terms of the Lost, returning to the fold. I will speak to Uncle Doc in the morning, I bet he will feel within the Symm and see what gift Mike might have. He is not yet 20 and I know of some of my friends who didn't show until very late, but he will have one, you can be sure of that."

"A pity that you're too old for a gift Lisa, they might have given you a bloody good singing voice, so we can get rid of the cotton wool from our ears." Dave was standing in the doorway, listening to what had been said.

Luc got to his feet "I think it must come with the territory, Dave, my mother can't hold a tune either." He chuckled as Dave moved out of the way allowing him to exit the room and go downstairs.

"Holding up, love?" Within seconds Dave was holding Lisa and he didn't for the life of him know how they got to be standing up in the middle of the room and holding each other, but they were.

"Yes, I think so, oh Dave, what a night eh!" Lisa turned her head resting it on Dave's chest.

"I'm so sorry love!" he felt devastated that he had given Dali to Aileen all those years ago, but had he any real choice?

"Don't be, you gave me the best gift you could. I got to raise Rosie, which I shall always treasure. Ailleen had the hardest job, she knew Dali was close to death and wasn't hers, but she kept him safe anyway."

"Yes she did," he pulled her closer in his arms, "and you know what? Jack told us just now what Ailli had said, after all we heard was, 'How sweet!' from Rosie. Ailleen had told her that she called our son Dali, because it was the first two letters of our names, so he would always carry a part of us with him,"

Dave watched the tears slide down his wife's cheeks. "She never forgot us love, and to be honest, neither did I ever forget her, I saw her every day in Buddy's eyes."

"I used to wonder where the hell that colour came from." She smiled up at him "Mind if I sleep here tonight sweetheart, I want to be close to her, just in case she wakes up in the night and she needs me." she whispered.

"Well there does appear to be a rescue meeting downstairs that might need my help. So go on girl, get your nightie on, I'll see you in the morning!" Promptly kissing the top of head, Dave went back out of the room and downstairs.

Chapter 26

Safe and Sound

"Bet you didn't see this coming Juniper?" Kawiti laughed, walking away from the exit, holding her hand and helping her over some of the debris.

"Actually no, and it feels very strange for me! It's as if I am still blocked in some way. I was told that all intuitive abilities would be cloaked, so I would not have an advantage during the contest, but now we are free, I'm still not picking up any vibes at all," she deliberately turned her head round as if looking for an indicator of some kind. "Something is obviously messing with my radar, even now!"

"Perhaps, it was just the fear factor. It has been a shock for all of us and anxiety is a great leveller when it comes to feelings!" Amitola took her other hand and helped Kawiti lift her over the entrance gate that was now knocked to the floor. "Maybe it's just a delayed reaction. The more you worry, the harder it will be to see."

"Maybe!" Juniper again looked behind her. "You might be right?"

Turning the corner into the street, they were assaulted by a sudden rush of recognisable family members coming bowling towards them.

"Mum?" Amitola was the first to see who they were.

"Dad?" Juniper leapt forward to be gathered in her father's arms.

"Parents arriving!" Kawiti yelled to the group behind them, letting them know that their relatives were on their way.

He scanned the group for his own parents, but not catching sight of them, as complete chaos ensued when the adults arrived in an unparalleled wave and in seconds it was hard to find a body that wasn't being hugged or kissed. Including those who didn't even belong to any of the families.

"How did you find us?" Laura asked her dad, hardly believing her eyes, as Stan hugged her tightly to him.

"Nick's little gem guided us here. We sent the older youngsters ahead as they were able to get through the hole easier than us!" Jacky Springer said as she pushed her husband out of the way and fell into her daughter's grubby arms.

"Hole?" Laura asked.

"Yeh, it was big enough us little un's, but wasn't big enough for Freddy, and it needed all of us to push and pull him through before the ceiling collapsed" her father added.

"Dad got stuck?" Kawiti began to smile, as he heard the last part of their conversation.

"I'm here now runt, so don't think you got rid of me that easy!" A familiar voice came from behind him.

"But, stuck Dad, really?" his face beamed at seeing his father in one marvellous piece, "Where's Mum?"

"She's just coming! Oh, is she, going to live off of this story for years." Freddie said. He picked his puny offspring off the ground and tried to swing him round, but with so many other children in the vicinity, reverted to squeezing him until Kawiti finally reached an unhealthy shade of puce.

"Freddy, let him go! Let him go!" his wife pounded on his muscled arm and he realised what he was doing and dropped Kawiti, still gasping for air, to the floor.

Amitola helped him up "I think they missed us!" he

whispered.

"You think?" Kawiti wheezed, holding his chest and taking deep breaths, then flew into his mother's arms and Nyree grabbed an arm, not bearing to let go of her brother either.

King Nick and Queen Sophie were talking to Noelia and Thorlief, as Juan came round the corner, followed immediately by Raul, both stood scanning the faces only stopping when Noelia called out their names.

"Papa!, Juan!"

They both turned towards the sound, saw her at the same time, and made their way over.

"Oh Papa!" she called, Thor stepped out of the way but gave a nod to Raul, and Juan, who gave him a man hug in passing before Sophie took this opportunity to grasp Thor's hand, as he stepped into her open arms and each trying not to imagine a life without the other.

Before any other conversations were started however, King Lenny's voice boomed over the small crowd.

"Look all of you! I think we are going to have to move from here, a little quicker. I don't like the sound of the building. Let's make our way to the Crystal Gem Palace hotel." He scanned the area and mentally counted the group around him.

"I reserved the whole of the top floor and actually, the floor below too. So plenty of room for everyone and only about a five minute walk from here, we can get cleaned up and they have an onsite doctor. I'm sure he will be able to fix what needs fixing and Nick and I can find out what is happening!" The two kings nodded at each other.

With this announcement everyone moved, as fast as they could in the circumstances, but following the distinguishable royals, who along with their bodyguards were also helping or carrying the injured. The rest of the uninjured assisting the lesser wounded, which luckily were not many.

It was difficult to move as lots of people were also trying to get away from the auditorium, and hindered by the usual morbidly curious section who had arrived to discover what had happened.

Luckily the hotel was just a stone's throw from where they had exited the building, with not such a mad crowd slowing their pace as they made their way across a couple of well lit London streets that led them to their own refuge.

It was only just over an hour before they were all finally gathered and were seated in the living room of King Lenny's suite. He had arranged with the hotel management to send up new clothes for them, from the fancy shops in the hotel lobby. Along with a number of extra chairs, stools, and floor cushions so they could all be together, once they were showered and dressed.

The rest of the violet competitors had been given accommodation on the floor below and allowed rooms under the protection of hotel staff and their companions, until relatives were contacted and a reunion could be arranged.

Everyone in the suite were far too hyped up to close their eyes just yet, they included all the families at the restaurant, with Raul, Juan, Noelia and Sarah. The three youngest children were asleep together in a room next door, exhausted from their own adventure.

Chapter 27

Tom, Lizzie and the Magpie

Tom opened his eyes to a room he had never seen before, and immediately closed them again, as he shook his head, thinking he was dreaming. Seconds later reopening them, he felt the crush of disappointment cover his whole body, realising straight away that it wasn't a dream.

Looking round at the walls in various shades of white, yellow and green, on which exceptionally lifelike paintings of birds flying either, one way or the other, were hung in abundance.

There was also a large window, barred of course, but as he lay on the bed, he could see the sun in the distance and hear waves gently lapping on the rocks below him.

The journey here, wherever here was, was not unfortunately, a memory to him.

When he saw Whitet come towards him in Covent Garden, his only thought was to lead the magpie away from Rosie. He had even turned to strike, but then heard a gunshot and Walt's order to run, both at the same time. The moment he took to turn his head, he saw Walt fall to the ground, with blood pouring from his shoulder. In that split second Whitet grabbed his arm, he felt his whole body promptly freezing and a voice in his head telling him to walk away, or watch his guardian die. He closed his eyes as the second shot rang out and its deathly ricochet pierced icily through his heart.

"What a bloody fool, after all these years!" he

thought and the memory made his stomach churn violently.

This had him pushing himself up from the king sized bed he was laying on and swing his legs over the edge. Endeavouring to see things objectively, although in truth he was furious with himself for being caught and heart rendering, to the very pit of his stomach, sad, because his friend had died trying to save him. A rush of self-pity coursed through him, as he suddenly realised what it would also be meaning to Ellie and to his whole family.

Sitting back up, he cast his eyes around the room and if he had not been a captive, he probably would have liked the size and modern furnishings. It was even bigger than his room back home, but then that one didn't have bars at the window, which in itself gave this one, a slightly claustrophobic feel to it.

"Why didn't anyone tell me he uses a mind link, together with physical skin joining?" he yelled out loud.

"Because only a magpie knows, and he isn't going to tell anyone, now is he?" A returning voice said clearly, and he actually looked around the room expecting someone to be in there with him.

He thought for a millisecond that it was Kristy, but this voice he realised was softer, younger and had an Irish lilt. Hoping it was his little sister did not make it so, and he realised then that the girl's voice was in his head and he shook it as if it would clear the jumble of thoughts within.

"Who are you?" he thought the words, but got no answer, in return to his question.

"I don't read minds, if that is what you are trying to do. I'm an oralan, you have to speak, for me to hear you" she added petulantly. "Even Dali's better than you!"

Tom cottoned on pretty quickly.

"An oralan! Wow, well done you!" he shouted, he was honestly amazed.

"Hey, don't patronise me!" the voice came back, "and you don't have to yell!"

"Sorry, I'm not belittling your gift, truly!" Lowering his voice to its normal speaking level, Tom instinctively pushed himself up and away from the bed to begin searching the room for any sign of spy cameras or hidden microphones. Lifting lamps and looking behind the paintings for bugs, but continued talking, "and as I can only assume I'm the one locked in this room, I'm grateful for the company." His voice not in anyway, betraying how much that particular fact actually hurt.

"Me too, and yes you are locked in, but even if you weren't, there is no place to go!" her voice stated in matter of fact way. "Unless, you happen to be, a long distance swimmer?"

"If only!" he thought, and his mind raced back to the last time he ventured near any water and nearly drowned. It was only because Walt had pulled him out of the ocean by his hair, did he survive that ordeal. So no, he was not a fan of the sea in any form.

"What's your name?" he asked her quietly. She sounded very young.

"Lizzie Meaney," she whispered. She said it as if she hadn't said her name for a long time, which in point of fact, she hadn't.

Tom stood still, the name was somehow familiar to him, but where had he heard it before.

"Hi Lizzie, I'm Tom Osmundsen." He spoke firmly, but friendly.

The silence that followed from Lizzie was deafening

for Tom, his stomach churned.

"Lizzie, are you still there? Please talk to me!" he called out to her.

"Yes, I didn't know it would be you who was chosen." Her voice echoed with the respect that his rank gave him.

"Chosen, what do you mean chosen? Chosen for what exactly?" At the back of his mind, he finally realised exactly what Lizzie was talking about, "Lizzie how old are you sweetheart?"

"16," she whispered again.

"Were you 16, recently, as maybe on 21st June?"

"Yes!" Again she whispered the reply.

"Oh Lizzie I am so sorry!"

This had never been a good situation to be in, but on hearing this news it was probably the worst scenario, he could have imagined.

"Don't be, I am honoured, it's nice to have someone else to talk to apart from Dali, Viggo and Ailleen," she stopped talking, as if musing over her new predicament. "He always told me he was going to find you, it was something in the way he spoke, he was obsessed with getting you here, especially now. The competition and the fact that I am now a woman and not a child, spurred him on I think!"

"Not more so than the fact I am 20, in a few months time and would be lost forever to him."

The irony was certainly playing out for him today, he thought.

"You're 19! Oh you're so old!" she said it in such a derogatory way, as to make him snigger.

"Thanks a lot!" Tom burst out laughing.

"Dali is only 16 and we share the same birthday!" she confided.

"Oh, so I have competition!" he returned gently.

Again she didn't answer.

"Lizzie, I'm kidding! Please tell me about yourself. How you got here and what has been happening here over the last four years for you?"

"Of course, Osmun Azure!" her young voice again becoming, softly deferential.

"Call me Tom please, you will have to get used to it, if I am to stay here with you." Which he hoped upon hope, wouldn't be long.

"I know, I'll just have to make the best of it then won't I!" Came her cheeky reply, "I just don't know where to start."

"How about, where you were born? Tell me all about your family."

"Oh yes I have a big family. I thought they would have found me by now, but Ailleen says I mustn't give up hope, she hasn't. I was born in Ireland and me Da and Ma live just outside Bantry, Cork and I have three brothers and a sister. I was the oldest, then there is Sean he'd be 14 now, Tim 12, Maggie 11 and little Patrick he'll be seven next week. Paddy was a darling boy, always had a smile on his face. We spoilt him, but he was just naturally happy."

"You had a good childhood then Lizzie, I'm glad." Tom said "I did too and I have good memories."

Suddenly it hit him where he had heard her name. "What date were you taken from Ireland, Lizzie?"

"December, almost four years ago and a few months after my 12th birthday. Ma had bought me a new dress then and was taking me to see my cousin, Siobhan in Cork, for her birthday party so I could wear it again, I was really looking forward to that."

"December" he thought, just two months after he

managed to bring back Elsie-jai, the Enever Emerald from Whitet and the last time he had had any contact with the white magpie. So another responsibility had been thrown his way, he was responsible for Lizzie being taken, because Elsie-jai had been saved.

"What's it like here?" Tom asked, changing tack.

"Okay, I guess!" she mumbled "I miss my family, but I can play with Dali most days and Ailleen teaches my lessons."

"Who are Ailleen and Dali and I think you mentioned a Viggo?"

"Well Ailleen and Viggo were taken when they were younger, but are married now and they have Dali. They are all Majestet, like us."

"Did they give Whitet their gifts voluntarily?" Tom asked, this would be an astonishing thing, if they had.

"I think so, but I don't think they had much choice, as Dali was ill when he was born and seemed to have no gifts, which made Whitet so angry that he was going to take him away, before he reached his first year. Ailleen and Viggo, said they would work for Whitet for the rest of their lives to keep Dali safe and well. It is really nice to have them here. I can talk to Dali all the time without anyone knowing and I see Ailli every day, and she is a very good cook."

"I won't starve then!" he answered.

"Oh no, Whitet takes care of us, especially if you can read for him!" she added.

"I just bet, he does." thought Tom.

"Do you read for him often Lizzie?"

"Nearly every week, but it was almost two weeks, until he brought you back, so I had a holiday."

"Oh, so I was good for something then!" Tom laughed out loud.

290

"Yes, you were, thank you, now I can ...." she broke off quickly. "Watch out, he's coming. I'll speak to you again when he's left."

Tom let out a long breath and leaned against the wall looking out of the window and trying to see beyond the bars. Could things get any worse?

Within seconds the sound of the door opening behind him had him turn slowly, from the window to see his captor.

Oh damn, it could it seemed, as he briefly caught sight of two guards outside taking position either side of the door, as the man himself closed it behind him.

Whitet was taller than average, but it was his eyes that stood him apart, shining out from his ashen face, they were almost white themselves, being the palest pink he had ever seen. His short pure white hair was a mass of tiny curls, no wonder he was given the name Whitet.

Although he knew what he looked like from photographs, being in the same room made Tom's skin crawl. This was the first time they had been face to face, the closest other encounter was 20 something feet, across a choppy sea.

"So we meet again, Whitet, but it seems you have lost some of that tan I saw you with last time!" Referring to the fact that disguise in their world, was not just a one way street.

"A joker you seem to be Osmundsen, but not laughing now though are you?" he answered with a humourless smile and wandered over to join him at the barred window. "How many times have we nearly met before?"

"Oh, enough to ruffle a few feathers, I think." Tom would have smiled if his position were not so precarious, but he could see his words had hit the mark and

Whitet's face actually gained a reddish hue.

"It seems now I've been caught at my own game, but honestly I could do with the rest. I've been working far too hard lately, especially with all the wedding plans." He tossed lightly to the man.

"Ah, yes I had heard, congratulations are in order. I hope you have invited Lokkint Blue and Enever Emerald to the wedding, it will be nice to see them again." He turned around and was walking back towards the door.

"What are you implying?" Tom levelled a surly stare at Whitet's back as they were now standing either side of the room. "There is no way in hell I would allow you into my home."

"Really! Allow me eh?" Whitet smiled maliciously, "You are in my house now, Osmun Azure and may I remind you, there are no choices as to what you will, or will not do. If you attack me, as I can see you would like to, one touch and I have control of you, body and soul!"

"You may have my body, but my soul is my own and always will be!" Tom responded bravely. "I will fight you Whitet, by any means available."

"You are a fool, boy! I can do anything I want with you and you can do nothing about it!" his smile now ingratiating and his pink eyes began to turn a deeper rose "You have been a thorn in my side for the last five years, but the status quo now appears to be in my favour, does it not young man. I will never allow you to return to your former existence. I shall make that my goal, I assure you!"

"Not heard of pride coming before a fall Whitet? You can never, say never!" Tom jumped back on the bed, plumped up the pillow and put it behind his head. "Some things are just not meant to be!"

"Oh, but I have great plans for you, and trust me,

you will co-operate; believe me you will!" he rubbed his hands together in what was an obviously slimy Uriah Heep practiced piece.

"Perhaps so, but life does the damnedest things. Everyone has choices and mine is not to be intimidated by a greedy psychopath like you!" Tom's grin was as convincing as it could be, under the circumstances.

The explosion he was hoping to ignite unfortunately didn't occur and he watched as the older man's pale face turned smugly confident.

"Nice try, but I'm not biting, you will be contained in this room and although it might be considered, a gilded cage, I doubt you will ever leave this island, voluntarily."

The room went quiet, neither man deeming to start another conversation and Tom surreptitiously glancing round his prison cell. His stomach turned a little and desperation clutched at him again, like a vice gripped around his throat. He couldn't let it get the better of him, he was in too precarious a position, so he closed his eyes and took a few deep breaths to calm himself.

"Well, if there isn't anything else, I'd like to go back to sleep, it's been a long day," he blustered.

"Do that! We have all the time in the world to catch up, Majestet!" But there was no respect in the title, he said it almost as if it was a dirty word, and he was so self-assured it turned Tom's stomach, yet again.

Ironically, Tom realised, he was now one of his Stolen, and like them didn´t even know where he was, but then what did that matter, there was no one out there to rescue him, now Walt was gone.

His father would do his best to find him, but that would take time, time he didn't have. The hollowness in Tom's middle, grew to fill his entire chest, there and then, he vowed he would not let this tragedy carve his future and he wouldn't cling to old dreams or bemoan a past that couldn't be changed.

Once Whitet had left the room, Tom threw a few scenarios around in his mind of where he might be, how he could assault Whitet without touching him and how to save Lizzie if he did get out. Not one had any substance of worth and he curled in a ball on top of the bed, frustrated and yes, even a little frightened.

Only one thing pleased him and that was that Whitet obviously didn't know about Rosie. He had been the prey today and no one else.

Again there lay the problem, how on earth did Whitet know where he was, he had said to Kristy that it could be a trap, but Rosie was an innocent and certainly not bait for it. If Whitet had known about Rosie, she would have been a far easier target, although with their past history, he could only surmise that revenge outweighed any gain, unless now he was imprisoned here, Whitet could go after her.

Without conscious thought, his heart began to beat harder, finally picturing Nicky in his mind. She was so precious to him and was the love of his life and he made a solemn vow to himself that they would be married before his gift was taken from him forever.

A tear of frustration fell onto the pillow, as he closed his thoughts and calmed down enough to go back to sleep, suddenly feeling drained and not even waking when Lizzie whispered in his head, asking if he was all right.

His sudden loud snore had her giggling.

"He's noisy!" she said to her teddy bear, a gift from Aileen when she arrived and cuddled him possessively, "I like the sound of his voice, but I like Dali's more!"

Chapter 28

Rosie

Moving forward in the lounge, Dave turned off the side lights, one at a time. Jack was sleeping on the sofa, as he had given up his bed to Ellie and Kristy, and Terry was asleep on the floor in an old sleeping bag of Mike's from the loft. Lucas had left with Mike to see Vicki to her home, at the end of the street and they were to carry on round the corner to Dave's brother Rob's house, to sleep. Bert had gone there earlier to help make up the spare beds and was to stay there himself, in what used to be the large family home, before he had downsized to the bungalow, when his Vi couldn't manage the stairs.

Closing the living room door quietly, he made his way into the kitchen, where he found Rosie holding a cup of hot chocolate. She'd only had about three hours sleep.

"Quite a night, dad eh?" she still looked tired, but the nap had obviously done its job. "I woke mum up and told her to go back to your bed as the bunk isn't good for her sciatica. You'll never believe it, but she went as quiet as a mouse!" she smiled up at him

"Blimey, that'll be a first!" Dave smiled back.

"Mm, I know!" Blowing onto the drink's surface to cool it a little, and then swallowing a mouthful.

"Buddy, do you forgive me, for carrying you away like I did?" Dave shook visibly at the question.

"Dad! Oh Dad" she banged her mug on the breakfast bar and flew into his arms, "you didn't take me. Ailleen gave me to you for safe keeping, and you, mum, Nanny Vi, Grandad Bert, Mike and even Jack did a fantastic job. I've had a wonderful childhood."

"But what I did to Dali was wrong, so wrong!" he sounded devastated.

"You thought he had died Dad! Ailleen must have known he was too ill to wait for the ambulance, when she left the house and her instinct was to protect me at all costs from something that could not be changed. It must have been overwhelming for her. I think she did it for all of us. Remember, she thought Dali would have no gift, so she could keep him safe and he was never going to be used like I would have been. I expect she thought at some point in the future, he and I would be swapped back again."

"No gift like yours, what is this gift you have Buddy? I still don't understand!"

"She can't tell you Dave." Ellie stood in the doorway, "as she doesn't really know herself yet!"

"You know though don't you Ellie?" Rosie looked at Tom's cousin and she could actually feel the Symm energy course through her while they stared at each other.

"No I honestly don´t. I think the best person to speak to is Dr Bush, he seems to be the one who knows the Symm personally."

"It all seems so strange, yet so familiar" Rosie, sat on the bar stool, pulling Dave onto the one next to her.

"That audio thing is weird" Dave commented.

"Yes, I supposed it is even for us, but tonight I seem to have got used to it really quickly. I now recognise that Dr Bush is special and Luc tells me that he is also an Elder of the Symm Council. Which means that his abilities are far greater than any Majestet, but regrettably even with his skills, Luc says he can't latch onto Tom, although he has tried several times to reach him. He is being blocked!"

"Look, forgive my ignorance, not being of the Symm and all, but what is this Majestet, I keep hearing about?"

"Majestet is the name of a group of families in the Symm who are, I suppose you would call them, royalty, kind of, or more like of an honoured family. They have the deepest respect within our culture." Ellie answered.

"There is royalty in the Symm world as well. Thorlief, King Nicolas and Queen Sophie's son, is a Season Royal, so is that why Tom is Majestet too, and being related surely you and Kristy are too?" Rosie got up and put on the kettle to make a cup of tea for the other two, as Ellie sat down on the bar stool next to Dave.

"I don't know what happens in the Symm's world, but yes, Tom is Majestet and he also has a little gem, and Kristy is only second born like my mum, but she is also a quarter day. Walt and I, are both from Majestet families, but even though we are first born and Walt is a quarter day, we are not actually Majestet in the same sense. We do however, have an acute awareness to our families needs and are known as Guardians." She got up and put the kettle on. "Walt knows more about magpies and squirrels than anyone in the world. He has a data base that keeps tabs on the ones we know, and has an idea where the rest are hiding. So after a good night's sleep, he should be on board with a lot more information."

"Then Rosie is Majestet, because both her mum and dad are, but my sons you said were Majestet too, but obviously I'm not." Dave pointed out.

"Actually Dave, you have to be, I think!" Ellie smiled at the incredulous face Dave was pulling as he paled at the thought.

"Your family must have been, back in the day. It was a bit like Lisa, her ancestors she knew were lost in World War II, but even more families were lost in World War I. Thousands of young men who were first born and their brothers, who would have been Majestet and Guardians, were killed before they reached 20 and a lot were probably even older, who still hadn't passed their gene on because of the war. Many men would have reached their 20th birthday realistically without being able to continue the line. Similarly after that war the country was ravaged by the epidemic of Spanish flu, which did not discriminate between men and women and many young gene passing youngsters also died. This further disrupted the Symm and it has taken many years to build families back up again." she smiled at him "Actually it is very rare that someone Majestet, doesn't marry within the Symm."

"Oh Dad, that's so cool!" Rosie's eyes widened.

"The one thing that has troubled me though Dave, I don't understand how your line was joined as your Dad must have been many years over the gene bearing age when you were born how many years older was he, to your mother." Ellie questioned.

Rosie looked at her Dad, "Ellie's right dad, grandad is eighty and I always assumed that nanny was a lot younger when she had you and the twins, Aunt Susan and Uncle Rob, but I remember Mum telling me she was three years younger than grandad, when she passed away."

"Never thought about it, they always looked so youthful, it never crossed my mind that they were different in any way to any of my friends parents!"

Suddenly the front door bell rang, making all three of them jump, and Ellie immediately stood guard at

Rosie's side.

"I'll get it, it's probably only Mike" Dave grumbled. "Can't understand why he hasn't used his key, he'll wake everyone up!"

Opening the door gingerly, he poked his head round, only to find a brunette and a blond, slightly bedraggled young women, standing in the porch under the bright security light, looking up at him.

"Frankie, how did you find us?" Ellie peaked from around his back, then stepped to one side, "Dave this is Tom's fiancée, Nicola Swenson and my sister Francesca."

"Come in, come in, both of you." Dave stood aside and closed the door behind them.

"She wouldn't wait until a more reasonable hour, Ellie, sorry!" Frankie rolled up her eyes, as she passed her sister.

"Dad piloted the Cessna to Biggin Hill for me when we heard. I couldn't stay in Oslo waiting for any titbits of news." She genuinely looked devastated, "Have you heard anything new?"

"Yes Nicky, I think we have, and by a very improbable link." Ellie took her hand, and brought her forward, so both Rosie and Nicola would come face to face.

"Let's talk in the kitchen" Rosie spoke up, looking at Tom's fiancée and suddenly feeling deep down Tom was her special friend and this woman in front of her was his destiny. "It will be less noisy there."

"No it's all right, we're awake. Go in the lounge, I'll make us some tea." Jack said, rubbing sleep from his eyes as he walked passed them, in nothing more than low slung pyjama bottoms.

Terry was standing behind him and took a step back,

to allow the girls to go through the doorway, his face mirroring his thoughts of bewilderment, at their arrival. This was the longest day he had ever known, but he doubted it was finished just yet.

"Kettles just boiled Jack" Ellie called after him as Rosie led Nicola by the hand into the room, where, she suddenly came to a halt, staring into Nicola's eyes.

"Rosie what is it?" Terry stepped forward swiftly and helped her into a chair as she tottered forward.

"I'm fine, honest, I had a weird flash, I finally realise something about my story. Thor had a message that was not only intended for him, but was also meant for me. We are the other group Juniper can see, I know this sound's crazy to you all, but it is so clear to me. Jack get me a pen and paper" she called.

As she wrote, everyone hung on every word.
"Thorlief was given information before the competition, in my dream, Tom is his sentinel you see, and the message read: *'Both must lead:*
  Six to bridge the rainbow, but not the
  Five to regain the blue,
  Four to seek their terra crystal, but not the
  Three who travel a route and see below,
  Two to mend the network, but there is only
  One who can free the legacy.'

I didn't realise when I wrote my chapter that it was also a message for me. Although I must admit, every time I tried to change the word 'Both' to 'You', my laptop changed it back and in the end, I gave up and left it in. I thought it was part of my story, but just now, I felt Nicola's overwhelming love for Tom, it made me realise the message is about him. He is the blue in the message and I hate to say this guys; but it sounds like five of us, have to go and get him."

Chapter 29

The Bodyguards

"Well now we know what happened!" King Nick held up his hand to cease any further conversation. He had played director to a very large play, over the last hour, which had carefully led them to the finale of being in this hotel room, safe and sound.

He smiled widely at all the youngsters, as he halted the overlapping explanations, but had let them vent their own stories in turn.

"I would just like to say we are very glad you are now with us again and you all got to the same level as we did 20 years ago. I am just disappointed that the contest ended as it did."

"Not to worry though, I have been told by the elders that you will be able to take the ABL test next week!" King Lenny added. "You can stay ...!"

"We won't be here next week, Dad!" Juniper piped up,

Her father and most of the rest of the company looked gob smacked. Only Stargazer, Sarah and Billy Kane, gave a nod of understanding, at this disclosure.

"You have to comprehend what is happening to us here." She stood up and looked round the room, "All of us, including Maddison, Alfie, Noelia, Juan and Tristan, have to be in several different places, to help with a mission. We have been called to be advocates, by our Father Sun, and this is nothing to do with Rainbow House, other than it was a way of getting us together. He is determined that we will lead Mother Nature's world towards something, but I just don't know exactly what yet?"

Before the understandable outburst could erupt, she held up her hand.

"All of us need to go! Don't even think this is not going to happen!" Juniper's voice quivered with determination.

"She is right, I too have known about this expedition, for some time." Stargazer stood up beside her.

"And I have been arranging things for the journey at this end!" Billy Kane moved forward in his fluid gait to stand next to Juniper on the other side. "That was why I was late." he admitted.

Sarah looked uncomfortable, but Stargazer nodded at her and she came to stand with them.

"I'm not admitting to anything, I just know I had to be here," she smiled at her group, "but, I didn't know things were going to get so out of hand, the way they did!"

"The tornado?" Thor asked, realising Juniper may have seen more info, than she was telling.

"It was released to destroy all of us, before we even started, and unfortunately, it now appears we are not to travel this path alone!" she smiled back at him.

"Great! Just great!" Kawiti said, "Well, they certainly mean business then, don't they?"

"Yes they do!" Stargazer gave a little smile, "But then so do you!"

"Well I'm not letting any of you go!" Stan Springer stood up, "Especially not all three of you?" he looked at his children with fierce determination.

"It isn't up to us Stan." Stargazer said, gently releasing Juniper's hand to take Stan's in her own and stroking the back of it to calm him a little. "Anyway they have guardians who will defend them with their lives, just outside the door, ready to take on anyone that would care to harm them."

"They do?" he looked bemused as did almost everyone in the room and she smiled at the obviously distraught parents.

"They have arrived, please let them in, Sarah!"

Sarah, gave a knowing smile back at her and did as she was asked. Walking over to the double doors and opened them wide to allow their new guests to enter.

The gasps of surprise and some with fear, were loud as the champions came just a little way into the room and stopping just beyond the threshold.

Yellow Sarah, was escorting Sun Ya's, Lyka Sham and Amur, her snow leopard walking sedately on either side. "Come here my babies," Sun Ya called to them, and they immediately sped across the room to her.

Red Sarah, had Amitola's Shirley and Clive, his humming birds on her shoulder and holding the hand of his mountain gorilla, Monty.

Green Sarah, was next and Laura smiled at the fact that Twix the fox and Spud her llama, galloped to her side, immediately on entering the room.

Orange Sarah, laughed out loud as Juniper sat down with a bump and opening her arms to her family of Meerkats, she called the MK's, who were hitching a ride on her leatherback turtle, Kelly.

Silver Sarah, came forward with Grumpy9. Thor was overwhelmed at seeing him safe and sound. His falcon, Speedy, flew straight onto his shoulder.

Blue Sarah, had hold of Goldie, Paul's tree kangaroo and his vampire bat Spook who flew straight up to the curtain and hung upside down near his head.

Indigo Sarah, came up at the rear of the procession with Kawiti's fabrications, Mally his Honey badger and

303

Poison Dart Frog, Chaz, who majestically rode on his back, enjoying the ride. "He wasn't too keen on the lift," she smiled at Kawiti, who immediately looked sadly at the badger, but she whispered, "not Mally! Chaz!"

Definitely the best bodyguards in the world, every one of them formed with love and devotion, and they would need all of this and more on their adventures, but then so would the adventurers.

The Stolen Window

Part Two of the Symm Saga

Autumn

Prologue

"Nobody here! Ruddy English magpies, knew I shouldn't have trusted them. Skipper warned me, but would I listen?" Vented Toni Willis out loud.

A sniffle from the girl standing next to her, filtered up through the noise of London Heathrow's arrivals hall. She looked down eyes blazing, still confounded that this 'Stolen' child was so conveniently like her in looks, it was amazing.

"Shut up! You'll be meeting your new Mum and Dad soon. Cheer up why don't you?" her voice rebounded around the girl, who cringed visibly.

"I don't want new ones. The orphanage was good, I liked it there." Rubbing her tired eyes, with her fisted hand. She was small for her age of 13, dressed in blue jeans and a loose kangaroo print t-shirt and her aboriginal ancestry shone like a beacon from her beautiful face.

"Yeh, you keep telling me!" Toni moaned.

Still looking around trying to remember what the lady Magpie looked like. Her transactions were with both of the magpies in Sydney, but it was the woman who dealt with picking the girl. The man dealt with Skipper and the money side of the trade, but that was five weeks ago.

Georgie Kalms was standing at the barrier and watching the multicultural passengers come through into the arrivals hall. Her mobile began to vibrate in her pocket, as she would never have heard the ring-tone, in such an overcrowded environment.

"You only rang a minute ago, Trev!" smiling lovingly, as she spoke.

"I know, but you would think that having aboriginal ancestry they would be easier to find."

"Look love, I still haven't seen them yet, so keep looking yourself!" Georgie turned her head and caught sight of a woman with a young girl walking slowly and pushing a trolley piled high with luggage. "Hold on a minute, what was she wearing again?"

"White t-shirt and red jeans, Gill said. Do you see them?"

"Yes, I think so. I can only see their backs, but they are heading towards the tube with their two red cases each. The woman is in red jeans and a red jacket."

"It's not them! Gill said, they only had hand luggage, remember. They would probably have come through by now with no suitcases."

"Damn it! We were here in plenty of time too!" her voice now tinged with regret.

"More than enough!" A gravelly voice said in her ear and Georgie swung round.

"Keep looking my sweet, we will find her?" Trev spoke as he reached the taxi rank outside the terminal and ready to finish his call.

"Not if I can help it, Kalms!" A male voice spoke into Georgie's phone just before he switched off the connection, then threw it onto the floor and kicked it under a chair.

"Georgie!" Trevor called her name before pocketing his phone and began to run back to the arrivals hall cursing himself for leaving Georgie alone.

He had to fight his way through the throng of passengers leaving the hall, but he knew she wouldn't have left the spot he had placed her in and looked hopefully for that position as he got closer.

She wasn't there, but as he scanned the local vicinity, he saw a woman sitting with her back to him in one of the seats further down the hall.

"Georgie?" he called, but the woman didn't turn towards him and he had to wait until he was closer to see that it really was his wife.

"Georgie?" he sat next to her, but her eyes were vacant and he could see she was struggling to think of who he was.

"Darling, it's me Trev. Take your time." Holding her hand gently within his own, he could feel his symm draining from him and into her. Grateful that he could see the colour flooding back into her cheeks and her eyes squinted twice, before he saw recognition again within them.

"Oh Trev!" she gasped, "he took my phone and I could hear him telling me to walk away and sit here, even though I didn't want to. I feel sick!"

"Quiet darling, we'll sit here and wait until you feel better and then I shall take you home".

"The girl, I saw the girl she was with a woman and they walked off together, but we lost them Trev." Georgie began to cry.

"Hey, it wasn't your fault sweetheart, we'll get her back, I promise." His eyes still scouted round for Adelaide Coates, the Australian Stolen, and he would make it his life's work to find her, as he had never broken a promise to his wife, not ever.

Other books from WordPlay

Precinct Murder
by Various Authors

New York: the city where killers never sleep. For those that like their murder stories potted, this is the perfect coffee table crime anthology.

WordPlay ShowCase
by Various Authors

A collection of works by a series of writers, for some of whom this represents their first time in print. The anthology covers a whole range of writing: factual, fiction, social commentary, and poetry.

My Gentle War (Memoirs of an Essex Girl)
by Joy Lennick

This is the true story of a young girl whose family is wrenched apart by the heartache and tragedy of World War II. Community spirit and togetherness see her through the worst of times, and welcomes in the best of times.

Losing Hope
by Nikki Dee

In 1995 a small girl vanished from her home. No trace of her was found though her family never stopped looking. In 2010 a damaged and vulnerable young woman is rescued from a burning building. Can this possibly be that long lost child and, if so, where has she been and why?

The Cardinals of Schengen
by Michael Barton

Jack Hudson, the UK Government's Foreign Secretary, is assassinated in his own home. In attempting to discover his brother's murderer, Peter Hudson finds himself in a race against time to save Europe from a secret society determined to see Europe become the Fourth Reich.

Divine Damages
by Georgia Varjas

This is a collection of ten elegant stories about the ends and means women will go to get even. Justice and sweet revenge has never been served quite so divinely as it is in this mischievous, ironic, and downright satisfying read. Bound to leave you fulfilled and gratified.

Shorts for Autumn
by Various Writers

The winner of the 2012 Writing Magazine UK Writers' Circle Anthology Award, this is ideal accompaniment to an autumn evening spent by the fire, or that morning coffee break when you need to unwind and relax, Shorts for Autumn is a collection of fiction to suit all tastes, whether they be murder, romance, ghostly tales or just a little light humour.

Keep Write On
by Ian Govan

Published posthumously, *Keep Write On* is a

collection of Ian's musings on life and, in particular, writing. There is wit, tinged with, perhaps, a little life cynicism here and there, that will make you giggle inside. All royalties from sales will be used by WordPlay toward 'encouraging writers to write, and then getting them read'.

Fallyn and the Dragons
by K J Rollinson

A magical adventure that sees Allan, Eileen and Martin called away from the 'real world' to a medieval 'dream world'. There, Allan is known as Lord Fallyn, and he and his friends go to the rescue of King Rudri's dragons and battle against Prince Bato who seeks to depose his brother.

Fallyn in the Forbidden Land
by K J Rollinson

In this second book of the Fallyn trilogy, Fallyn and company again meet fascinating characters, including a mysterious race of little people called Chougans and their dragons.

Are the Chougans responsible for the band of red dragons attacking Nashta? Or are the red dragons led by Prince Bato?

All books are available on Amazon and kindle.

Made in the USA
Charleston, SC
15 May 2014